PARTICULAR PASSAGES

DECKED HALLS

Table of Contents

A Creature Was Stirring

by
Arlen Feldman

A Creature Was Stirring

Wrapping a dozen appendages around the chimney stack, it sent a spindly tentacle exploring deep down into the chimney until it felt heat. There was a fire far down below.

That wasn't a problem for *it*—it could handle ridiculous temperature extremes. But the package wouldn't survive. Closing most of its eyes to concentrate, it started to extrude a chitinous membrane from one of its larger body segments. After a few moments, the package disappeared into it, leaving a slightly incongruous set of right angles in its otherwise curvy and sinuous body.

Climbing headfirst into the chimney, its body automatically thinned out to fit into the narrow space. It had to compress the package very slightly to get through one section, but it was within the tolerances of the item.

When it reached the bottom, it allowed a small, eyeballed tentacle to drop below the lintel.

Empty.

Careful to avoid the ash that could leave smears in the room, it slid out and along the wall until it could plop down onto the floor. It took longer to retract the membrane back into itself, leaving a very slight pink area on its mostly gray body. The feeling was very slightly unpleasant, but it was used to it.

It used three tentacles to position the package under the Christmas tree and a fourth to absorb back bits of the slimy substance that had attached to the bow. There was a little bit it couldn't get without risking damaging the delicate ribbon, but by morning the coating would harden and brush off like dust.

While doing this, other tentacles were exploring the room. On a small table, there was a hand-drawn picture of the human-perception of what a "Santa Claus" looked like, along with an even more unlikely drawing of a heart, both done in red crayon. It tasted the waxy surface with the tip of one of its many tongues.

Next to the drawing was a glass of cow mammary fluid, which it drained off appreciatively. There were also three irregularly shaped baked goods. The rules said that it could only eat one. The cookie disappeared into another mouth.

Then it flipped itself over and slid back up the chimney, going much faster without having to worry about damaging the package.

On the roof, it picked up its sack, which was made of the same chitinous material it had extruded earlier. Then it inflated its body into a canopy-shape, waited for a gust of wind, and hurled itself upwards, reshaping itself like a sail to guide itself towards the next rooftop.

It liked floating like this. If it could, it would have just let the wind take it wherever it wanted, but it had many more deliveries to make that night. Its many millions of siblings would be helping, but it was still responsible for dozens of packages.

The next roof was flat, but there was still a chimney. There was something strange about it, though. It tasted the chimney tentatively. Titanium. In hundreds of years, it had never encountered a titanium chimney.

But things changed. It used to be wood and stone homes. Then concrete came, and high-rises. Fortunately, high-rises tended to have intricate ventilation systems that were easy to navigate.

It slipped into the opening, two packages held in a bundle of tentacles as it made its way through the many turns of the chimney. Inefficient, it thought. Too many turns and a chimney ceased to function. It expected to run up against an electric heater—which would likely mean going out and finding a different route in. But no, there was simply an empty fireplace.

It dropped two eyes down this time and looked all around. White walls, no furniture. But there was an undecorated artificial tree against the far wall, its built-in LED lights flickering on and off.

Very slowly it dropped down out of the fireplace, leaving a handful of tentacles still running up the chimney. But the tree was too far across the room. It had to let go. It moved quickly, filled with an unquantified sense of unease. But it still took time to position the two packages neatly.

Several eyes had stayed pointing at the fireplace, and it saw the movement a moment before it heard the sound of metal-on-metal as a solid barrier crashed down, closing off the fireplace. It had started moving almost immediately, but it was too late. It slammed into the barrier, causing minor damage to several tentacles.

It tasted the barrier. More titanium. As strong as it was, it couldn't break through titanium. It reshaped tentacles to their thinnest possible size and tried to insert them underneath the barrier to lift it, but there was not the slightest gap.

It was trapped.

Unpleasant stress hormones started flooding its bloodstream, and it quickly synthesized a mild tranquilizer to calm down. Then it started a systematic examination of the room.

All the walls were made of titanium. There was a slight indentation that might have been a door, but there was no crack big enough to exploit. There were also cameras everywhere, but that didn't really matter since its kind didn't show up on camera unless they chose to. But it had missed the pressure plate under the tree. The weight of the packages must have triggered the barrier.

It moved itself into a corner and stretched out as far as it could, changing colors slightly to match the wall. There was nothing else it could do but wait.

The worst thing was that it still had so many packages left to deliver.

The rumbling didn't come from the fireplace, but from one of the side walls. Several dozen eyes watched as a section of the wall slid away to reveal a window. On the other side was a man, staring right at it.

"I can see you," he said.

It kept perfectly still, wary, and slightly afraid.

"I knew it! All these years, and finally I've proved it."

The man was short, with thick glasses that made his eyes look like they were bulging. Or perhaps they were. To it, he looked very slightly deranged.

The man started taking pictures, then looked down at the screen on his digital camera with dismay.

"Why don't you show up?" Then he looked at it directly in one of its larger eyes. "If I can't get a picture, I'll have to get proof another way."

It couldn't help it. It panicked. The window was an obvious weak spot. It propelled itself with all its considerable strength towards the narrow opening, its skin pulsing red and orange, and slammed into the glass.

It bounced off, landing heavily on the floor, several tentacles bent at strange angles.

It managed to point a few eyes towards the window. The man had disappeared, but a few moments later, he climbed back to his feet, breathing hard.

"Phew. I knew the titanium would hold you, but I wasn't quite as sure about the plexiglass."

It spent a few moments straightening itself out, then slid along the floor and positioned itself underneath the window. It still couldn't get out, but at least it could no longer be seen by the man.

"Hiding won't do you any good. I've waited too long for this. And I have *contingencies.*"

It didn't have vocal chords, so it couldn't speak as such, but it made several tentacles into strings and ran a rigid tentacle over it.

Who are you? The words sounded like a wheezy piano speaking but were understandable.

"You don't remember me. No reason why you should. My name is Devin Cartwright. And we've met before."

It searched its memory. It *did* know the name.

You were dying.

"I was alive enough to see and remember you, even if absolutely nobody believed me."

Exactly forty-three years ago. It had come down a chimney to find a boy being beaten by his drunken father. It had snuck up on the father and knocked him out, then had resuscitated the boy with chest compressions, while dialing the rotary phone and calling for an ambulance.

"After *everything* happened, I spent years in foster homes, going to therapy. But I knew what I saw. There are monsters coming into everyone's homes. It's been my life's work to prove it. And to find out why..." His voice suddenly got small. "Why you saved me."

It said nothing. It had apparently not occurred to Devin that any creature that spent Christmas Eve delivering gifts to children was unlikely to allow a child to be harmed if it could prevent it.

Devin didn't say anything for a while. It had snuck a small tentacle up to watch him, but the man was just standing there, looking like a lost little child.

But it had also looked towards the Christmas tree and the two small gifts sitting below it. It had delivered them because there were two children at this address, and neither of them had the name *Cartwright*.

Why are there children here? It thrummed.

Devin looked up, almost like he'd forgotten why he was there. "I've done research, you see. You've been seen lots of times. There's lots of references in old books and online. If you know where to look."

It hadn't been seen very often, but in a family of millions, it was inevitable that there would be sightings and stories. It was unlikely that any human would be able to tell them apart. It was a huge coincidence that it happened to be it who Devin had captured.

The children?

Devin's face sagged. "I had to. Don't you see? You only come to houses with children, and I don't have any children of my own."

It felt genuinely sorry for Devin, but that didn't matter now. Devin was no longer a child, but there were children here who needed its help. Assuming it could figure out how to get out of this room.

It did have one option, although it would be uncomfortable. Carefully it extruded out a section of its stomach into a long purple tongue-like extremity, then, with a quick, squelchy movement, wiped it across the glass, leaving a coating of stomach acid.

"What was that?" Devin was looking panicked now, and it was worried that he would close the panel over the window, but instead he pulled out a small remote and hit a button.

Current arced through the floor and walls, sending it flying, pain shooting through its limbs. It landed across the room in an amorphous blob.

"Don't try to get out," Devin warned. "You're trapped."

Very slowly it managed to form itself back into shape. As it did so, it tasted the floor. Titanium, yes, but also copper. Titanium was a poor conductor, so Devin must have embedded a grid of copper.

Even as it lay there shuddering, it wondered what was wrong with Devin—what had driven him to this. He'd obviously become obsessed. Maybe it should have checked on him after what had happened, but there was little that it could do—other than deliver gifts.

Keeping its upper surfaces as still as possible, it carefully started to shift its weight away from the grid and onto dozens of tentacles that just fit within the space between the copper wires, all the while pointing an eye towards its captor.

Devin had put down the remote and was now trying to take pictures again, probably hoping that the electric shock would make it show up. He looked at the camera's screen then looked down at it through the window.

"I don't want to hurt you," he said, his voice almost pleading. "But I have to have proof. Have to show them..." He picked up the remote again and hit the button. When nothing happened, he hit it again, looking horrified.

It hoped that enough time had passed. It bunched itself up and then drove at the window. The plastic, weakened by stomach acid, warped, then gave way. It had to grab Devin to stop him from being hit by the flying chunks of plastic. Then, as gently as it could, it knocked him out.

The bedroom door was locked. It slid a tentacle into the lock and reshaped it until the pins clicked and the tumbler rotated open. It peered into the room through the tiny eye on the end of the tentacle.

There were two children—a boy of five and a girl of six. They were playing with toys that Devin had obviously put out for them, but there were tear tracks on both of their faces.

This was going to be tricky.

It reshaped and hardened a few tentacles into bells, then started to ring them softly. It was the sort of sound that the bells on reindeer might make. The little girl looked up, frowning.

Ho Ho Ho. It had a lot of practice with that one, and it genuinely sounded like a large man laughing, albeit with a bit of a stringy wheeze behind it. Now, both of the children were staring at each other.

Time to go children. A bit wheezy, but plausible. It opened the door slightly, then slipped down the stairs and waited. It took a few minutes for the children to build up their courage, but finally the door pushed open, and they stood there, holding hands.

There was a light over the stairs, and with a quickly shifted pair of tentacles it made a shadow on the wall—of a large man with a beard, and a sack over his shoulder. In previous centuries, that figure would have been terrifying, but today it was one of the most recognizable shapes on the planet. The children started down the stairs.

Just before they got to the turn, it slid away and opened the front door, then rolled at high speed to the neighboring house. This house had children and beautiful decorations. It must be safe. It pounded on the door.

There are children in danger. Help them.

The children were just coming out of the front door. With enormous effort, it puffed itself up into the shape it had shown as a shadow earlier, forcing bits of itself to color in a red body with white boots and a white beard. If they were even a little bit closer, the illusion wouldn't have worked, but from a distance, it was *just* good enough. It beckoned to the children, and they ran towards him.

Just then, the front door of the neighbor's house started to open. It used the distraction to thin itself out and turn gray before shooting up the wall. It waited until police cars and an ambulance pulled up at the house, then let itself float away.

The following year it was happy to see the two children back at home, apparently none-the-worse for wear. It delivered two especially large gifts under their tree, sucked up the cow mammary fluid and ate a cookie, then went on to finish its deliveries.

But instead of returning home, it travelled far upstate to make a final delivery.

Getting into the building was surprisingly easy. It entered through a disused coal chute, then worked its way through the vents until it found the right place.

Devin's room was not exactly a cell, though it was locked from the outside, and there were bars on the window. Even the children's parents had thought that a psychiatric hospital made more sense for him than a prison, and the prosecutor had not pushed the issue.

He'd started to decorate the walls with hand-drawn images of uncanny creatures with lots of eyes and tentacles, as well as with maps of sightings, drawn from memory. Some of these drawings had been used at his trial.

It had to wait for Devin to finally fall asleep before unlocking the door with a tentacle, dropping the wrapped present on the table, and then withdrawing, locking the door after it. Technically, presents only went to children, but it could make its own decisions about when to break the rules, and Devin hadn't really had a proper childhood.

It slithered back into the vents. It was done for another year.

Devin didn't notice the parcel at first, then gaped at it, afraid it was a trick. Then he thought that it *really* was a trick—something to silence him, perhaps. But the monster had had an opportunity to do that a year ago and hadn't taken it.

But it was a bit pointless. The only thing he'd ever wanted, he'd never get. Still, it was Christmas. He picked up the package and opened it.

It was a framed photograph. At first, it just looked like Santa Claus, but if you looked really closely, you could see that it wasn't Santa Claus at all. The shape and the colors weren't quite right, and what should have been buttons and bells were actually eyeballs.

Devin stared at the picture for several long moments. Then, for the first time in years, he smiled.

About the Author

As well as writing fiction, Arlen Feldman is a software engineer, entrepreneur, maker, and computer book author—useful if you are in the market for some industrial-strength door stops. Some recent stories of his appear in the anthologies *Museum Piece*, *Particular Passages 4*, and Kevin J. Anderson's *Gilded Glass*, and in *Little Blue Marble* and *Nocturne* magazines, with more coming out soon. He lives in Colorado Springs, Colorado.

His website is cowthulu.com.

Mastodon: @cowthulu@mastodon.social

The Key to Christmas

by
Josh Morrey

The Key to Christmas

*S*adie pushed the stool against the cabinet in the kitchen and climbed up to peer onto the countertop. Her goal was the large tray of toffee Mommy had made that afternoon. Sadie was hoping to snitch a piece before the toffee got divided up for the Christmas plates Mommy was making for friends and neighbors.

To her disappointment, the counter was bare. No treats, no candy, not even cookies. All she found were some crumbs, a few Christmas cards, and a strange little object lying beside one of the cards. Curious, Sadie stretched out her little arm, straining to reach the thing. Her tiny fingers were just able to touch it, and she dragged it across the counter towards her. Prize gained; Sadie climbed down before examining it.

She thought it was a key of some kind, but it was different. Not like the keys Mommy and Daddy used for the car or the house, this one was long and skinny, with a fancy handle on one end and three big teeth on the other. She'd never seen anything like it, and she wondered what it was for.

A racket sounded from the nearby stairs as Sadie's oldest brother Steven bounded down, jacket in hand.

"Hey, kiddo," Steven said. He tousled Sadie's hair as he passed, stopping to pull open the fridge. He was tall and skinny, with brown hair like Sadie's, and bright, happy eyes.

Sadie smiled as she watched him. She liked Steven, and not just because he was her brother. He was always nice to her—unlike Simon, who could be really mean sometimes—and Steven was old enough to drive! She wanted to be just like him someday.

Sadie looked at the key in her hands again. If anyone knew what it was for, Steven would.

"Steven?" she said, walking over to the fridge.

"Hmm?" Steven mumbled. He shut the door and looked at Sadie. A large, red apple was jammed into his mouth. Sadie giggled. He pulled the apple out with a big bite. "What's up, kiddo?" he said as he chewed. "I have to go soon."

Sadie held up the key. "What's this for?" she asked.

Steven looked at the object, then at the cards on the counter, then back at Sadie. A tiny smile tugged at the corners of his mouth. He crouched in front of her and took the key, looking at it closely.

"Oh, this is important," he said.

"It is?" she said.

"Yup. You found the Key to Christmas."

"The Key to Christmas? What's that?"

"It's *very* special. Don't lose it." He returned the key and stood back up.

"But what does it do?" she asked, turning it over in her hands.

"That," he said, bopping her on the nose, "you'll have to figure out for yourself. Now I gotta run. Love you, kid." He kissed her on the head and hurried out the door to the garage. It was Saturday, which meant Steven had to go to work.

"Love you, too," she muttered quietly as she stared at the key.

The Key to Christmas.

What was that? She'd never heard of it. Granted, this was only her sixth Christmas, so maybe she still had a lot to learn, but no one had ever said anything about a key before. What did it open? A door? A treasure? Did it have something to do with Santa? Sadie really wanted to know. Why hadn't Steven explained it better before he left? She decided she would have to ask someone else, so she left the kitchen to find Mommy or Daddy.

In the family room she found Simon playing a racing game on the TV. Simon was ten, and was around a lot more than Steven, since he couldn't drive. His hair was red, like Mommy's, and his face was covered in freckles. Daddy liked to tease that a strawberry had sneezed in Simon's face when he was a baby. Simon was usually nice to Sadie, but sometimes he said mean things. He always said sorry later...when Mommy or Daddy made him.

"Simon, do you know what the Key to Christmas is?" she asked.

Eyes glued to the screen, Simon said, "The what?"

"The Key to Christmas."

He mashed the buttons on the game controller. "Oh, that's easy. It's all the presents."

Sadie stared at him. That didn't even make sense. The key is presents? No, it's not, it's a key. The presents are wrapped and under the Christmas tree. The key is in her hand. Maybe he didn't understand her. "But—"

"Shh!" he hissed. "I'm winning, and you're gonna mess me up." He leaned to the left as his car went around a corner.

Sadie shut her mouth, scowling at him. He probably didn't really know what the Key to Christmas was anyway. She left him to his game and went looking for Mommy.

Mommy was in the laundry room, pulling a pile of clean clothes out of the dryer when Sadie walked in.

"Mommy?" Sadie said.

"Hi, honey," Mommy replied. "What are you doing?"

"I'm trying to learn what the Key to Christmas is."

Mommy put the last of the clothes in the laundry basket and opened the washer. Like most Saturdays, she wore a pair of Grampy's old overalls, with holes in both knees, and her faded, but brightly colored "chore shirt" as she called it. "The key to Christmas? Where did you hear that?" Mommy asked. She pulled out wet towels a few at a time and shoved them into the dryer.

"Steven told me."

"I see. So, what did he tell you?"

"Nothing, he just left for work. Do *you* know what the Key to Christmas is?" Sadie held the key up, but Mommy didn't look.

"Well, to me, the key to Christmas is helping people who are less fortunate than ourselves. It's about serving others."

Mommy's answer made less sense than Simon's. Sadie was about to ask more when the doorbell rang.

Mommy slammed the dryer shut and pushed the button. The dryer hummed to life. "That's probably the pizza guy," she said. "Go tell Grampy it's dinner time, okay?"

Before Sadie could reply, Mommy hurried out of the room. Sadie tucked the key into her pants pocket, though it was so big the top stuck out. Maybe Grampy would know what the Key to Christmas was.

Sadie walked down the stairs to the basement where Grampy lived. He'd moved in with them after Grammy died. Sadie didn't remember Grammy; she was just a baby then. But she sure loved Grampy and played with him almost every day.

Grampy was sitting in the big, soft chair in his bedroom, reading a book, like always. His white hair and beard made him look like Santa Claus, except that he was too skinny. He sure was jolly enough, though. Grampy looked up when Sadie walked in.

"Well, hello, darlin'," he said, his eyes lighting up. He slipped a piece of paper into his book and set it on the table beside the chair. "Come here."

Sadie climbed up into his lap. He wrapped his big arms around her and squeezed until she giggled. He smelled like spice cake.

"What are you doing down here, little one?" Grampy asked.

"I want to know what the Key to Christmas is, but everyone keeps giving me weird answers." Sadie snuggled into Grampy's warm sweater.

"The key to Christmas, eh?" Grampy said. "Seems to me you already know the answer."

"I do?" Sadie said, looking up at him.

"Sure, you do. Whose birth do we celebrate at Christmas?"

"Baby Jesus."

"That's right. He's the reason for the season, as they say. Without him, there would be no Christmas, no atonement, and no resurrection."

Sadie pursed her lips. "What's *rez-nur-ecshun*?"

Grampy laughed. "Well, that means we all get to live again, and see each other again, after we die."

Sadie sat up. "So…you'll get to see Grammy?"

"That's right." Grampy nodded. "And it's all because of what Jesus did for us. That's why we celebrate his birth. Without him, we would all be lost."

"So that makes him the Key to Christmas?" Sadie asked. She still didn't understand what that had to do with the key poking out of her pocket.

"Well—"

"Dad?" Mommy called from upstairs.

"Oh!" Sadie gasped. "I was supposed to tell you the pizza is here."

"*Pizza?* And you didn't tell me?" Grampy tickled Sadie. As she squealed with laughter, he shouted. "We'll be right up!"

Grampy stood, threw Sadie over his shoulder, and carried her upstairs, tickling her all the way. She didn't even mind that the key kept poking her in the side.

In the kitchen, Mommy and Daddy were getting plates and cups out while Simon sat at the table playing a game on Dad's phone. Grampy dropped Sadie into her seat and sat next to her. Daddy passed the plates around while Mommy set the pizza in the middle of the table. It smelled like cheese and pepperoni, Sadie's favorite.

"Let's say a prayer," Daddy said, snatching his phone away from Simon, who gave a whine.

Sadie started to fold her arms, but the key was still poking her in the side. She quickly pulled it out and set it on the table next to her plate.

"What's that, Sadie?" Mommy asked.

"It's the Key to Christmas," Sadie replied.

"Wait," Simon said. "*That's* what you were talking about?"

Sadie nodded. "I found it on the counter. Steven said it was the Key to Christmas, but I don't know what that means, and no one will tell me."

"No one will tell you?" Daddy said. "Who did you ask?"

"Everybody," Sadie whined. "Simon said the Key to Christmas is presents, Mommy said it was helping other people, and Grampy said it was Baby Jesus. I just want to know what it opens."

Mommy and Daddy smiled at each other. Simon laughed. "It's just a tree ornament, dummy. It came with the Thornocks' Christmas card this year. It doesn't open anything."

"Simon!" Mommy snapped.

Simon looked away and slid down in his seat. "Well, it doesn't."

Daddy gave Simon one of his *you're in trouble* looks, then looked at Sadie. "Well, sweetie, everyone is right."

Sadie didn't understand.

"Sometimes words have more than one meaning," Daddy said. "Like the word 'bark.' It can mean the stuff on the side of a tree, or—"

"Or the sound a dog makes!" Sadie said, grinning.

Daddy smiled. "That's right. Well, it's the same thing with the word 'key.' It can mean an object that unlocks things—like the one you have—or it can also mean the most important part of something. So, while you were asking about a physical key, everyone else was telling you what they thought is the most important part of Christmas. Do you understand?"

Sadie stared at her little key. "I think so."

"To Simon, the most important part of Christmas is *giving* presents, right Simon?"

Simon shrugged.

"And to Mommy, the most important part of Christmas is serving others. And to Grampy, the most important part of Christmas is our Savior, Jesus Christ."

"What do you think is the Key to Christmas, Daddy?" Sadie asked.

Daddy looked around the table. "Well, I agree with everyone else's keys. But I think there's one more I would add...you."

"Me?" Sadie said in surprise.

Daddy laughed. "All of you. My family. The ones I love the most. I think the key to Christmas is love."

Mommy reached over and squeezed Daddy's hand. Grampy nodded. Simon even sat up straighter in his chair and smiled at Sadie.

Sadie looked at each of them, thinking about what Daddy said. "Well," she said after a moment. "If the Key to Christmas is love...then maybe what it unlocks is our hearts."

Daddy smiled bigger. "I think you're right, sweetie."

Mommy wiped a tear away from her eye.

Simon looked at her and snickered. "Are you *crying*?"

"No," Mommy said with a sniffle. "Of course not. Now, somebody say the prayer, the pizza's getting cold."

Everyone laughed.

"Wait," Sadie said. She grabbed the key from the table and climbed down from her chair. She hurried around to the living room where the Christmas tree stood tall and beautiful, with twinkling lights and ornaments hanging all over it. She thought about hanging the key on the tree—Simon had said it was an ornament—but it would just get lost among all the other decorations.

Instead, she walked over to the little table beside the tree; the one that held the figures of Mary and Joseph and the shepherds. Sadie gently placed the key in the little manger, right next to baby Jesus.

Then, she ran back to have pizza with her family.

About the Author

Josh Morrey loves a good story, in any format. Whether it's novels, short stories, video games, movies, TV, bedtime, campfire, or anything else that tells a captivating tale of what it means to be human. He's been writing stories of his own for nearly twenty years. Most of those were submitted to Writers of the Future and, when they didn't win, were forgotten about in some subfolder or another on his computer. Six of those submissions earned Honorable Mention in Writers of the Future, and one a Semi-Finalist. The struggle continues. In the meantime, Josh has finally started searching for homes for these long-forgotten tales. He lives in Utah with his wife and four amazing kids. Find him online at www.joshmorrey.com.

Time to Remember

by
Katie Kent

Time to Remember

Your sister would have loved it here."
I push the half-eaten slice of carrot cake to the side of my plate, my appetite suddenly gone as my stomach churns. "Why do you have to do that, Mum? We were having a nice time. Why do you have to ruin things?"

She sighs, looking into my eyes and reaching for my hand. "We can't avoid mentioning her forever, Vicky. I'm sad too, but she would want us to get on with our lives."

I pull my hand out of her grasp. Sad? I'm not sad. I'm angry. Really angry. How could Kerry do that to me? I'd always thought we were close.

"We need to go." The temperature suddenly feels too warm, the lights too bright, the chatter too loud. I'm struggling to breathe, feeling lightheaded. I want to stand up and leave, get some air, but I don't trust my legs to carry me out of here.

Mum reaches across the table for my hand again, but I pull it away. Pins and needles are shooting through my body. "Vicky, talk to me."

Her voice sounds far away, as if I'm in a dream. I wish I *was* dreaming. Since Kerry died, my life has been more like a nightmare. I went to bed one day thinking everything was fine, and when I woke up the next day, Kerry was gone. I can still hear Mum's screams in my ears.

"What can I do?" Mum asks.

Nothing. Unless you know how to bring her back.

Mum calls one of the waitresses over and asks her for a glass of water. "My daughter isn't feeling very well," she says.

I'm fine. It's your other daughter who wasn't well. And no one knew. She didn't even leave a note. When I heard the paramedics mention suicide, I'd almost laughed. Kerry wasn't depressed. She'd always been one of those people who was always happy. She was a glass half-full kind of girl, always telling me to be more positive. But then Mum told me she'd found her with the empty pill bottle next to her. There was no denying the evidence. At the inquest, they said that Kerry had taken her own life. It was an open-and-shut case. It wasn't just my sister I'd lost. I'd also lost everything I thought I'd known about her.

The waitress comes back quickly with the water. Mum thrusts the glass in front of me and encourages me to drink. Soon, I am feeling a bit more normal.

"Are you going to finish that?" She points to the remainder of the cake on my plate.

I shake my head. "You have it if you want. I'm not hungry." It's not quite the truth, but I doubt I could keep anything down now. I'd actually had my eye on the red velvet cake, but that had been Kerry's favourite, and I didn't need reminders.

Mum gives me that look, the worried one that I've seen a lot of lately, but luckily, she seems to realise that now isn't the time for another argument.

After she asks the waitress for the bill, I stand up. "Gotta pee," I announce, taking a few paces in the direction of the toilets.

She touches my shoulder with her hand. "I should come with you. What if you have another funny turn?"

"I'll take my phone." I retrace my steps, take my phone out of my bag, and slip it into the pocket of my jeans.

As I walk past the other tables, I see the big Christmas tree with the tinsel wrapped around it, the lights sparkling and the angel standing proudly on the top, and realise that Mum was spot on. Kerry *would* have loved it here. She always loved Christmas; it was her favourite time of the year. The thought hits me like a sledgehammer and I shake my head to try and dislodge it. This is Mum's fault, bringing her up like that. I keep trying to forget what happened, but Mum seems determined to remind me at every available opportunity.

After using the toilet, I look at myself in the mirror and wince. My blonde hair looks lifeless, my skin blotchy. There are dark rings under my eyes—I've not been able to get a good night's sleep since it happened. When I do drift off to sleep, I'm often woken again by nightmares of Kerry. I dream that she's drowning and that no one is there to rescue her.

Not once did she tell me she was struggling. I could have helped. I could have talked her out of it, reminded her of what she had to live for. But she didn't give me the chance. Whatever was going on in her head, she chose to hide it, chose to pretend that everything was fine.

You don't get to do this to me. When she made the choice to take the pills, she ruined not only her life but also mine. I take a deep breath, trying to dislodge Kerry from my mind, then turn around and walk back to Mum.

She's looking around the room when I enter, a wistful look on her face. I clear my throat, and her expression immediately rearranges itself into a smile. "Ready to go?"

I nod, and she stands up and gathers her things.

"What shall we do now?" she asks when we get outside. It's a cold December day, and there's frost on the ground.

I pull my coat around me, put my gloves on and shrug. "I don't mind."

"How about we go over to Harrods? We could buy some new Christmas decorations." Her eyes don't leave my face as she makes the suggestion.

"No." I know what she's doing, and I'm not having any of it. I don't want to celebrate Christmas this year; too many bad memories. We should never have come here. "Let's just go home."

She sighs again, and I feel a sudden stab of guilt, but I can't do this. The lid is threatening to come off the bottle I've tightly bundled my emotions into. "Okay," she says. "If that's what you want."

"It is."

We walk in silence until we come to the outdoor ice rink. Kids and adults glide around on the ice, laughing gleefully. I glance at it and start to walk in the other direction, but Mum grabs hold of my sleeve.

"Want to have a go?" she asks. "We've got time."

"No."

"Vicky…" she begins. "You and Kerry used to love ice skating."

"Used to." I try to push away the image of me and my sister on the ice. As the eldest, she took it upon herself to teach me how to skate. Later, we went skating together, trying to outdo each other to complete a lap of the rink first. She always won, although sometimes I came close.

"She always wanted to go to an outdoor rink. Do you remember?"

I feel like steam is shooting out of my ears, just like in the cartoons. How many times have I told Mum that I don't want to be reminded of Kerry? But she keeps on bringing her up, over and over again.

"I want to go home." I take off before Mum can argue again, striding as fast as I can towards the train station, my head down so that I don't have to see any more happy people. How I wish I could turn back time, be one of those people who are looking forward to Christmas. Mum struggles to keep up, but I don't slow down—until we get to a street performer.

People are in my way, and I am naturally forced to slow my pace. As I push through the crowd, I turn my head to the side. A small guy dressed as an elf is street dancing to pop songs. He's not bad, actually. Music is booming out of an old-fashioned ghetto blaster. As I pass, one song ends and everyone breaks out into applause. Then 'Last Christmas' starts, and it stops me in my tracks.

There's a lump in my throat as a flashback of Kerry singing along to this song hits me. This was always her favourite Christmas song. Tears are pricking at my eyes, and I swallow. There are stars in my vision.

"Vicky, are you alright?" Mum has managed to catch up to me.

"No, I'm not okay. I miss her, Mum." The tears finally start to flow, then. I'm sobbing so hard that people are looking at us and whispering.

I feel Mum's arm around me, and I manage to manoeuvre myself—half walking and half being led by her—to some steps up to the nearby market. I flop down onto the step, still crying. Now I've started, it's like I can't stop. I'd cried when I'd found out Kerry had died, of course, but not since I found out *how* she died. I didn't even cry at her funeral. I was too angry with her. I'd felt really out of it whilst Mum had cried next to me. I hadn't even tried to comfort her or anything. It was like I wasn't even in my own body, like I was watching it from far away.

It's a few minutes before I notice that Mum is crying, too. Not like me, but there are tears rolling down her cheeks as she sits next to me on the step.

"Mum?" I manage to get myself under control. My voice is croaky, my face wet.

"I'm sorry," she says, sniffing. "For bringing you here. But you were so closed off, so detached about Kerry's death—I hoped all the Christmas things might trigger something."

I clench my fists. "That's not fair."

Mum's face pales, but she continues speaking. "I just wanted you to admit that you needed help." She shakes her head. "I think about what Kerry did every day. I wish I'd noticed there was something up. I can't help but feel responsible."

"That's how I feel." I sigh. "How could I not notice that she was so depressed?"

Mum tries to smile. "Whatever your sister was going through, she kept it to herself. There was nothing either one of us could have done. And we'll never know why she did it. That's hard, but we have to find a way to move past it."

I lower my head.

"It's too late to help Kerry. But I don't want to lose another daughter. I could see you struggling, and I couldn't bear to sit by and do nothing. I wanted to suggest counselling, but I knew you weren't in the right headspace for it. Maybe now?"

I trace a shape on the step with my foot. "Yeah, maybe. I've been trying to forget her. I thought it would be less painful that way. That's why I got angry when you kept mentioning her name. But I don't want to forget her, Mum. I want to remember my sister."

Mum reaches out her hand and puts it on my shoulder. It's comforting. "What happened to Kerry, it was shocking and tragic, but let's try and honour her memory by thinking about the good times we had with her. Especially at Christmas. She'd want us to do that. Remember how excited she always got when we put the tree up? She'd dance along to the songs as she hung the decorations up."

I nod. This year, our house is bare. I had refused to help Mum with the tree last weekend; it would have been too painful. I take her hand. "Is it too late to go to Harrods? Perhaps we could buy some new decorations. Maybe purple ones. And when we get home, let's put the tree up." Purple had been Kerry's favourite colour.

"I think that would be lovely." Mum's voice wavers, and I squeeze her hand.

I pull myself to my feet. "It's time to remember Kerry."

About the Author

Katie Kent is a writer of fiction and non-fiction living in the UK with her wife, cat, and dog. She likes to write stories, mostly for a YA audience, particularly about LGTBQ characters, mental illness, time travel and the future—sometimes all in the same story!

Her stories have been published in *Youth Imagination*, *Limeoncello*, *Breath and Shadow* and *Northern Gravy*, amongst others, and in a handful of anthologies including *The Trouble with Time Travel*, *Summer of Speculation: Catastrophe*, *Growth* and *My Heart to Yours*. She won second place in *Writing Magazine's* 2022 'Love Story' competition.

Her non-fiction, mostly mental health-related, can be found in publications including *The Mighty*, *You & Me Magazine*, *Ailment*, *OC87 Recovery Diaries* and *Feels Zine*. You can follow her on Twitter @uniKH80 and visit her website at: www.katiekentwriter.com

Holiday Singles

by
Donea Lee Weaver

Holiday Singles

As she drove through the snowy roads to Claire's boutique, Sam tempered her urge to glare at the tinsel-strewn Christmas trees and candy cane decorations the city had posted on every light pole along Main Street. She didn't have time to obsess over the fact that this was the first Christmas in twenty years that she would not spend enjoying a month-long collection of whimsical Yuletide activities with her husband's family. That all she had planned for was the usual Christmas Eve dinner with her sisters and their families, and now she'd be the only "single" there.

She had a dress to buy.

Because there was this one other thing...

"A Christmas mixer for single, newly divorced people who have nothing better to do for the holidays, huh? Could be fun." Sam's best friend, Lena, snickered as she pointed at an open parking spot in front of the boutique.

"You're hilarious." Sam's response was dead-pan sarcasm, but she couldn't help grinning. "I do need to stop feeling this way, though. You're right. It could be fun. Funner than whatever Tom has planned."

"That's the spirit." Lena gave her that bright smile of hers and nodded. "But, I get it, hun. You don't have to explain it to me. This will be a rough season."

"I know you do." Sam reached over to give her best friend's hand a squeeze. "God, I love you."

"I know." Lena winked, and then got out of the car.

Sam followed suit. Really, she'd had choices here. But her daughters made her promise to go to this thing, and to look "bomb," whatever that meant, and she didn't want to break a promise.

As they walked to the storefront, a silver fox strutting down the sidewalk distracted her from where she was stepping. The ice, clearly, was out to get her.

"Oh, noooo..." Her voice lilted in tune with her body as her right foot slipped up in front of her, and she seemed to fall in slow motion. She could see Lena reaching out to her, their fingertips barely missing each other's. She clenched her eyes shut, waiting for the inevitable.

And then, like a lucky dream, she felt a strong hand on her back, and when she opened her eyes, she was greeted by piercing blue ones with long dark lashes and salt-and-pepper eyebrows.

"Woah, woah, woah. That was almost some kind of fall," Mr. Silver-Fox said.

"On my ass, almost." *What* was she saying?

Lena muffled a snicker as the man righted Sam and lead her to a safe spot on the concrete. He seemed to be suppressing a good laugh himself.

"Well, then. I think you'll be good here." He nodded to both of them with a handsome grin on his face. "Ladies."

Sam's gaze lingered on the guy's backside for a good three seconds before she realized she hadn't thanked him. "Oh. Thank you!" she called after him.

He waved a hand but didn't look back.

"Good one," Lena said, letting go of the giggle.

Whimpering, Sam's glare returned as she pointed at the boutique window. "Maybe I'll go with that red dress. It will match nicely with my face."

Singles party. Oh yeah—she'd do great.

Spence couldn't keep the smile off his face. *That* woman today. Wow. Her bright green eyes dazzled as she stared at him and uttered those ridiculous and charming words.

"Ass." He chuckled. "Hilarious."

"What are you smiling at?" his sister asked, as she smoothed a holly printed tablecloth over another table.

"Nothing," he said, picking up another box of gifts to put under the tree. But then he stopped and put the box on the table. "Well, okay. There was this woman."

"Oooh. A woman, huh?" Sally winked. "Attractive?"

"Oh, yeah."

"Did you talk to her?"

He scratched the stubble on his chin. "Kind of. I saved her from slipping on the ice in front of Claire's."

"So, knight in shining armor then? Nice. Did you get her number?"

Spence shook his head. "You do know I'm an idiot, right?"

"Since birth." She gave him another wink.

"Thanks, sis."

He picked the box back up and trudged over to the tree: a bushy seven-foot blue fir Sally and her husband had chopped down themselves in the Uintas. His sister's decorations were spectacular, all ice-blue and silver, with punches of red here and there. Thank goodness she oversaw all that. If it had been him, the tree would have looked like someone ran by and just chucked ornaments on there in passing.

"Tree looks awesome, Sal. As usual," he called out to her.

"Thanks! I do have a knack for it, don't I?"

He nodded, knowing she couldn't see him.

"Well? Don't I?"

"Yes, of course."

Sally and Jack had hosted a divorced singles holiday mixer every year for the last seven years. Spence never had occasion to attend, until this year. His ex had graciously waited until *after* Christmas last year to confess she was leaving him for her Pilates instructor. A woman, to boot. Well. Whatever made her happy.

Spence still hadn't wanted to come to the mixer this year either, until Sally roped him into helping her plan the whole darn thing, since Jack would be out of town on business with a new job.

Glancing at his watch, he realized that by this time tomorrow, he'd be pulling out his not-so-sick dance moves among a throng of equally sad and abandoned divorcees, all hoping to make some kind of connection before the big day came around—December 25th. Maybe they wouldn't be alone on Christmas after all. Maybe they wouldn't have to stroll up to the family dinner by themselves. Maybe they'd have a plus-one again. Maybe…

"Divorce sucks," he muttered, as he placed the last gift under the tree.

The house was aglow with multi-colored lights, strung along the eves. Lovely snow-flake shaped torches bordered both sides of the walkway that led from the street to the front door. And the host had the cutest Santa sleigh and reindeer décor staked out on the east side of her lawn. It was charming.

When Sam reached the front door, she was charmed again. The wreath... Wow. Beautiful, stunning, all the good words. She was both awed and a little ashamed. She hadn't even put a tree up yet. It seemed pointless in her downgraded space she lived in all alone, except for her mini dachshund, also named Sam. Although, the girls would be home soon from college for the holidays. Maybe she'd do something...

But then, the home she had shared with Tom never had Christmas lights strung outside either. He'd never wanted to bother with it. Smoothing out her dress—and yes, it was red— she pulled out a mirror compact to check her matching lipstick before knocking on the door.

A gorgeous woman in a sparkly green dress answered with a smile. "Welcome!"

Sam nodded. "You must have a wonderful husband."

The woman looked confused for a moment. "Umm, well yes. He is."

Not again. "Oh, and thank you. Yes. Sorry. I appreciate the invite." *Quit talking.* She stuck out her hand. "I'm Sam."

Her lovely host lifted a slender finger. "Oh, yes. You must be Maddy's and Justine's mom." She grabbed Sam's hand and welcomed her in. "Nice to finally meet you."

She hated the way her brain didn't work sometimes, but yes. She knew this woman. Or at least had heard her daughters' best friend talk about her mom lots of times. It seemed ridiculous to her that they'd never met in person before. Though Tom was never much of a social person and never wanted people at their house. It'd been a small miracle he'd agreed to his family's holiday shenanigans. But those were only once a year.

"Oh, my goodness, you're Tara's mom. Sally, right? It's so nice to meet you. Sorry for the..." Sam waved a hand over her entire being. "You know, all this awkwardness. I'm kind of mess most of the time."

"Honey, aren't we all?" Sally gave her a side hug. "No worries. And I hope you have fun tonight."

"Thanks." Sam grinned as she took in the interior of Sally's house with all its festive décor. "Your home is beautiful."

"Ah, thanks. I think it turned out pretty good myself." Another knock at the door, and Sally excused herself.

Sam wandered farther into a living room space that seemed too big for most houses but easily accommodated a few festive tables for the guests. There was a makeshift bar in one corner, a stunning decorated tree in another corner, and maybe a dozen people milling around the middle of all of it. Though their faces were muted other than the one tall, fit, and familiar looking silver fox among them.

Sam's whole body shivered, and she pulled out her phone.

He's here! she texted her best friend. Quickly dropping her phone back into her party clutch, she tried to look anywhere but at him. *Oh, dear God. He was here.*

Lady in red. Wow.

Spence noticed her the moment she sashayed in. How could you not? The woman was stunning—her long black hair a perfect accent to that dress and those lips. Wow, wow, wow, just wow. And when she met his gaze, he knew what he had to do.

"Excuse me, please." He left the group he'd been chatting with and made his way over to her.

He couldn't keep a grin contained as her eyes first went wide and then darted around for an escape route. He knew the feeling well. Hopefully she didn't do this because she didn't want to talk to him. But, as he drew closer, she returned his grin and pointed at him.

"It's you!"

"It's me."

Her lovely mouth dropped open to say something else, but no more words came out.

He thumbed over toward the bar. "Would a drink help?"

She gulped and nodded. "I actually think it would."

He offered his arm, and she took it, and the bartender/helpful-next-door-neighbor greeted them warmly as they approached.

"Happy holidays," he said. "What can I get you?"

"Anything the lady wants. Put it on my tab."

The guy with the drinks bit his lip and leaned in. "Um, the drinks are free."

She giggled beside him and the sound of it made his heart light. "I think he's joking."

"Oh." The bartender laughed. "Good one."

"What would you like...um?" He cringed as he realized he hadn't properly introduced himself.

"Sam," she said, grasping his hand and shaking it. "And you are?"

"Spence."

"Nice to meet you, Spence."

Boy, did he love the way his name sounded from her mouth. "Really nice to meet you, too."

"And I'm Jordan." The bartender said, offering them both a knowing wink that made Sam blush a little. "We've got eggnog with a twist, if you know what I mean. Or the other boring stuff."

"I'll take an eggnog," they said in unison.

With drinks in hand, Spence and Sam found a loveseat away from the crowd and sat in their respective corners. They sipped their eggnog in silence for a moment.

"So," Sam said, between glugs. "How do you know Sally?"

Spence was a little surprised she didn't already know the answer but shrugged it off. "I'm her brother."

"Oh." Sam's expression dimmed.

"But I am also divorced."

"Oh!" It brightened up again. "Gosh, no. I didn't mean that to sound like I thought it was a good thing. Although, you know..." She blushed again and flicked herself in the forehead. "My words get away from me sometimes."

She laughed the most adorably awkward laugh and Spence found himself grinning like an idiot again.

"If you're Sally's brother, then you probably know how this whole thing got started?"

He nodded. "Yes. Well, Sally's husband's brother got divorced about eight years ago. It was a mess. He was a hot mess. Sally said she'd never seen a grown man cry that much."

"Oh my."

"Exactly." Spence straightened for a second and panned the crowd for his sister. As he expected, she was entertaining her guests with a round of caroling. If he strained his ears a bit, it sounded like "Let it Snow." "Anyhow, they decided to throw this thing to cheer him up. He'd been trying the dating apps and all that good stuff, but most of the ladies he went out with were single, never-been-married, and I think the dynamic there is just different?"

Sam scooched closer to him and draped one arm over the back of the loveseat, so her fingertips were almost touching him. "How do you mean?"

How did he explain it? "They asked, so what'd you do wrong? A lot. Like it was his fault. Of course, this is Sally telling me his story. But it seems that once he was with other divorced people around him, the conversation changed."

Sam nodded. "Makes sense. I have one single friend. Bachelorette for life. And she said something similar to me, although it was more like, what did Tom do wrong? Though, it's not necessarily that he did anything wrong."

"So, if you don't mind me asking, why did your marriage end?"

She'd just taken a drink of eggnog and choked. He leaned forward to pat her back. "I am so sorry. None of my business?"

She covered a cough with her fingers. "I mean, you're getting straight to it. But that's okay." The grin she gave him let Spence know that she didn't take offense. Thank goodness. He was blunt, sometimes, but also just curious. "I guess I took a long time to realize that he just wasn't my person. Emotionally unavailable hermit. That's Tom. You?"

"Lesbian."

"Ah. Got it." And then she snort-laughed. "Oh my gosh, no. I'm sorry. I don't know why I'm laughing."

Spence started up too, couldn't help himself. And when they leaned forward at the same time to set their glasses on the coffee table, because they knew they'd spill if they didn't, they started laughing even harder.

"Shoot—now I'm crying!" Sam leaned forward, probably so the tears wouldn't mess with her eye makeup and Spence offered her the cocktail napkin he'd almost forgotten he'd grabbed and shoved into his pocket.

"I'm crying too." He laughed some more.

Dabbing at the corner of her eyes, she offered him an apologetic grin. "I'm so sorry. I don't know where that came from. I mean, good for her."

He quirked an eyebrow, and she quickly leaned closer to squeeze his hand.

"I mean, not good for you, of course. But she's living her true self now, so…" Sam sighed. "I should probably shut up."

"No, no. You're totally fine. And right. She is free to be herself now, and in the long run, I guess I can't really be mad about that."

"Spence!"

They both looked as Sally approached them, her face bright and shiny with a thin sheen of sweat. "So sorry to interrupt, but I need my brother's assistance for a minute."

"Of course." Sam leaned back into her corner of the loveseat.

Spence stood and grinned down at her. "I'll be right back."

And he would. Couldn't wait.

Sam sighed as she watched him walk away. Oh, she hoped he meant it—that he'd be back. That she hadn't somehow totally scared him away with the usual awkward garbage that came out of her mouth. Had she really laughed at the lesbian reveal? She rested her forehead in her hand, mortified. What was she thinking? She loved lesbians. Heck, she'd be one if she was attracted to women. But no. She was attracted to men. This man, Spence.

Shaking off her shame, she grabbed her eggnog and drained down the rest of it. Then promptly stood up to go get another one. *Sigh.*

"Ah, you're back," Jordan greeted. "Loved the eggnog, right?"

"Yes. It's delicious. Calories be damned." She handed him her tumbler and he filled it full. "Old family recipe?"

"Not sure. Sally took care of the catering. I'm just here to serve."

"And you *are* serving, honey. Yes, you are." A buxom blonde, in a tiny black dress that left little to the imagination, bounced up to the bar and patted Jordan on his cheek. "Can you give me a bourbon, neat? Pretty please?"

Sam couldn't decipher the look on Jordan's face.

"Yes, Ally. Coming right up."

She tried not to stare, but did this Ally person have a bit of mistletoe sticking out of her cleavage?

Ms. Curves snapped a look at Sam, giving her a quick once-over, and then offered a toothy smile. "I'm Ally."

"Sam." She tried hard not to do it, but her eyes panned down to the mistletoe again.

Ally plucked it from her bosom. "Oh, this?"

"Got big plans for it, do you?" What was she saying? Sam cleared her throat. "I'm sorry. That's so none of my business, and I didn't mean to stare. I mean, they're really nice." She waved a shaky hand over her own chest. "I'm a little jealous." Forcing a laugh, she cringed inwardly and died a little inside.

Jordan seemed to shrink a little as he slowly pushed Ally's drink toward her. Clearly, he didn't want to be any part of this conversation and Sam didn't blame him.

Ally just chuckled and then swigged down her drink in one long, glorious swallow. She hiccupped when she was done, and then pointed a sharp fingernail at Sam. "You're a little odd. But I kind of like it. And to answer your question, I do have big plans. Wish me luck?"

Sam just went with it. "Good luck."

Winking, she tapped her glass on the bar and turned to leave. "Thanks!"

Sam took a glug of her own drink and then pulled her phone out of her party clutch. She'd completely forgotten about her earlier text to Lena, or if Lena had texted back. The screen flashed on and, true to form, her bestie had been blunt with her advice.

Don't eff it up.

"Too late." She typed back. Was it, though?

Aside from the time they spent with family, Tom and Sam had barely socialized outside their home in the last twenty years. She was always turning down invites to holiday parties, birthday parties, anniversary parties, any kind of party in general. Except family ones, because those were easy and your family had to love you no matter what, right? Of course, she always encouraged her daughters to put themselves out there and enjoy their lives to the fullest. To be absolutely nothing like their mother.

And, to her relief, Maddy and Justine were well-adjusted social butterflies. But her?

She gazed around the room at the other divorced singles there, eating, laughing, singing, even a few dancing to "Jingle Bell Rock." Had Spence not immediately pulled her aside and started talking to her, would she be out there with them? Would she be giggling at that bald guy's stories like everyone else around him was? Would she be able to eat appetizers prettily, without spilling something on herself? Did she even remember how to dance?

"Mistletoe!"

The word, spoken so loudly and suggestively, pulled everyone's focus, including Sam's. And as she lifted on tiptoes to see over a mob of people in the middle of the room, she saw Ally holding the wretched plant over Spence's head. And before she could blink, that big-breasted woman laid a hard kiss on the would-be man of her dreams. The singles whooped and hollered, and Spence didn't seem to be struggling to get away.

Turning from them, Sam pushed the remainder of her drink away from her. "Thanks, Jordan. Happy Holidays."

And then she ran from that house as fast as her shaky legs would carry her.

Stunned, Spence felt his body go rigid as Jack's overly flirty cousin smooched the heck out of him. She did this every year, he'd been told. Picked who she deemed the most attractive guy in the room and pulled out her magic mistletoe. This year, apparently, it was him. He should probably be flattered. Instead, he hoped beyond hope that Sam wasn't watching this.

Pushing her away as gently as he could, he backed up a few steps. "Um. Thanks?" And then he shoved his way through the crowd and back to the loveseat. His shoulders sank when he found it empty. He glanced toward the bar. She wasn't there, either. Spence paced through the room, his chest tightening with every step, looking for the woman in red who'd stolen his heart.

Gone.

Finding his sister at the bar, her eyebrows crinkled with concern when she saw his face. "What's wrong?"

"Sam. Do you know where she went? Did she leave? Maybe she's just in the bathroom or something?"

Jordan snorted. "No, dude. She bailed. Right after she saw Ally kissing you."

Crap.

Sam had taken Friday off work to get ready for the party. Today was Sunday. The dress still laid in a pile on her bedroom floor, and she'd been slumped on the couch for two days straight, stuffing her face with gingerbread and candy-cane ice cream. Luckily, the girls were visiting their dad first this weekend. Poor baby Sam. The little guy had been left alone to deal with her depression and bad food choices.

"Here buddy," she said, offering the dog the gingerbread man's leg. He chomped it down happily, and then snuggled up next to her side. "At least you really love me."

Oh, she was ridiculous. It's not like she'd even been dating since the divorce. And then she meets one random guy, has one random conversation with him at a party, sees him kissing some other chick and suddenly her life is a craptastic hellscape?

Yes. Sounded about right.

There was a knock on her door, and she groaned.

"Let me in, Sam. I know you're in there."

Lena.

Sam wanted to let her in, but she wanted to not move at all whatsoever even more. "You know where the key is," she shouted.

When her bestie came in and saw the state of her, she stood in front of the couch, arms crossed and glared at Sam with no sympathy in her eyes at all. "Are you serious?"

Sam licked the last of the ice cream from her spoon. "Leave me alone."

"Nope. Not gonna happen." Lena plopped on the couch next to her. "This is like last December all over again."

It was just about a year ago that her divorce had been final, and although it'd been for the best, it was still twenty years of her life gone. "This isn't remotely the same situation."

"You're right. I think you're even more pathetic now."

"Gee, thanks."

"That guy must really have been something."

"You saw him." Sam nudged her friend.

"In passing, but I didn't have a conversation with him. Didn't share a drink with the man. That was you."

Sam closed her eyes, sinking further into her couch, remembering the sound of his voice and the way he gazed at her over his glass of eggnog. Sparks. There had been undeniable sparks. She didn't even remember feeling something so strong, so immediately, for Tom all those years ago when they first got together. This guy was something special, and she'd totally blown it.

"I think it's too late. He must have thought I was a crazy person."

"Wrong." Lena handed her a slip of paper.

Sam sat up, confused, and took the note from her. "What's this?"

"Read it, silly."

She did. And she smiled for the first time in forty-eight hours.

He didn't know how Sally had managed it—something about her daughter telling Sam's daughters to tell Sam's best friend to get her ready for, well...whatever this was about to be. A date? He was just happy Sam had agreed to meet him. His sister's Christmas party ended up quite the fiasco.

But as he waited at the entrance to the town's Christmas village, he shivered with anticipation. He couldn't wait to see her again.

"Spence?"

Startled, he turned to see a beautiful pair of bright green eyes staring back at him.

"Sam." His first impulse was to go for a hug, and he started leaning that way, his arms widening to draw her in. Was it too soon? He started to back away, but she leaned in herself and embraced him.

"It's so good to see you again," she whispered in his ear, as she hugged him tight. "I'm sorry I left so abruptly the other night."

Man, he could swim in this hug for a lifetime. When she pulled away, he fought hard to suppress his disappointment that the hug ended.

"It's okay. That scene isn't for everyone. Trust me, I know."

Her smile was infectious. "Yeah, not sure what happened there. But I promise to stick around this time."

"Perfect."

Ice-melt crunched under their feet as they huddled together for more warmth and strolled through Christmas exhibits and all manner of lights. It was colder tonight than it had been, temperatures rumored to hit below thirty-two and the town might even get snow overnight. Sam's nose and the tips of her ears turned pink, and all Spence wanted to do was warm her up again.

"Hot chocolate?" he suggested.

"Ooh, I'd love some."

He ordered two large ones from a vendor cart on the corner, and they found a bench to sit on. Funny or not, their seating just happened to be under a string of mistletoe lights. He didn't think Sam noticed, at first. That was probably a good thing. But as she sipped her warm beverage, her eyes took in everything around her, eventually shifting upward.

"Mistletoe!"

People startled around them at the shouted word and Spence spewed all the drink he'd had in his mouth.

Sam snorted and just laughed and laughed and laughed. Wiping his mouth on his sleeve, he opened it to say something, but she held a finger up.

"Nope. That's not how it goes."

She put her drink down, and he followed suit. She angled her body toward him, and he did the same. Then Sam leaned in and started to close her eyes. His eyes widened. And then they blinked—fast. He couldn't make it stop. As she puckered those beautiful lips of hers, he so wanted to do the same. What was stopping him? The closer she got, the more his heart raced. And when she was millimeters away from kissing him?

He swerved.

When her lips met rough stubble, her eyes popped open, and she realized what had just happened. He'd dodged her kiss. He'd dodged her kiss? Well, if her ears had been cold before, they were enflamed with embarrassment now.

She pulled away. "Sorry," she mumbled, grabbing her hot chocolate from the bench.

He didn't say anything.

"I thought it'd be funny, you know. Because of the other night." Still nothing. "Clearly, I was wrong." She moved to stand up, but he grabbed her arm.

"Sam," he started. He was clearly struggling with an excuse. "Look, I'm flattered, but…"

"You can stop there. It's okay. Too soon, right? We barely know each other."

He shook his head, his eyes looking mournful. "That's not it, exactly."

Oh, God. Was it something worse then? Did her breath stink? Was he not attracted to her after all? Was he just being nice, here?

"I just haven't kissed a woman since Nicole. My ex."

Sam's eyebrows crinkled. "Um. The party?"

"Ally doesn't count. What I mean is that I haven't kissed a woman I've actually been interested in. I just want to make sure it's right first. Does that make sense?"

"Sure." She bit her lip. *Actually, no.* "It's fine. I get it. I didn't read it right. It's fine."

He sipped his drink, then sighed. "It's not that I'm not interested in you."

He wasn't exactly saying that he was either. Shoot. The urge to buy another gallon of candy-cane ice cream grew strong.

"It's fine," she said for a third time. If he was as smart as he looked, he would know that it wasn't fine. Not by a long shot.

Spence stood and offered his hand. "Would you like to look at some more displays? I hear there's a great one at the other end of the park, of the North Pole."

Dismissing his offered hand, like the child she was on occasion, she stood and shrugged. "Sure."

Sally glared at him over her kitchen table, after he gave her the recap of his date with Sam.

"Oh, that poor woman," she said, shaking her head at him. "What is wrong with you?"

Spence slumped further down into his chair. "I don't know."

Rubbing her eyebrow, his sister's expression got more bewildered as he imagined all the things going through her head.

"I mean, you do like her, don't you?"

"Yep."

"And you're attracted to her?"

"Oh, yeah."

She held up three fingers. "And you said she was funny. Good sense of humor."

He wanted to sob laugh. "Great sense of humor."

Sally wadded up her napkin and chucked it at his head. "Bro. You're an idiot."

"It's true."

She reached over to stack his empty plate on top of hers and then took them over to the kitchen sink. "So, what are you going to do about it?"

That was a very good question.

Another week went by, and Sam hadn't heard a peep from Spence. Not that she really expected to. Well, at least it was over before anything had really started. The sad truth? She'd hoped that she wouldn't be alone for Christmas. Sure, she'd have her girls with her, but it was a different kind of alone. If she was being completely honest with herself, as much as she'd fought against going to that divorcee Christmas mixer, she'd kind of hoped that

49

she'd come away from it with a…not necessarily a happily ever after. But at least a happily for now kind of thing.

If it didn't last, that would have been okay. She'd at least have someone around…for a little while.

Though, Spence wasn't exactly an HFN. He was the type of man you wanted to spend the rest of your life with.

"Justine. Maddy," she called. "Come help me wrap these presents, will you?"

Her girls padded out into the living room, all giggles and light and full of life. Maddy leaned down to give Sam a hug and kissed her cheek. "You know you're the best mom ever, right?"

Sam smirked. "It's true, of course. But I feel there's an ulterior motive here."

The girls looked between themselves, wringing their hands together in that way they did when they didn't want to tell their mom something.

"Spit it out."

Justine sat in the chair next to her, scooting close enough that the legs were touching. "So, remember how we were at Dad's last weekend?"

"I'm old, not senile."

Her daughter nervous-giggled. "Right, right."

Sam looked up at Maddy. "What's going on? Just tell me. I'm sure it's fine."

There was that look again.

Maddy sat in another chair and scooched in close so that Sam was now sandwiched between them. Each girl took one of her hands and Sam started to get nervous. This couldn't possibly be good.

"So…Dad's been dating this woman."

First she'd heard about it. "How long?"

Maddy shrugged. "Six months or so."

Sam snatched both of her hands away and clasped them together. "How long have you known this?"

Justine shrank away from her. "Six months or so."

"Oh, my goodness. Girls!" Sam backed away and stood up. She started pacing around the table. "Why didn't you tell me?"

They clung together, looking pathetic and apologetic. "We knew it'd probably hurt your feelings. You've been so sad lately, and when he told us, it was right around your birthday so that didn't seem like the right time, and when they got engaged…"

"He's engaged!" Sam sat down again, but on the opposite side of the table.

Justine cleared her throat. "Yeah, earlier this month. On the one-year anniversary of your divorce."

Sam clenched her eyes shut for a moment to think about how she could react to this news. There was one of two ways. Shooing anger away, she shrugged. "Well, good for him."

Maddy's eyes narrowed. "Really?"

Sam reached across the table to grab her daughters' hands again. "Sure. I mean, I don't want to be married to him. But, if someone else does, more power to them."

"Well, they are getting married." Justine confirmed.

Sam's neck kinked.

"The day after Christmas," Maddy said. "In Vegas. And they want us to be there."

Fantastic. Now she really would be alone on Christmas.

Spence slogged through the aisles at the grocery store. His heart had been heavy since he last saw Sam. Heck, everything had been heavy. And he hadn't had a good night's sleep for almost a week. It's what he deserved, honestly. Not only had he let her down with that attempted kiss, but he also hadn't even bothered to check in with her since.

Yep. He was some kind of jerk.

He drew a crumpled list from his jeans pocket and smoothed it out to read it. What had Sally asked him to buy again? More cranberry sauce?

He turned a corner and his cart bumped up against another one, making a hard clinking noise that made his headache worse. "Oh, sorry."

"Sorry," she said it at the same time.

Sam.

"Oh, it's you," she said. It was the most annoyed he thought he'd ever heard a woman sound in his presence.

Smiling, because he wanted to give her one, he pulled his cart out of the way. "Sam. Hello. How are you?"

She dragged her purse over a pint of ice cream. "I'm good. You?"

"Oh, good. Yeah, you know. Just picking up a few more things for Christmas dinner with the fam." He shrugged.

She grinned at him, but it seemed forced. "Oh. Well. Good luck with that."

She pushed past him, before he could say anything else, and it crushed him.

Yep. Jerk.

Utterly alone at her family's Christmas Eve dinner, all she could think about was Spence as she shoveled a second helping of scalloped potatoes into her mouth. Justine and Maddy were in Vegas with their dad. Little Sam was at home, probably curled up on the couch, waiting for her to come home. Although, she didn't know why. She hadn't exactly been a sugar plum to be around lately.

She gazed around the table at her three sisters. Somehow, they had all managed to find "the right one" the first time. They drank merrily with their significant others, and laughed, and leaned into each other for little smooches here and there, and it kind of made her want to vomit.

No. Dang it. She was happy for them, really. Of course she was. And she loved Christmas. She always had. It was, normally, her favorite time of year. She loved the snow, and the lights, and getting presents and giving presents, and spending time with people she loved. She loved the music and the tangible spirit of the season.

"Excuse me." No one really paid attention as she left the table. They were wrapped up in their holiday merriment, just like they should be. She ran to the bathroom, locking herself inside and took a long, hard look at herself in the mirror.

"So," she whispered at her reflection. "What do you want for Christmas, Sam?"

She didn't want the tears that threatened. No. She was stronger than that. She needed to quit looking at her divorce as a bad thing. Tom had given her the opportunity to start fresh. Just like he was doing. So, what did she want?

"Spence."

"Sam? Hun? You in there?" her sister Keely asked.

She cleared her throat, took a deep breath, and smiled before opening the door to her sister.

"You're not hiding in here, are you?" Her sister pushed her way inside and grabbed Sam in a side hug. "I'm sorry, sis. I guess I didn't realize how hard today would be for you."

Sam hugged her back. "It's a little hard. But...you know. I think I'm going to be okay."

Keely pulled away for a moment to study Sam's face. "You sure? I can make some excuse for you if you want to leave?"

"And miss out on Kate's dessert? I'm divorced, not crazy!"

Keely snort-laughed and hugged her again. "I love you."

"I love you, too."

After gifts and two big helpings of her sister's famous Dutch apple pie, Sam drove home on quiet streets and the snow began to fall. The way the flakes glowed under the streetlights was magical. It lifted her spirit, a little more. Yes, it'd been a hard year. And these holidays had...well, they were just different. But she had more candy-cane ice cream at home, and all of this would pass. Eventually. It'd get better. It would.

She turned the corner to her condo and blinked. Hard. Gazing around at her neighbor's houses, she made sure she recognized the neighborhood, because the home she was headed to didn't look the way she'd left it. Brilliant white lights were strung along the front eaves and around the door. She parked and got out to inspect things. Along with the lights, there was a gorgeous white poinsettia in a sparkling red pot, sitting on her welcome mat.

And then a man emerged from the shadows.

"Spence?"

He looked cold, shivering in his blue flannel and navy jacket. "Hey."

Her heart zinged. "What are you doing here?" She pointed around at the lights. "Was this you?"

Tilting his head to the side, he gave her an adorable half grin. "Yeah. I came by to drop off the poinsettia and noticed you didn't have any up, so…" He shrugged. "I hope you don't mind?"

"Mind?" All thoughts completely left her head and she stumbled a step.

He rushed next to her and gently grabbed her hands. "You look absolutely beautiful tonight. And I'm so sorry about everything. This divorced dating-again thing is weird, and that's no excuse for how I treated you, and…"

Coherence finally back, she stopped him with a gloved finger to his lips. "You're forgiven. Want some hot chocolate?"

His whole body visibly relaxed. "I would love some."

Spence tried hard to quit staring at Sam, but he couldn't help himself. She was a vision in her ugly Christmas sweater and mom jeans. She'd be a stunner in a holiday paper bag. He was just happy she was here. With him. With his family. And that neither of them was alone for Christmas.

Sam and Sally laughed in the kitchen as they dished up pecan pie for everyone, and he wondered if they were talking about him. Hopefully his sister was doing him a solid and really talking him up. Hopefully. Sam met his stare and his heart grinned. She winked at him, before heading over with two slices of pie.

"Warmed and with ice cream, right?" she said, handing him a plate.

"It's the best. Honestly. Sally is kind of famous for this pie."

She sat beside him, scooching in close, before taking a bite. And then she moaned, and it set something inside him on fire. "Oh, my goodness," she said, her eyes rolling back into her head for a moment. "This might be one of the best things I've ever had in my mouth."

"Right?" He took a bite himself and nodded satisfaction. "So good. I look forward to this every year."

She leaned into him and gazed around the room. "Your family is awesome. Thank you, so much, for inviting me over today. I…" She paused, her eyes glistening. "Just, thank you."

"I do have something else for you."

"Oh, yeah?"

They abandoned their pie for the moment, and he took her into the hallway, far from the prying eyes of his family. Notes of "White Christmas" filtered through the air, and he sucked in a breath, to gather his courage. Man, did she smell great. Like warm gingerbread.

Her smile was warm enough to melt snow, as she gazed up at him. "So, what is this mysterious thing you got for me."

Please let this work. He pulled something out of his pocket, a little smashed but still identifiable. Raising it high above her head, he leaned close to her ear.

"Mistletoe."

"Finally."

As her lips met his, all warm and soft and pulsing, he pulled her in tight, their bodies melding together perfectly. Kissing Sam was better than pecan pie, and the best Christmas present he'd had in a long time.

About the Author

Donea Lee Weaver is a perpetual daydreamer who has been creating and telling stories since her elementary school days. When she's not writing about the things she loves (all things romance, fantasy, sci-fi, and yes, even a little horror) you can probably find her planning her next vacation, playing games with the girls, reading, taking the scenic route or cuddling on the couch, with her family and dog, binge-watching a favorite show. She was born and raised in Utah and earned a BA in English from Weber State University. She's also a member of The League of UT Writers and attends a variety of writing conferences every year.

Feel free to connect with her at: www.donaleeweaver.com or on Facebook at Donea Lee Weaver Author.

Christmas Confession

by
Emily Martha Sorensen

Christmas Confession

*B*less me, Father, for I have sinned," a man's voice said from the other end of the screen. It was a kind voice, grandfatherly, of a type that made one think of cookies and warm cocoa. "It has been five hundred years since my last confession."

That gave the priest pause.

"…Five hundred years?" he repeated.

"Approximately." There was an embarrassed chuckle. "I'm afraid I haven't kept track of the decades."

The priest sighed internally. He made it a point to treat every parishioner with respect, to listen patiently and without condemnation. But privately he dreaded those confessions from senior citizens that were really just rambling and seeking for company. Particularly the senile ones whose "sins" were clearly muddled imaginings or dreams.

But his desires for a quiet Christmas Eve, in which he reread the early chapters of Luke, sipped peppermint tea, and fell asleep under warm blankets with snow drifting softly outside the window, were unimportant. His purpose was to aid others, not to see to his own comfort.

"Please continue," the priest said.

The man was supposed to say *I accuse myself of the following sins* next. But he didn't. Instead, there was a creaking sound as the figure on the other side of the confessional moved to scratch a beard.

"You see, Father, I'm worried."

"About what?" the priest asked.

"About the fact that I'm being worshipped instead of God."

The priest suppressed a sigh. He tried not to be judgmental, really he did, but why had God seen fit to bless him with three senior centers within walking distance of his church?

Perhaps it was to teach him to improve his patience. If the mere promise of a long and wandering confession on Christmas Eve had the power to dissatisfy him, then the priest had many sins he needed to repent of himself. Perhaps he was a far weaker man than he had ever suspected.

"Go on," the priest said, humbled at the realization.

"I asked to be allowed to tarry, in order to help people. I asked for the privilege to give gifts to those whom God was willing to bless. Not presents, you understand, but *gifts*. But the more I look at how I am regarded today, the more I feel…despairing. I am mixed with pagan legends and an ad campaign from Coca-Cola. I am used as a symbol of avarice, rather than selflessness. Children who do not believe in the God I worship *do* believe in me and treat me as some kind of a replacement. Why am I being worshipped, Father? Why? And what can I do to stop it?"

Behind the screen, the bearded man began to weep.

The priest was silent for a long moment. For some reason, his doubts about the man's sanity now seemed to have flown. He didn't quite dare to venture a guess about whom he was speaking to, especially since he was not supposed to know the identity of the one who was confessing. But he wondered…he wondered.

"Perhaps the Virgin Mary feels the same way," the priest said softly. "And all the saints. There are those who treat God's mighty warriors as an idol. But is that *your sin*? No. You cannot choose how others choose to venerate you, even if they do so wrongly. All you can do is to keep honoring God, and hope that, at a proper time, He will set everything straight."

There was silence on the other end of the confession booth.

"Thank you, Father," the man on the other end said softly. "I see now why I was sent to you."

The priest took a deep breath. "Have you any other sins to confess?"

There was a wry chuckle on the other end. "Oh, many, Father. Many. The last time I confessed was after I slapped a heretic in the fourteenth century. I've learned to be a bit more patient since then. But tonight is Christmas Eve, and you deserve some peace and quiet. I will come back another time."

There was a sound of someone getting up, and boots plodding out of the room. The church doors opened and shut.

Once he was sure he was alone, the priest got up and left the confessional. He walked to the front doors, opened them, and was about to step out to head to the rectory.

Then he paused, looking down.

There was no other exit or entrance to the church. He had clearly heard the front door open and close.

Yet there were no footsteps in the pristine sheet of white snow.

A bubble of laughter rose up in the priest's throat. He laughed loud and long.

It wasn't that he'd needed a sign. But it was a rather fun gift to receive one.

About the Author

Emily Martha Sorensen writes fantasy and science fiction books with realistic paths to a happy ending. She considers all her books clean, with zero swearing and not much violence, but the romance between married couples can be PG-13. She likes clever characters with unique personalities who charge straight through her plot and spend it spinning wildly off the rails. (Those brats.) She likes magic systems with strict rules and intriguing limitations. She likes romance after the happily ever after. That's where the relationship begins! She likes plot twists that will make your jaw drop. She likes hope and fun and humor. She likes darkness that exists only to help characters grow towards greater light. She likes— Wait, where did those uncooperative protagonists put the plot this time? They just ran off with it, cackling maniacally!

Well, she hopes they'll leave you grinning. You can find her books at www.emilymarthasorensen.com.

Christmas in Bringle Gulch

by
Shannon Fox

Christmas in Bringle Gulch

*L*et me have a turn, Lowell."

Seth's voice cut through the cold, still air as Lowell swung his axe at the tree. The blade bit deep, opening a pale gash in the wood. Chips of pine bark fell into the snow.

Lowell had known the child's request was coming. Seth had supervised the felling of the tree by the creek in relative silence, but his blue eyes had the hungry light of a boy eager to prove himself a man.

"Lowell—" Seth started.

"I heard you." He rested the blade of the axe on the ground. "And the answer is no. I like having somewhere to stay on Christmas. If I let you do this, your mother will turn me out on my ear without a second thought."

The boy scrunched up his nose. "She wouldn't. Not after everything you've done for us."

Victor, the other man with them, snorted. He held an axe of his own and wore a black eyepatch that did nothing to brighten his habitually sour expression. His one good eye was on Lowell, but the man's words were for Seth as he replied. "Then you don't know your mother very well, boy. She loves you a whole lot more than she likes him."

Seth made a disgruntled sound and scuffed the toe of his boot in the snow. It'd only been a few weeks since Lowell and his mother, Becca, had told him about their relationship. While the boy liked Lowell and seemed happy for his mother, he'd also reacted the way children do—with an equal amount of disgust at the prospect that he might turn a corner in the boarding house and find them kissing.

A cold wind sprang up, carrying the distant sounds of voices and hooves crunching along the snow-covered road that ran in front of the boarding house. Lowell looked in the direction of the noise and cast threads of his magic toward it. His gift responded at once, surging through him like a hound with a scent. Eager to find and identify the metal, to whisper a story of who was there.

Judging by the iron horseshoes and the nickel bit, it was a solitary horse and rider come to call. Then Lowell's magic brushed against a familiar pair of spurs.

Catching Victor's eye, he jerked his head in the direction of the house. "Sheriff's here. Let's go see what he wants."

The dark-haired man nodded and leaned his axe against the tree beside Lowell's. Seth cast a last, longing glance at the discarded tools before falling in with the two men as they trudged across the yard.

It was considerably warmer inside the house and the scent of beef stew welcomed them as they stepped through the front door. Sheriff Larson was seated at the dining room table with Becca. He'd removed his black hat and laid it on the wood alongside the garland Becca was endeavoring to sew from scraps of unused fabric.

The sheriff greeted them as they walked in, his deep voice loud in the enclosed space. Lowell winced as he thought of Emmeline upstairs. Victor's pregnant sister was fond of taking late-morning naps, and he hoped the sheriff's voice hadn't woken her.

"Did you find a tree?" Becca asked. The corners of her green eyes crinkled as she smiled at Lowell.

"We found one," he replied. "It's still standing though. Seth picked the sturdiest one it seems."

"Well, hopefully the tree will keep until tomorrow," the sheriff said. He brushed a hand through his sand-colored hair, as if embarrassed by what he had to say next. "I need your help again."

Lowell gave him a look. The last time the Sheriff of Bringle Gulch had asked for his help it had ended with him getting mixed up in a war he'd had no intention of fighting.

The man raised his hands in a placating gesture. "The town's not in danger. Not today anyway. I've just got this small request and the truth is, there's no man better for the job.

"There's a mare that's gone missing. She's due to foal any day now. Apparently, she's worth a nice sum of money and her owners are desperate to find her."

"Did somebody take her?" Lowell asked.

"It looks more like she broke through the fence and wandered off in the night."

"Tracking a horse in the snow shouldn't be difficult," Victor said.

"It shouldn't be," the sheriff agreed. "But the snow thins out about a hundred yards past the barn and her tracks disappear."

Victor grunted. "This story doesn't make a lot of sense. Who'd risk a valuable horse's life by foaling her in the winter and then leave her outside at night?"

The sheriff's reply was terse. "I didn't say her owners knew a lick about horses. Only that they wanted her back."

"What is it you need my help with?" Lowell cut in.

"That mare was wearing horseshoes."

Lowell stilled. He still wasn't used to the fact that people in Bringle Gulch knew what he could do. Not only that he had the ability to transfigure ordinary metals into gold, but also that he could find metal anywhere he went. Sheriff Larson wasn't the first to come seeking Lowell's unique abilities. He was simply the latest.

"Lowell's not an errand boy," Becca said. Her words were edged with steel.

"Now Miss Anderson—" the sheriff started before she cut him off.

"It's Christmas, Horatio. Let these people find their own horse. She can't have gone too far."

"It's not Christmas yet," Lowell said. "And it probably won't take more than an afternoon to find her."

Becca glared at him, and his lips twitched with a suppressed smile. He liked this protective side of her.

"If you really mean to help, I'm coming with you," Victor said. "You might be able to sense metal nearby, but I've seen your poor excuse for tracking."

"Can I come?" Seth asked. The boy had been so quiet during the conversation Lowell had forgotten he was there.

"No," said his mother. "What you can do is run over to Mr. Augustus and ask if he can spare any men to cut that tree down for us."

"I'll finish it tomorrow," Lowell said. "First the horse, then the tree. It's not even Christmas Eve yet. We have plenty of time."

She shook her head. "I can already tell you it's not going to be that easy."

Two hours later, Lowell had to admit that Becca was right. The forest around Bringle Gulch's eastern valley was thick, and the rugged landscape proved challenging in the snow. The last thing they wanted was for one of their horses to step into a concealed hole and break a leg.

The sun was slipping toward the spiny ridge of mountains that stood over the town. They had maybe an hour of good daylight left and very little to show for it.

Lowell placed an affectionate hand on Murphy's flaxen mane. The horse snorted and crunched the bit in his mouth. Though the little palomino had been eager to get out of his stall, his energy was flagging after a couple of hours of slogging through the snow.

"Anything?" Victor asked. He was mounted on his own horse, Gunner.

Lowell shook his head. "Nothing like a set of horseshoes anyway. Lots of nails and discarded tools."

"Let's head back. We can try again in the morning."

Victor turned Gunner in the direction of the road and Lowell followed. They'd make better time back to the boarding house if they got out of the deep snow.

Though night was descending, the forest was coming alive. Owls hooted and creatures moved through the underbrush as they rode past. Lowell smelled woodsmoke on the wind, its scent mingling with the pungent aromas of pine needles and horse sweat.

"Do you have something for Becca yet?" Victor asked. He normally wasn't very talkative, so Lowell was surprised that he'd initiated conversation.

"For Christmas," the other man clarified.

"I have an idea," Lowell replied. "Though it depends on whether we can get that tree cut down in time."

The concept of putting up a Christmas tree was new to Lowell. Becca was from Kansas, and he'd thought maybe it was a local tradition until Emmeline had assured him it was growing in popularity along the East Coast, too. He supposed he'd been on the road too much in recent years to take much notice of the way the holiday traditions were changing.

"I need to get something for Emmeline still," Victor said. "Though I'm not sure what."

Lowell stayed quiet. He suspected this was the real reason the other man wanted to talk and waited for him to continue.

"What do you get someone who is grieving?" Victor asked. "All she wants is her husband back."

Emmeline's husband, Roland, had passed some six weeks ago and the young woman was deep in her mourning.

Lowell shifted the reins in his hands and flexed his fingers to put some feeling into them. The cold was seeping through his gloves and chilling him down to the bone. He'd be glad to be back in a warm house.

"I'm sure Becca would have a better answer," Lowell said. "However, I think you should get your sister something for the baby. Help her look ahead at the future instead of back toward the past."

Victor grunted and Lowell wasn't sure what he thought of that answer.

"What sort of things?" the other man said, after a moment's silence.

"Clothes. A swaddle. Cradle. A christening gown if she means to baptize the baby."

"Baptism." He rolled the word around in his mouth like it had an unfamiliar flavor.

"You should ask her," Lowell said. "I assume you'll be the baby's godfather, after all."

By the look Victor gave him, the thought hadn't so much as crossed his mind.

Lowell felt a sudden tug of iron across the snowy woods. Four small pulses in the gathering darkness. Horseshoes.

"I felt something," Lowell said, gathering the reins in his hand. He pushed Murphy up to a trot. "Might be the mare ahead of us."

Bringle Gulch sprawled across two valleys, ringed by high mountains and divided by an impressive, soaring peak. The road from Deadwood cut the town north to south, with businesses lining the wide street. A second road ran along the north end of town, from the Golden Providence mine in the west to the smaller, eastern valley where Lowell and Victor had concentrated their search. Gold had originally been found on the east side, though the topography of the land meant there wasn't room for a proper town, so the founders of Bringle Gulch had built to the west. A few people had their homesteads in the eastern valley, though most had settled closer to town.

The throb of iron grew more insistent as Lowell and Victor rode. A set of horseshoes and nothing more. Lowell's heart beat a little faster. It sure seemed like a horse alone without a rider. Otherwise, he'd surely feel a bit or the metal rings on the saddle.

When they rounded the next bend in the road, disappointment snaked through Lowell's belly.

It was a horse all right. But not the one they were looking for.

A horse and rider stood in the crossroads at the edge of town. The stranger raised a hand to Victor and Lowell as they approached. He had no gun on him, nor any kind of metal that Lowell sensed. No spurs or bladed weapons. Instead of a bit, his horse wore a hackamore bridle, the heavy band of rawhide snug across the stallion's nose.

"Evening to you," the stranger said. "I'm looking for a place to stay the night. Shelter from the storm blowing in."

"You can come with us to the boarding house," Lowell said. "We're headed there ourselves."

"I'd be much obliged."

The man fell in alongside them. Up close, it looked as though it'd been a long time since he'd had a decent meal. His face was all sharp angles, and his frame did little to fill out the long duster coat he wore.

"You say a storm is coming?" Victor asked.

"It's to the north of us now," the man replied. "Looks like we're in for heavy snow in the next day or so."

Lowell and Victor traded glances. It would certainly complicate their search for the mare.

Music and laughter spilled from Bringle Gulch's twin saloons as they rode three abreast down the main street. Most businesses had closed for the day and the men had drifted in seeking conversation as much as a pint of ale. With so many far from home and without family, loneliness had a way of creeping in and eating at you if you let it. Lowell knew what that was. He'd spent most of the last years of his life alone with only Murphy for company. It'd been his choice, but still. People weren't meant to be alone.

As they rode up to the boarding house, Seth came outside to greet the men. Though seeing a stranger among them, he promptly went back inside to retrieve his mother.

When Becca came to the door, the man introduced himself as Martin. He put the emphasis on the "I" in his name in the Spanish way. Lowell looked at the man again. He hadn't taken him for Mexican at first glance. There was no trace of an accent in Martin's voice, though Lowell supposed time and practice might have relieved him of it.

Once Becca and Martin had agreed on a price for one of the empty rooms upstairs, the three men went to the barn to put their horses away for the night.

The morning dawned bitterly cold. Storm clouds had rolled in from the north during the night, obscuring the mountains in a thick blanket of gray. A light snow was falling, though Lowell expected it to pick up as the day went on.

He and Victor left early to resume their search. It was Christmas Eve and neither one of them wanted to be caught in a snowstorm.

"You really think the mare is still near the house?" Lowell asked.

Victor nodded. "We looked in the wrong place yesterday. Went too far."

They were about half a mile from the farmstead belonging to the mare's owners. The road ahead of them was empty, covered in a layer of pristine white snow. Lowell knew Sheriff Larson and the other men he'd recruited to help in the search would be along at some point in the morning, though they'd decided not to wait for them.

"We were all over those woods yesterday," Lowell said. "If she was there, I would have felt her."

"Maybe something got in the way. Made you overlooked her."

There had been a fair amount of metal objects out in the snowy woods. Lots of discarded tools, iron-rimmed wagon wheels, and yes, horseshoes. Though nothing that had spoken to him the way the four horseshoes belonging to Martin's horse had, like pinpricks of light flaring in the darkness. Still...

"There's a place I want to check again," Lowell said. He closed his legs around Murphy and the gelding immediately complied, breaking into a fast trot. Victor's horse, Gunner, picked up the pace as well.

When the farmstead came into view around the next bend in the road, Lowell slowed Murphy to a walk and turned him off the trail. The snow was deeper here, and the gelding was soon up to his knees in it.

Yesterday they'd meandered through these woods, Lowell's magic scouring for any hint of metal while Victor tried to pick up the mare's tracks. Now, Lowell headed straight toward a large rocky outcropping they'd passed the day before.

Murphy's ears pricked up as they drew close to the rock. His muscles tensed as he lifted his head and nickered.

Lowell held his breath as he strained to hear anything beyond the sound of hooves crunching through snow. To feel something.

A faint, answering whinny came on the wind. It was accompanied by a singular pulse of iron.

"Let's go," Lowell said, nudging Murphy forward. He guided him around the side of the rocky outcrop, looking for a place large enough for a horse to hide.

Behind the face of the rock, they discovered that a narrow cleft cut through the stone. The snow was thin on the ground here, the channel protected from the worst of the wind by its sheer, high walls. It was an ideal place to shelter from an approaching storm.

They found hoofprints a few feet in. The drifting snow must have covered the marks leading to the mouth of the passage. Lowell's heart beat faster as they pressed deeper.

A bit further on, Gunner lifted his head and nickered. This time, the whinny was louder.

The men looked at each other. Victor lifted the rope he'd hung on his saddle horn. Lowell had a rope, too, though Victor had the better aim. If the mare ran, Lowell and Murphy would cut around in front of her, keep her close so Victor could get the rope around her neck.

They found her just past a bend in the passage. She was standing beneath a rock overhang lined with icicles. She was a pretty horse, even with her thick winter coat. Her fur was entirely white apart from several large black spots on her back and belly. A splash of black covered one eye. Her mane was long, and wind-tangled.

The mare wasn't shod on all four feet. That was a detail Sheriff Larson had had wrong. She must have only been wearing horseshoes up front in the first place, but sometime after she'd escaped, the mare had stepped on herself and ripped one of the shoes off. She wore only one horseshoe now as she regarded the two men and their horses. Lowell had felt a whisper of iron in this area the day before but had shrugged it away as being nothing more than a thrown shoe, discarded in the quiet woods. He'd had no reason to believe it might lead them to the mare.

"She's foaled," Victor said, quietly.

Lowell's eyes went to the streaks of brown on her hind legs, dried blood on fur. He didn't see the foal, but that didn't mean the baby horse wasn't there.

Murphy took a step forward and the mare pinned her ears back in warning.

From the corner of his eye, Lowell saw Victor put both hands on the rope. He eased it into a loop, his movements slow and precise. No need to spook the mare before he was ready.

When Victor finally did throw the rope, Lowell held his breath as he watched it sail toward the mare. That it slid easily over her head was a testament to the other man's skill. She'd tried to jerk away at the last moment, but somehow, he'd anticipated which way she'd go.

The mare took a step back, tightening the rope around her neck. She shook her head and tugged harder.

"Easy," Victor called. The rope was taut in his hands.

"She won't leave her foal," Lowell said.

He dismounted Murphy, his boots sinking lightly into the undisturbed snow. He patted the gelding on the neck and then started toward the mare.

She pinned her ears at him as he walked up, but he ignored her. Victor had her. All he had to do was stay clear of her teeth and hooves.

He spied the foal lying against the base of the rock wall. With his dark brown fur, he blended into the stone. The colt lifted his head as the man approached, but he didn't attempt to stand.

Lowell kept one eye on the mare as he moved closer to her baby. He'd watched his father foal a few horses back home in Vermont. Judging by the dried blood on the mare's legs, she'd foaled very recently. Perhaps the colt was having difficulty in standing and nursing.

Taking off his own jacket, he rubbed the foal vigorously with it. Protected as they were from the worst of the falling snow, it was still cold out here. They needed to get these two back to the farm and inside a warm barn.

The mare didn't take kindly to Lowell touching her baby. She squealed her displeasure and struck out with one foreleg, but Victor did an admirable job holding her back.

After a few minutes of rubbing, the foal came out of his torpor. He made a move to get up, planting his tiny hooves against the frozen ground. Lowell let him try it on his own, but when the foal failed to rise, he gently helped the colt get to its feet.

Standing for what was likely the first time, the foal looked around at his mother, the other two horses, and the men. He took his first wobbling steps toward the mare, tail twitching. Lowell stayed back. He would not interfere again unless absolutely needed.

Step by step, the colt crossed the snow until he reached his mother. Then, he bumped his nose against her udder and nursed.

When they returned to the farmstead with the missing mare and her foal, only the wife was at home. The woman was overjoyed to see them, and tears sprang to her eyes when she spied the new colt.

Her husband was still out looking with the sheriff, so they helped the woman settle the mare and foal in the barn. As the sheriff had intimated, she and her husband were nice people, just not entirely experienced with horses. Lowell gave her a few instructions about caring for the new foal and promised to come back after Christmas to help the couple secure their fences so they didn't lose any more of their horses.

She insisted on paying the two men for their trouble, which they refused. As it turned out though, the couple owned the new furniture store in Bringle Gulch. When they turned down her offer of payment, she suggested they take their pick of something in the workshop instead. Victor got a curious look on his face, and then surprised Lowell by agreeing to go look.

Lowell stayed behind with the horses in the barn. Already, the colt had improved since they'd found him in the snow. His eyes were brighter, and he was nursing as a new foal should. The mare half-dozed while the colt ate, all tension gone from her body.

He was glad they'd helped find the horse, even though it had meant not being able to finish cutting down the tree for Becca. Some of Augustus's men had done that in his stead, so they'd have a Christmas tree tonight after all. Still, when he'd returned to the boarding house the previous evening, Lowell hadn't been able to tell if Becca was irritated with him or not.

If she was, he hoped his Christmas gift would be enough to make it up to her.

Lowell stepped back from the tree to admire his work. The sun had long set, and the front parlor was illuminated by candles. He nodded to himself as he took in the effect of the lighting on the tree. He couldn't wait for Becca to come downstairs and see it herself.

Outside, the storm raged. The wind made a mournful sound as it blew past the house, kicking snow against the windowpanes.

The glass was already frosted with so much ice it made it difficult to see outside, but Lowell imagined everything was covered in a fresh blanket of snow.

A door opened upstairs, and female voices spilled into the hall. Becca and Emmeline coming down for Christmas Eve Dinner. Becca had spent much of the afternoon preparing the meal and the house smelled of meat, roasted vegetables, and the plum pudding she'd made for dessert.

Both Becca and Emmeline had put on their best dresses for the holiday, Emmeline in a red taffeta gown that perfectly complimented her olive skin and dark hair. It was Becca, though, that drew Lowell's eye. Though her dress was not so dramatic as her friend's, the blue fabric was no less striking. She'd done something with her hair, too, pinning her reddish curls up and away from her face. It was a nice style for her, though undoubtedly Emmeline's handiwork.

Becca's eyes found Lowell's and she smiled at him before her attention shifted to the room behind him. She gasped and reflexively drew a hand to her mouth. Lowell grinned and turned back to look at the tree himself.

While he and Victor had been out looking for the mare, Becca and Seth had decorated the branches with whatever things she found in the house. Colorful ribbons, the garland she'd made, baubles, and bits of tin. It was to this last that Lowell had applied his talents, changing the lesser metal into gold. Illuminated now by candlelight, the tree seemed to glow with an ethereal, golden light.

"It's beautiful," Becca said. She came to his side, and he noticed her eyes seemed a bit glassy in the low light. As if she were about to cry.

"I didn't know what to get you," he said, "So I thought maybe I could make this Christmas more memorable instead."

"Well, you managed that," she replied.

They were soon joined in the front room by Emmeline, Victor, Seth, and Martin, who hung shyly back near the door. Whatever the traveler thought of the tree's transformation, he kept it to himself. Truth was, Lowell knew the rumors of magic were spreading beyond Bringle Gulch. He'd have to deal with them eventually. But not now.

Victor took his sister's elbow and guided her over to the present he'd placed under the tree earlier, the large, cloth-wrapped item he'd brought back from the farmstead. Though Lowell had asked several times, Victor refused to answer any questions about what it was.

Emmeline tugged at the ribbon and nudged the folds of fabric aside now to reveal a handsome wooden cradle. Its smooth sides gleamed in the candlelight. Victor pushed it gently, to demonstrate its rocking ability. Emmeline let out a soft sob, then embraced her brother. Lowell looked away to give the siblings their privacy.

"Did you have something to do with that?" Becca whispered.

"I might have suggested it."

"It hardly seems like something Victor would have thought of on his own."

"You underestimate him," Lowell said.

"No. I just know you very well."

She held his gaze for a long moment. Once, it would have scared him, to let someone that close to him again. To let anyone know him at all. But not now. Coming to Bringle Gulch and meeting Becca had changed his life in unimaginable ways. The man he'd been the previous summer would hardly have recognized himself now.

And he wouldn't have it any other way.

"Merry Christmas, Becca," he said, taking her hand.

She tightened her fingers around his and smiled up at him. "And Merry Christmas to you."

About the Author

Shannon Fox is a San Diego-based writer of fiction spanning multiple genres. She grew up in the foothills of the Colorado Rockies before relocating to California to attend UC-San Diego, where she earned a B.A. in Literature-Writing. She misses the rugged natural beauty of Colorado, but definitely doesn't miss the wind.

Her short stories have appeared in the *Monsters, Movies & Mayhem* anthology, the first *Particular Passages* anthology, *DreamForge Anvil*, and *Air and Nothingness Press*, among others.

Besides writing, Shannon has a passion for horses. She has competed at the international level in the sport of dressage. Shannon also owns a digital marketing company that works primarily with small businesses and real estate agents.

To learn more about Shannon and her forthcoming stories, visit her website: www.shannon-fox.com

Mr. and Mr. Claus

by
Kay Hanifen

Mr. and Mr. Claus

*D*ear Santa,
    As requested, I've enclosed the list of people I saw being naughty at the Stanford Mall. For your convenience, I've organized them by behavior: rudeness, theft, and callousness. What is it about the mall at this time of year that makes people such—and pardon my language—jerks? It's not the underpaid minimum wage worker's fault that the toy store is out of Furbies or Happy New Year Barbies or even Tickle-Me Elmos. Why can't people just be nice to each other every once in a while?

Sorry. I don't mean to melt your snowman. Besides, I know it's not all doom and gloom. The two Santas that the mall hired for Santa's Cottage are super sweet. One's even named Nicholas (though he prefers Nick). How perfect is that? The other is named Michael, and they're both just like you: round, jolly, and with massive, snow-white beards. And they're both so good with the kids. Even the nervous ones can't help but smile at them. We haven't had a crying Christmas photo yet!

But there is something off about them. Their smiles sometimes get so sad when they think no one's looking. Michael told me that he's a widower. He lost his wife to cancer five years ago. Nick has never mentioned family to me at all—no wife or husband or children or brothers or sisters.

I think they're lonely.

But I've been watching them in the breakroom and when they're switching shifts. Nick, who is usually warm and outgoing, goes shy, and I swear that he's blushing behind his big, bushy beard. And Michael is just as bad. He giggles and finds excuses to talk with Nick.

Santa, I know you've said that I'm not supposed to meddle in the affairs of humans—just observe and report—but our job is to make people happy. Michael and Nick are both good people. Don't they deserve a little Christmas magic?

I'll keep you updated on the situation.

Love,
Stella the Elf

Dear Santa,

I've been watching the movies that humans call romantic comedies. They aren't really for me, but they're giving me ideas. I've created a step-by-step plan that will end in those two kissing under the mistletoe for the rest of their days and I have begun step one already.

Step one is to get them talking to me about one another. I'm so grateful that we have your gift of gab. They'll be more honest, which is crucial for the plan going forward.

Nick had the morning shift today, so I talked to him first. Because it's a school day, the mall is pretty empty and slow, so we had time to chat. I leaned against his high-back chair while he reached down to where he kept his secret stash of snacks behind a cutout of a snowman.

"Do you have any plans for Christmas?" I asked.

He smiled and handed me one of his sleeves of crackers. "Not much, I'm afraid. I'm volunteering at the youth shelter nearby, but that's about it. What about you?"

Obviously, I couldn't just say what I did on Christmas Eve, so I hope you'll forgive a little lie by omission. "Christmas is the busiest time of year for my family, so I have a mile-long list of things to do."

At that, he chuckled, but it wasn't a happy chuckle. It was the nostalgic, melancholic kind, like when you're remembering someone you loved and lost a long time ago. "It used to be that way in my house too. My mom always baked our favorite cookies and decorated the house like the inside of a catalogue. Those were some of the happiest times of my life."

"What changed?" I asked.

He sighed. "They caught me with a boy. It was the seventies, and people didn't take kindly to folks like me. I'm lucky my parents only kicked me out. Dad might've killed me if I ever came back."

My heart broke for him. What kind of horrible people would kick out someone so kind and gentle just because he was a little different? I hope you permanently put them on the naughty list for this, Santa.

"Mom tried, though," he continued. "She was in poor health and would have left him if it wasn't for the fact that his insurance paid for all her medical care. So, instead, she looked after me from afar by dipping into her own savings to secretly pay for food and an apartment for me. I-I guess I do this because I want to feel closer to her. This was her favorite holiday, after all." He wiped his eyes with a wet laugh. "I'm sorry, Stella. Not sure why I dumped all this on you."

I patted his red velvet-clad shoulder. "It's okay. I have one of those faces that makes people tell me things. I want you to know, though, that you didn't deserve to be treated that way."

He smiled. "I know, but thank you for saying that."

"So…" I began, wracking my brain for a way to change the subject. "If you could have any gift for Christmas, what would it be? I mean, within reason, of course. Santa can't resurrect the dead or anything." (Okay, yes, I know you did it that one time when you were Saint Nicholas of Myra, but most people don't know that story.)

He gave me a funny look. "Why?"

"Well, everyone talks to you about what they want for Christmas, but no one ever asks Santa what he wants," I replied with a shrug.

At that, he let out a big, booming laugh that made his belly shake like a bowl full of jelly. "Fair point." Sitting back in his seat, he thought for a moment. "You know, I've always wanted to learn how to bake like my mom, so maybe some cake pans and recipe books?"

I smiled. "I'm sure that can be arranged."

"What? You've got a direct line to the boss man or something?" he asked, his eyes twinkling.

"Or something," I replied with a wink.

A harried looking mother with twin toddlers in her stroller appeared. All three wore matching sweaters patterned with reindeer.

Duty called.

The pair stared at Nick like he was some kind of monster even as he let out a hearty "Ho, ho, ho," and beckoned them over. I knew that panicked look. The waterworks were about to start, so I somersaulted to them and ended with a silly face.

"Merry Christmas! I'm Stella the Elf. What's your names?" I asked, putting a little bit of our magic into my greeting.

The mom shot me a grateful look while the boys giggled. "That's Eric and Peter."

"Those are great names," I said, kneeling in front of them. "Do you wanna take some pretty pictures for your mommy?"

She unbuckled them, and I led the pair to Nick. While the kids babbled in toddler speak about what they wanted for Christmas, I set up the camera. Waving a hand, I got their attention. "Say cheese!"

And with a sprinkle of Christmas magic, all smiled radiantly. Another perfect picture. The printer hummed and out popped their happy faces. Satisfied, the family paid and left, so we could talk again.

"You're amazing with kids," Nick said.

I leaned on the wingback chair. "You are too. If you wanted, I bet you could make a career out of playing Santa. Michael too."

"Michael is pretty amazing," he replied softly, his eyes growing distant. With longing? I hope it was with longing.

"I know he thinks the same about you. So…" I leaned in conspiratorially. "Do you have any misters waiting underneath the mistletoe?"

At that, he let out a hearty laugh. "I wish! The dating pool's pretty small here, especially once you get to be my age."

"But you'd be open to dating?"

"Aren't you a little young to be caring about an old man's love life?"

With a sigh, I rested my chin on top of the chair. "It's a slow day, and I'm bored."

He shrugged as "Santa Baby" began playing on the speakers. "Fair enough."

"What about Michael? Do you think he's cute?"

"Worse," he replied with a sigh. "I think he's straight."

"What if he was bi? Would you date him?"

Another shrug. A noncommittal answer is not a no, though. "Do *you* like him?"

"I do," he replied, "but I'm not sure he'd like me back." There was a pause, but then he snorted. "Okay, your turn. Have you got anyone?"

"I'm not really one for those kinds of ooey-gooey human emotions like romance or special sleigh rides…if you catch my drift," I replied, which was true. I love romance when it's happening to other people. Humans call it being 'asexual' and 'aromantic.'

He nodded sagely and replied, "Welcome to the family, then."

Technically, I'd been a part of the 'family' for longer than humans have been alive, but I couldn't tell him that. I just thanked him.

Michael was going to be a tougher nut to crack, but more because malls are busier in the afternoon on weekdays, and I was constantly keeping the line moving. We barely had time to say two words to each other, let alone to talk about the possibility that he liked Nick.

When Michael had first arrived during the midday break between shifts, Nick hung around eating his takeaway from the food court while Michael put the finishing touches on his Santa outfit. I listened from the corner, pretending to drink coffee while they talked. Apparently, both were fond of scary movies and Korean food, and spent the entire time recommending restaurants and films to each other. Like all their interactions, it was cute to see, especially the way Michael's eyes lit up as he made predictions for the newest Friday the 13th movie.

I didn't get the chance to talk to him until after our shift. As we took the final family picture, Michael got to his feet and stretched. "Man, my ass is numb from that chair."

"Try staying on your feet the whole time," I replied, because to have a petty complaint was a normal human response. I could have done another three days straight of this before I even felt an ache in my knees.

He twisted his waist this way and that, his spine crackling like old wrapping paper. "Fair point."

"So," I said as we made our way to the breakroom where we kept our things, "do you have any plans for Christmas?"

He shrugged. "Not really. My daughter is with the in-laws this year, so I think it'll just me and a box of those Pillsbury sugar cookies."

Lies for the greater good are not so bad, right boss? Because I know you'll frown upon what I said next, but it might help them find love. "You know, Nick told me that he's going to volunteer at the local youth homeless shelter and invited me to join."

Michael smiled fondly at the mention of Nick. "He would spend his holidays helping the needy. The guy's sweet like that."

And he's sweet on you, I wanted to say, but I had enough sense not to. I didn't want to scare Michael off Nick—or worse, make him angry enough to try to hurt him. People are unpredictable like that. Even the kindest, gentlest souls have a mean streak buried somewhere beneath the surface. If I was wrong about Michael and he was homophobic, I risked Nick's safety and even his life.

"I'm sure he'd love it if you joined us too," I said. "We can give these kids a real Christmas."

We reached the employee lockers, and I entered my combination. Inside was my decoy shirt and pants—clothing for regular humans so people would believe that I was heading home just like everyone else.

He paused at his locker, thinking carefully about the offer. "If you don't mind, I'd like to hear the invitation from him. I wouldn't want to intrude on his plans."

And now, boss, I'm beginning phase two of the plan. Operation: Get Nick to Invite Michael to the Shelter for Christmas. Wish me luck!

Love,
Stella the Elf

Dear Santa,

Phase two is going well. I talked to Nick today while we waited for kids to show up and get their pictures taken with him. I'm going to apologize in advance for all the lying, but it's for the best, I promise. And it's not like you don't lie sometimes, boss. I've caught you pretending to eat your broccoli at the table while hiding it in your napkin and sneaking cookies as a midnight snack even after Mrs. Claus told you not to. Nobody's perfect, after all.

It was another slow morning, so I got to chatting again with Nick again. "So, Nick, I was talking to Michael yesterday."

He huffed, his expression somewhere between amused and annoyed. "Is that so?"

"Just about his Christmas plans. His daughter is visiting the in-laws, so he's on his own. I told him about your plans to volunteer at the youth shelter, and he thought that sounded fantastic."

Nick arched an eyebrow. "Did he now?"

I tried to lean casually against the chair, missed, and straightened myself up like I'd mean to do that. "If you asked him, I'm sure he'd go too. It's better than spending it alone with a box of Pillsbury sugar cookies."

"Do you really think so?" he asked, scratching thoughtfully at his beard the same way you do when you're deciding who's naughty and who's nice.

"One-hundred-percent," I replied.

He chuckled, but I wasn't quite sure why. "I guess it can't hurt to ask. Maybe when he comes in for his shift." A small family approached, and his demeanor changed, becoming less ponderous and more jolly. "Ho, ho, ho, who do we have here?"

It was a bit busy after that, so we didn't get to talk much until it was time for the shift change. But Santa, he didn't do it. He said he would, but then he didn't. Instead, he took one look at Michael and bolted. Humans can be so frustrating sometimes.

On the plus side, Michael brought in a different backpack than usual. This one was covered in pins with art and pithy sayings like "Squatch Squad" with Bigfoot in the center. At the top, though, I spotted a round pin striped with blue, purple, and pink. Bi pride, Santa! I was happier than a reindeer in a carrot patch, but I had to make sure.

"I like your backpack," I said to him as I nibbled on my lunch, a slice of pizza from the food court.

He laughed, looking a little embarrassed. "Yeah, my usual broke, so I had to dig my old one out of the closet." It wasn't just the bag that he brought out of the closet, Santa.

"Did your wife know?" I asked, pointing to the bi pride pin.

He smiled sadly as he ran a thumb across it. "I figured it out after she passed. This was a gift from my daughter when I came out to her."

"That's so sweet," I replied with a mouthful of pizza. "She sounds lovely."

He put the bag away. "She really is. You remind me of her, a little bit. Like you, she always knows how to brighten my day."

And if that isn't the sweetest thing a human's ever said to me, Santa, I don't know what is.

Yours always,
Stella the Elf

Dear Santa,

I swear this was an accident. Cross my heart, mistletoe kissed, lest I be on the naughty list. But I may have locked Nick and Michael in the breakroom together today. The door locks automatically to keep customers from going where they're not supposed to (you'd be surprised how often they ignore Employees Only signs) but I guess I must have been thinking a little too hard about how I just wanted them to talk to each other, and I kind of, maybe, accidentally…enchanted the lock until they talked. I know, I know. It's bad. But it's also good.

Because it worked.

Kind of.

I didn't realize I'd done it until I was halfway down the hall to grab something from the food court for lunch. The moment I heard the door rattling, I realized my mistake. So, I did what every elf knows to do at the first sign of trouble. I went invisible.

"Stella! Stella, let us out!" Nick yelled on the other side of the door.

"Stellaaaaa!" Michael cried in an impression of Marlon Brando in *A Streetcar Named Desire*, and then they both laughed.

"I can't believe she did this," Nick said, still chuckling. "How did she even know how to lock it on the inside too?"

"Maybe it wasn't her. Maybe it's just a freak accident," Michael suggested.

I watched through the window as Nick sat on the threadbare couch. "Come on. She's been trying to set us up all week. This has to be her."

Michael took a seat beside him. "So, you noticed too?"

"She's as subtle as a trainwreck."

I was a little insulted by this assessment of my people skills. I've kept the biggest secret on earth from them for weeks now. I can be subtle if I want.

"I was going to ask—"

"I was wondering—"

They began speaking in unison, stopped, and laughed. "You first," Nick said.

Michael shook his head. "No, you."

With a groan, Nick buried his face in his hands. "I was going to ask if you wanted to come to the youth shelter with me this Christmas. Most of the kids have been kicked out by their families, and they need some holiday love and cheer."

Michael put his hand on Nick's knee. "With or without the red suit?"

"Your choice," he replied with a booming laugh.

And they were going to say more. I know they were going to say more—or even kiss—but then our boss knocked on the door. I didn't even hear him coming because I was so excited about this development. Mr. Dundee, the manager, called in a voice that sounded remarkably like Piglet's from *Winnie the Pooh*, "Mr. Corwin, where are you? We have a line almost a mile long."

Michael replied, "I'm so sorry, Mr. Dundee, but the door seems to be stuck, and we can't open it."

Mr. Dundee turned the knob and opened the door with ease. "Are you kidding me?"

"We swear, it was locked a minute ago," Nick said, and I took that as my cue to leave and get lunch. The Auntie Anne's wasn't too busy, so I grabbed myself a pretzel and headed back, the picture of innocence as Mr. Dundee chastised the two men.

"Sorry I'm late. Auntie Anne's was pretty busy," I said, channeling all my elvish charm. "Is everything okay? The line at the cottage is getting long."

Mr. Dundee rubbed his face with a sigh. "Three more days. Three more days of this three-ring circus and I'll be free."

Until he said that, I didn't even realize how close we were to C-Day. I guess I need to head back up North. It's funny. I usually hate it here, but this time, I kind of don't want to go. At least, not until I learn if Nick and Michael get together. I guess there's always next year.

See you soon,
Stella the Elf

Dear Michael and Nick,

By the time you're reading this, I'll be gone. That sounds really dramatic, like I'm running away or something, but I'm only going home for the holidays. Before I go, though, I just wanted to say that I really enjoyed working with you this year, and I wish you both the best. I've left you both a tin of cookies. (An old family recipe. They're heavenly.)

Michael, I know you feel a bit guilty about finding love again but it's okay. Your wife would want you to be happy, and you aren't betraying her memory by loving someone else.

Nick, you've been hurt a lot, but that doesn't mean that everyone you love will abandon you. Sometimes, the scariest thing on earth is opening yourself up to others and feeling vulnerable, but I promise that it's worth it.

Hopefully, I'll be assigned to your mall again next year. For now, enjoy Christmas, have a cup of good cheer, and—maybe—kiss under the mistletoe.

Your friend,

Stella the Elf

P.S. Nick, I just wanted you to know that I pulled some strings, and this Christmas is going to be the best that the youth shelter has ever seen.

Dear Stella,

I don't know how this will reach you. When we asked Mr. Dundee where we might be able to find you, he said that the mall had no record of Stella the Elf on file. And there's no one in town by that name. Or even the county. The closest is a little old lady three counties over, not a teenage girl who is way too perky for a minimum wage customer service job. (Michael's words, not mine.)

So, who are you, Stella?

I keep thinking back on our conversations. You always steered it towards us, and never revealed much about yourself. You have a big family, you're busy at Christmastime, and you're ace and aromantic. That's it.

When we found your note and the cookies (which were as amazing as you promised), we were sad that you were gone. And then we were worried. We even contemplated calling the police to look for you. I'm not sure what I would have told them. We're concerned about our teenage coworker who apparently doesn't exist?

Michael jokes that maybe you are one of Santa's elves and you came down to make sure that mall-goers were all being nice instead of naughty. At least, it was a joke at first. Then, we arrived on Christmas morning at the youth shelter.

Throughout the year, I'd been collecting the perfectly good clothing, books, and trinkets at the mall that would otherwise have been thrown out because they didn't sell. It really is a shame how much we waste as a society, how little we value one another and the things we create.

The kids at the shelter are a little old for the Santa routine—most of them have been kicked out for being family like us—but they still love it. Double the Santas means double the Christmas cheer, so Michael and I both wore our costumes. The staff rarely decorates all that much, not when the money can go to other, more important things like food and healthcare, but this year was different. Instead of a plastic tree that the kids called the "Charlie Brown Tree" because it was scraggly and falling apart, there was a seven-foot-tall, genuine Douglas fir decorated with lights and ornaments. Underneath was a massive pile of presents individually addressed to each of the teens currently living there. The walls had been covered in garlands and lit with fairy lights, and the air smelled of Christmas cookies. It was breathtaking.

And at the center of the coffee table was a note addressed to me and Michael:

Hi guys,

I told you I pulled some strings with my boss. There's a present under the tree for each of you as well. And don't look up now, but you may be standing underneath the mistletoe.

Your friend,

Stella the Elf

We both stared in stunned silence for a moment before looking up. We were, in fact, standing underneath the mistletoe. No one was around just yet, so Michael pulled me in close and leaned in for a kiss. It was magical in the same way Christmas is magical, all joy and nostalgia and warmth in the coldest, darkest days of winter.

So, thank you, Stella, for bringing us together and making this Christmas magical.

Your friend,

Nick

P.S. I wanted to thank you for the bakeware you got me. I've used it to make a delicious cake for Michael's New Year's Eve party.

P.P.S. Michael says hi and that he wanted to thank you for the new backpack and pins. He hopes you'll come back again next year. We both do.

About the Author

Kay Hanifen was born on a Friday the 13th and once lived for three months in a haunted castle. So, obviously, she had to become a horror writer. Her work has appeared in over forty anthologies and magazines. When she's not consuming pop culture with the voraciousness of a vampire at a 24-hour blood bank, you can usually find her with her two black cats or at kayhanifenauthor.wordpress.com.

Twitter: twitter.com/TheUnicornComi1
Instagram: www.instagram.com/katharinehanifen

Swift Couriers on Their Appointed Rounds

by
Tony Covatta

Swift Couriers on Their Appointed Rounds

"Neither snow nor rain nor heat nor gloom of night stays these couriers from the swift completion of their appointed rounds."
–Herodotus, *The Persian Wars,* Book 8

*F*ew remember the three-cent letter, the penny postcard, twice-a-day mail delivery. Those who do will have no more than the usual difficulty recalling that the United States Postal Service hired bright-eyed college boys years ago to assist its couriers in the swift completion of their appointed rounds at Yuletide.

The post office has taken its lumps over the years. Deservedly so. I saw that myself during my stint as a Christmas relief letter carrier. Some want to privatize the service. I disagree. I still appreciate what I learned that Christmas, of good more than ill, in the employ of the USPS.

1963. Less than a year since I had left the seminary, re-entered what we call the real world. I was nineteen, emotionally about seven. Money and jobs were scarce. I was working my way through college, eager to make an extra buck. My ears perked up when a pal alerted me that the Post Office had holiday season openings. I took the two-hour qualifying exam for this august position. In only six or seven weeks, the results arrived, by ordinary first-class mail, of course. I had passed with flying colors. Thirsting for new experiences (not to mention cash), I eagerly awaited the call that might come from one of the local offices. And lo and behold, it did. I was posted to the Okolona Station.

Okolona was a suburb then being hewn out of the rural wilderness that surrounded Louisville, a weird gallimaufry of older farmhouses, single rural cottages, and clapped-together subdivisions, new and raw then, long since painfully showing their age. Now enveloped in urban sprawl, Okolona lies out Preston Highway, beyond the Louisville airport.

The post office building was a typical redbrick government installation with a small, low-ceilinged, public service area containing an inadequate number of barred, black turreted service windows. Behind the public area, a gray wall sported only a very recently installed picture of President LBJ. This barrier blocked the curious public from viewing a cavernous high-ceilinged hall replete with battleship-gray desks, gray tables, each gray table supporting a gray sorting rack, all lit by large, hanging commercial fluorescent fixtures. Front and back of the house, carriers and patrons alike shuffled back and forth over a black and gray, gritty linoleum floor.

That Yuletide, as for some years before, the Postmistress was a woman, Miss Betty. The outsized flour sack she wore as a dress ineffectually hid her ample girth. Miss Betty was an amiable, grandmotherly figure, graying brown hair pulled into a loosely packed bun on the rear or top of her head, as the spirit moved her. She oversaw her otherwise all-male battalion with pleasant good humor. She liked her postmen and responded to their rowdy greetings and jokes with a smile, good-natured laugh or withering rejoinder. She could be as raunchy as her troops.

In those days, the post office was not making one of its forlorn attempts to operate profitably. Time was not money. Miss Betty and her troops moved at a pace that suited them, They acted as if the work could get done without undue stress, and as we will see, they were correct. This post office was a fun place. The carriers were not vets down on their luck, subdued by anti-depressants, hounded by time-and-motion men. They were high school educated guys, always guys, country boys and mountaineers, devoid of ambition, who had found a pleasant berth to take them through to retirement. They saw a comfortable government pension waiting for them at the end of the line to fund a life of squirrel hunting in the Smokey Mountains and piloting the houseboat around Lake Cumberland.

My first morning on the job, after waiting outside a nervous, shivering time in the cold, I was admitted into the inner sanctum, the huge sorting hall. Ushered into her presence, Miss Betty welcomed me with a warm smile, then, strong hand firmly gripping my shoulder, steered me to Van Meter (last name only, first name unknown, never used). Van Meter was a tallish country boy, of rangy, middling good looks, including strong white teeth and a ready smile, forty-five or so, and prematurely gray. Over in Hope, Arkansas, a young man then growing up resembled Van Meter in looks and affect: William Jefferson Clinton. Van Meter had immigrated to Louisville from the Eastern Kentucky Mountains after high school, and shortly thereafter caught on with the post office. Van Meter couldn't spell nonchalant, but that was what he was. His manner was easy and offhand. He made people want to like him, without what seemed like trying. Another lad and I were to assist Van Meter with the crush of Christmas cards, presents, and the regular mail inundating our office.

Genial Van Meter introduced his fledgling assistants to the other regular carriers. The initiation apparently shocked my fellow assistant even more than me. He never said a word, then or after. Eager to welcome us, the noisy carriers enjoyed having college boys as their subordinates, to rib and poke fun at. They joked more with us than at us, told us their names and nicknames, tried out nicknames for us, and then shared one of the secrets of the lodge, inviting us to peruse the ample library of pornography and nudie photos confiscated over the years from Okolona's apparently sizable population of sex-starved citizens. The bolder fellows displayed graphic sample pieces to us, to the uproarious laughter of their fellows. Of course, we primly declined to participate, and started studies at Van Meter's knee.

Van Meter gave us a short dissertation on how he "cased" the mail, sorting it by hand into the racks that served as the back of his desk, one pigeonhole for each delivery address on the route. I didn't understand much of what he said. Either Van Meter's teaching skills were lacking, or I was just abuzz, unable to absorb all the new sensations.

I do remember that I was appalled by the behavior of Otis, who occupied the casing desk next to Van Meter's. Otis was as rough and caustic as Van Meter was smooth and pleasant. A short, paunchy guy with reddish curly hair, watery eyes and pimply complexion, Otis oozed anger. While sorting his mail, Otis savagely tore open and confiscated an occasional odd exemplar of the cheap, small cardboard boxes that came his way containing little kids' premiums—spacemen, toy trucks, decoder rings, and other trinkets that cereal companies had sent as prizes to their gullible, sugar-saturated customers. The whole cereal premium scheme engendered visceral hostility in Otis. When he chanced on a prize that raised his ire to the boil he chortled wickedly and stored it away in a paper shopping bag below his desk. Who knows for what or why—a black mass, perhaps? Otis's volatile temper repelled me. I turned away, trying to focus on Van Meter's voluble but impenetrable lecture.

Once he had completed his dissertation, Van Meter was scrupulously fair in dividing up the work. He would case the mail and we would "help him" with delivery. He had said his route was divided into ten loops. That much I had caught. With a straight face, he assigned the other acolyte (never seen again) five loops, and five to me. Ten loops minus five minus five equals zero. Not a word from our leader as to how he was going to spend his time. I didn't dare ask.

It was a cold and damp morning as I trudged out of the post office into the parking lot laden to the limit with my half of Van Meter's route, manfully if shakily clasped in both arms. As I passed Otis's pickup truck, I could not help noticing him fortifying himself against the cold and damp with a healthy swig from a half-pint of Early Times, a cheap but serviceable bourbon.

In those days, after driving by private car to his route, each carrier delivered the mail on foot. Every couple of loops or so on the route stood an olive-green storage box. Before starting individual deliveries, the postman strategically stored the mail for later loops into the requisite storage boxes, to avoid lugging the whole day's mail the whole way. I drove my ancient jalopy through the neighborhood, finding and stuffing mail into the (hopefully) proper storage boxes.

Then delivery could begin. At the start of the first loop, I nudged the strap over my head, hoisting my dirty shopworn postman's bag, relic of Christmases past, onto my waiting shoulder. The bulging bag was heavy, awkward. The bottom banged against my hip. The strap cut into my shoulder blade, promising pain to come. Even so I was exhilarated, shaking not only with cold but excitement, out on my own, slogging over the soggy tundra that underlay the lawns of Okolona, Kentucky.

"A hard time I had of it," to paraphrase T.S. Eliot in a slightly different context. The atmosphere was damp, the ground not quite frozen. All during those days, the temperature hovered just below or above thirty-two degrees Fahrenheit. As the day wore on and excitement wore off, the temperature went up a notch or two. Ground moisture soaked through my tennis shoes, adding to the discomfort of the ungainly load. I had flatly refused to don the long underwear my mother had bought me for the job and scoffed at her suggestion that I wear boots.

As Einstein predicted, time warped, stretching out ever more slowly with each weary step I took under my gravity-laden bag. I trudged across postage stamp lawns, through scruffy hedges, up and down steps of tiny front stoops and dark porches, overarched with brick and crumbling mortar. At times I peered into picture windows of bargain basement living rooms, curious but always on the lookout for the box or slot to deposit the instant load. Moving as if through a swamp of ankle-deep sludge, feet wet, back stiff, shoulder sore, knees aching, I was cold all over.

About four or so, part of one loop remained undone. Suddenly, Van Meter appeared out of nowhere. I sensed that he appreciated my discomfort and knew as well that my tardiness would count against him. Without a word of reproach, he gently relieved me of my burden. Awestruck, grateful, feeling guilty, I watched my leader, skipping up and down steps, deftly sorting the next house's letters and magazines while placing the current house's mail in its slot. Within minutes he did what would have taken me an hour.

Chastened by my ineptitude, and not wanting to disappoint Van Meter, whom I had begun to idolize, I vowed to do better. Over the next few days, I did. Clad in the scorned long undies and a pair of boots, I became more and more agile, completing the route more and more quickly. I learned how to handle the occasional time-eating COD or certified mail delivery that required me to ring the doorbells of the humble, compliant but bewildered customers. I enjoyed talking to them, however briefly, showing them where to sign or what to pay.

Only a few vignettes of those days remain alive in my memory. Approaching one house, something seemed vaguely familiar. The car parked out front—I had seen it before. I noticed that a certified letter needed signature and rang the bell. A reasonably attractive, youngish housewife answered, straightening disheveled hair and smoothing her open collared blouse. She was overdressed for a midweek late morning at home in Okolona—form-fitting pedal pushers, earrings, a bangly bracelet, lipstick—smudged? When she saw it was the postman, she smiled conspiratorially, almost smirked, and stepped back from the door. I could see into the living room, where Van Meter himself relaxed on the couch, shoes off, postman's tunic in disarray. Cigarette smoke hung in the air over a laden ashtray. Sinatra crooned enchantment from the hi-fi at the end of the living room.

Ever solicitous, never dismayed, Van Meter asked me with aplomb how things were going. Had I been quicker witted, I would have asked him the same thing. But my knowledge of the big bad world was very limited then. Savoir faire in short supply. I mumbled something inane, got my green receipt card signed, and beat a hasty retreat.

As Christmas neared, increasing skill and a lessening load told me my services would soon be unnecessary, if they ever had been. Van Meter and I were reduced to overt logrolling. One day, driving by what had now become my route, Van Meter knew that his faithful assistant would be finished by 11:30 or so. He instructed me to take a long, early lunch, and not report back to the post office before 2:30 or 3:00. "Or I'll have to go back to work!" This saved my job for one more day, an ugly one, and the last, Ms. Betty had decreed, for the temp Christmas carriers. Permafrost conditions had returned. By 3:30, I finished the final loop. A cold, fine, freezing rain had started, glazing everything with a thin layer of ice.

I made it back to the post office, wet and cold again. I said my goodbyes to Van Meter, Miss Betty and those met over the days. The vast sorting hall echoed with absence, as others were leaving or had already completed their farewells. Besides the weather, the leave-taking, and the loss of a paycheck, another somber thought weighed me down. My beat-up, elderly car's heater did not work. No heat, no defroster. I would not be able to make it home down Preston Highway in the freezing rain with rime constantly rebuilding on my already coated windshield.

As I warily crossed the frozen parking lot, inspiration struck. Parked next to my jalopy was Otis's pickup truck, and I knew just where Otis stashed his half-pint of Early Times. This ex-seminarian experienced no moral dilemma at the time, not even a momentary one. Glancing furtively around the lot, I reached behind the driver's seat and extracted the bottle from the nest of shotgun shells, empty premium cartons, fishing gear, and girlie magazines that covered the floor. I was in luck. The bottle was more than half full, enough to get me home. Yes, I should have left a few bucks on Otis's truck seat to pay for the Early Times. But I didn't even think about that until I wrote this sentence. My bad.

I scraped the windshield and applied a measured coating of the bourbon. I drove at a conservative pace, seeing the route clearly enough, and stopped a couple of times to coat the glass anew. I made it home, although the car and I smelled like a neighborhood dive by the time I got there. Mom treated me to a lecture on drinking on the job.

And so ended my USPS career, my first foray into the larger world of commerce. In this brave new world, I had seen and committed petty theft, witnessed perversion of the public trust, dereliction of duty, trafficking in pornography, drinking on the job, had myself uttered false statements in writing, handing in palpably misleading timecards, and probably was an accessory to adultery. All in only a few days. The excitement and newness of it all must have dulled my moral sense for the moment. I am now and have been for many years a model citizen.

So why should this convince me or anyone that the USPS is worth saving? Those acts are in the past, whether for good or ill. The postal service abolished the Christmas courier boondoggle long ago. The sorry Okolona Station of 1963 no longer exists outside my fond memory.

And that fondness, based on what I saw and felt is why I think we should leave the post office alone. Naive as I was, I did not understand until I handled them that the cards and letters I distributed held the very stuff of life and death—love and longing, hatred and forgiveness, profit and loss, failure and triumph: checks, bills, letters, invitations, applications, rejections, acceptances. The patrons who came to the door were generally pleased to see me. The transactions relieved their daily monotony, gave them something to smile or worry about, connection with the outside world.

Also, there was—and is—artistry and athleticism afoot, efficient performance of a boring, difficult job. I will always remember Van Meter at the close of my first day—in the cold and gathering dark, gliding through his paces, hands, feet, eyes all in sync, ensuring timely delivery of the mails. Nothing kept this swift courier from completion of his appointed rounds, even his own very human minor perfidy.

The common endeavor is alive and kicking. I see it at the group mailbox where our building's occupants gather to get their mail and chat for a moment with neighbors and the mail person. In thousands of rural post offices like the one in the remote village where my wife and I vacation each summer, the P.O. is a mini community center, the closest contact for people with one another and their government.

I would trade all the decoder rings in all the premium boxes ever delivered for the feeling of community and fulfillment my time as a letter carrier brought and yet brings me, even today.

About the Author

Tony Covatta is a retired English Lit teacher and retired lawyer now trying his hand at writing short stories, full length, flash, and micro. To date he has been published or is forthcoming in *October Hill Magazine*, *The Opiate*, *The Headlight Review*, *The Literary Club Anthology 2021*, *Literary Club Anthology 2023*, *Friday Flash Fiction*, *Scribes MICRO Fiction*, *101 Word Stories*, *Fifty Word Stories*, *A Story in 100 Words*, *Bright Flash Literary Review*, and others.

He lives in Cincinnati with his wife of 48 years, has three good kids and four splendid grandchildren. The family puts up with three dogs of various and varying dispositions.

For more information visit: tonycovatta.com

Twitter/X – @TCovatta

Facebook – @tony.covatta.96

Drowning in Christmas Spirit
by
Julia LaFond

Drowning in Christmas Spirit

I'm just coming back from spreading some Christmas cheer when I hear someone screaming. It could be excited screams, but it sounds more like scared screams, so I run to see what was going on. Sure enough, there's a shulikun dangling a woman over a bridge.

"What do you think you're doing?" I hop onto the wooden railing, crossing my arms.

His chain mail rattles as he whirls, one hand going to his sword hilt. The other, mercifully, remains tightly wrapped around her ankle, so she doesn't fall. "She's my rightful prey," he replies defensively, adjusting his pointy helmet. "I've never seen less Christmas spirit!"

"I'M JEWISH," she shrieks, thrashing.

I wince at the lie.

"See? She's undoubtedly on your *master's* 'Naughty list.'" He utters the last two words with utter contempt. "Why should you care?" He peels back his pinkie finger, loosening his hold on her.

I raise my voice over the woman's renewed screams. "Drowning people isn't nice."

The shulikun roughly swings the woman back onto the bridge but doesn't let go. He covers her mouth. "Finally, some quiet," he sighs. "You." His eyes bore into mine. "If you want my prey, you must fight for it."

I gulp. He's three times taller than me, clad in chain mail, and wielding a *sword!* Walking away wouldn't be nice. It wouldn't be nice *at all*. But for once, I'm seriously considering the naughty list.

The shulikun, sensing my hesitation, drags the woman back over the railing. She goes completely limp.

"Wait, wait, wait!" I plant myself in his way, even though he could punt me over the edge with a flick of his metal boot. "It's a week to the 25th. What if I help her find the spirit of Christmas before then?"

"A battle of wills would certainly be more interesting than a contest of strength between us," he muses, depositing the woman on the bridge. "I accept. But when you fail—"

"If!"

"*When* you fail," he continues grimly, "you must take her place."

"It's a deal," I reply with a fierceness that surprises me. "Let's shake on it, Mister...?"

"Grigoriy Leonovich." He grasps my outstretched hand. "Your name?"

"Silverbell Warmhearth." I bob my head so the bell on my tassel jingles.

Grigoriy's face puckers. "Silverbell," he repeats disdainfully. "You have my word." He stalks toward his horse. "One week."

I turn to the unconscious woman. It's cold, so I summon my favorite wool blanket to wrap her in. When she still doesn't wake up, I check her driver's license. Hester Yew, white, female, 41, 5'7", 170 lbs., brown eyes, brown hair (with white streaks). More importantly, she lives at 1313 Mortbur Lane, Apt. 444. With a tap of my heels and a pinch of glitter, I transport us there.

My heart skips a beat as I take in her bedroom. Clothes scattered across the floor, a trash can overflowing with Styrofoam cups, and dust-covered particle board furniture. No wonder Hester's not festive if she comes back to *this* every night.

That's an easy fix. I roll up my sleeves, grinning as I work.

I'm drizzling syrup over Hester's strawberry pancakes when she shuffles out of the bedroom, moaning and rubbing her head. She blinks slowly, still clutching my blanket.

"Good morning!" I chirp, skipping by to set her plate on the table. "I was going to bring you breakfast in—" The beeping coffeemaker derails my train of thought. "Almost forgot!" I pour us both a mug of hazelnut blend.

Hester takes a deep breath, lowering herself into her chair. "Maybe Tom spiked the punch," she mumbles to herself. "He's creepy enough."

It finally occurs to me that she's probably never heard of a shulikun, let alone seen one. Between that and her fainting spell, no wonder she's confused.

"No, this is real!" I bring her the tray of bacon. "Here, eat. You'll feel better."

Hester takes a hesitant bite, immediately perking up. "Tastes real. Tastes amazing!" She sips the coffee next. "Did you make all this?"

"Yup!"

She stares at me, clutching her mug with both hands. "If this is real..." She rubs her eyes. "What happened?"

"A shulikun. They're Russian, originally. Mostly, they prank Christmas revelers by pushing them into snowbanks. But— W-w-well s-sometimes if s-someone doesn't have enough Christmas spirit they—I'm sorry, it's not nice at all—they'll drown them."

"Drown them," she repeats flatly, the color draining from her face.

"You're safe now!" I pat her hand. "Anyway, you fainted, so I took you home."

"He...won't come back?"

"Nope!" I'm about to tell her about the deal I made, then stop myself. It wouldn't be nice to pressure her. "M-maybe stay away from the lake, though. At least until Lent."

She shudders. "Don't worry, I'm *never* going back there." She swallows a mouthful of pancakes. "But—" She waves her fork. "What about everything else?"

"What do you mean?"

"You made me breakfast, cleaned, and...um...decorated..." Her eyebrows knit together as she surveys the artificial tree, the wreath on the door, and the gingerbread house on the counter. "Where did you even— Never mind. Why all this?"

"Because the best way to spread Christmas cheer is to do nice things for people!"

She stares at me for an uncomfortably long time. "Who are you?"

"Oh!" I stand on the chair. "Sorry I didn't introduce myself sooner. I'm Silverbell Warmhearth!"

"That's..."

"A mouthful, I know." I brush my bangs aside. "If you want, call me—"

"Sylvie?" she interrupts.

"Sure."

"You're…a Christmas elf?"

I nod vigorously enough to jingle.

"Right. Of course you are." Hester chugs the rest of her coffee. "Listen, Sylvie…I'm grateful for everything you've done."

My smile freezes in place. She's lying. What did I do wrong?

She glances at her empty plate. "I've never had breakfast this good before."

Her sincerity warms my heart.

"Thank you," she continues. "But I'm alright now; you can go. Besides, I have work."

"But it's Saturday!"

"Retail," she grunts, carrying her dishes to the sink. "When I get back," she mumbles.

As she's freshening up, I start doing the dishes, still wondering what I did wrong.

She sighs when she sees me at the sink. "You really don't have to."

"I want to!"

"But— Never mind. I don't have time to argue." She heads for the door. "Thank you, again. Just…make sure the door is locked when you leave?" One more tired sigh leaves her lips, devoid of Christmas spirit.

Alone, I survey the apartment. My hurried decorations are positively paltry. That must be the problem.

Lucky for me, I have all day to fix my mistake.

Hester drops her takeout, jaw hanging open.

"Merry Christmas!" I place her salad on the table, trying to hide how jittery I am. I hope it's good enough now. The train was tricky, since there was so little room for the tracks. The fake snow could have been thicker, too. My biggest worry is the snowman music box; it's not as loud as I'd hoped.

She collapses onto the couch, covering her mouth. "It's like a Christmas unicorn exploded."

"You don't like it?" My hat droops.

She rubs her head. "No. I hate everything Christmassy."

It takes a minute to comprehend her words. Only then do I realize I've made things worse. "I'm...so sorry." I join her on the couch. "Did...something bad happen to you on a Christmas?"

"No." She pinches the bridge of her nose. "Retail. Starting in November, the entire store transforms into *this*." She gestures around. "All day, I have to smile and wish people Happy Holidays, while inane songs play on repeat, and the customers are extra clueless and abusive because it's *Christmas*."

"Ohhh. I'll take everything down right away." I pack up the music box. "By the way, I made ham for dinner."

She blinks, wearily. "Thanks, Sylvie."

Un-decorating hurts, but I'm hopeful. They're only the trappings of Christmas. I'll just have to get creative to help Hester discover her Christmas spirit.

My first idea is family. Hester lives alone; she must miss them. Maybe a reunion would help.

When she catches me browsing her contacts list, she scowls and snatches her phone. "No surprise parties."

"I—uh—"

She pinches the bridge of her nose. "My *family* is fine. My *relatives* never miss a chance to lord it over me that my cousins are *successful*. Because it's *Christmas*, they'll get their chance." She storms off, muttering about wine.

My next idea is her not-nice job. She hates her hours, the customers, her co-workers, and most of all, her manager.

"Could you quit?"

"I wish," she snorts. "My other options are equally bad."

I invisibly follow her to work. I'm immediately struck by how un-jolly her manager is. Maybe if I cheer him up, he'll be nicer to Hester. When he happens to complain about his car's radiator, I know exactly what to do. I fix up his car until it's good as new. He beams at the "luck", humming as he drives off.

Then he forces Hester to cover more hours so he can celebrate Christmas with his family.

She needs a better job.

That's not something I know how to do, and I can't find much. I've almost given up when I stumble across some horror stories she's written. They're really good, even if the victims all look like her manager.

"Give that back!" She snatches the laptop away. "Enough! Stop. Just stop."

"But I—"

"I know you're only being 'nice' because you want to 'fix' me! I don't have 'Christmas spirit,' I never will, and I don't care! So, *leave already!*" She points to the door. "*GET! OUT!*"

Choking back tears, hat in hand, I do leave. The snow falls thick and fast when a familiar figure approaches.

"I warned you," gloats Grigoriy. "Shall we get this over with?"

I shake my head, crossing my arms. "I have until tomorrow."

But we both know it's inevitable.

Hester doesn't answer the door. She pretends she can't see me at work. When she goes home, she locks me out. So, I slip my apology card under the door.

The snow crunches underfoot as I approach the bridge. The cold bites at my skin, harsh and cruel.

"I admire your spirit." A smile cruel as the cold tugs at Grigoriy's lips. "But this battle wasn't much of a challenge, either."

I can't help flinching when he grabs my shoulder. So much for dignity.

"What's going on?" shouts Hester.

My stomach plummets. Did she follow me? Why would she follow me?

"I got your note, I should apologize, too, but— Why's he here?" She points a shaky finger at the shulikun.

"It's alright." My voice squeaks with fear. "Go home before you catch a cold."

Grigoriy grasps the hilt of his sword. "Or I change my mind."

Hester cringes back, eyes darting between us. "No. Your letter—you said things that don't make sense unless…" Her eyes widen with realization. "You're taking my place?"

The shulikun's grip on me tightens.

I nod reluctantly. She deserves the truth, no matter how not-nice.

"No." Hester takes a shaky step forward. "I can't let you do that."

"The deal is struck," Grigoriy growls. "Run home!"

"Sylvie, this whole time… You were just trying to…" She wipes her eyes as she strides forward. "I'm the one you want. Take me instead."

"Hester, don't," I croak.

"Do you want her sacrifice to be in vain?" presses the shulikun.

"I've only known her a few days, and she's already helped me so much." Hester plants herself in front of him, frosted breath drifting into his face. "I'd be a terrible friend if I didn't return the favor."

"What a *selfless* gift," he sighs.

Before I can blink, the shulikun scoops us both up, one on each shoulder. I squeeze my eyes shut, whimpering. "You promised."

"I did."

He hurls me into a snowbank. Hester lands next to me with an "oomph."

"Merry Christmas," Grigoriy grumbles, mounting his horse. "You won after all."

About the Author

Julia LaFond got her master's in geoscience from Penn State University. She's had short stories published via *The Librarian Reshelved* (Air & Nothingness Press), *The Future's So Bright* (Water Dragon Publishing), and *Alternative Holidays* (B Cubed Press). In her spare time, Julia enjoys reading and gaming.

Website: jklafondwriter.wordpress.com

A Ghostly Christmas

by
Dawn Colclasure

A Ghostly Christmas

When some people think of Christmas, they think of snow. But as someone who has lived in Southern California for my entire seventeen years, the only time I ever see snow is when we are out of town.

As I sat in my room, staring out at the rain falling, I was glad that at least snow wasn't such a big deal for me. I didn't need snow for it to be Christmas. For me, Christmas is all about the Christmas tree.

My aunt Lizette takes the Christmas tree thing a little further than most people, though. Christmas isn't just a season for her: it's an everyday thing. She keeps her house decorated for Christmas all year long, which I find strange since her daughter had died on that day.

Why would she want that kind of day to last if it was so sad?

Well, that was how she lived. And my mom was having none of it.

"We're going to visit with your aunt for Christmas," she announced one morning during breakfast, right after I had taken a bite of my cereal.

I almost choked on my food. "Really?" I asked, looking at her with surprise.

The last time we had seen my aunt was two Christmases ago, a year after that dreaded Christmas day when my cousin had fallen through the ice and drowned. We had stayed for a few days after Christmas, and when my mom had tried to take down the Christmas decorations, my aunt had protested. They had a big fight about it, and we left. We didn't visit the next Christmas and I had expected the same thing to happen this year.

But now my mom was saying we were going to visit her again.

"I was being silly staying away from her like that," my mom said. She took a sip of her coffee. "She needs her family with her."

"I don't know if I'm ready to see her again, Mom," I said, shifting in my chair.

She looked at me and reached across the table to squeeze my hand. "What happened to Claudia wasn't your fault, Juliet," she reminded. "And your aunt knows this."

I looked down, swallowing the lump in my throat. Images of my cousin screaming for help as she struggled to get out of the river flashed through my mind. I had grabbed her hand and screamed "Hold on!" but her hand had slipped, and she'd gone under.

I looked at my mom again. "I feel like it's my fault. I didn't do enough to save her."

"Sweetheart, you tried," my mom said. "Just remember what your therapist said, okay? 'Don't fight what you can't change.' Maybe visiting with your aunt will help you."

The drive out to the mountains was a long one. I gazed out the window of the car as my mom drove in silence. She was probably trying to decide the best thing to say to help her sister get over her Christmas fixation.

Well, as far as I knew, my aunt's fixation with Christmas was just that: a fixation. I don't know why she kept her Christmas decorations up, but as I thought more about it now, I thought maybe it was the only way to be close to her daughter.

My cousin had been 13 when she died, a year younger than me. She was so excited to get her ice skates on Christmas morning that she wanted to go out onto the ice to use them. I had declined to join her on the ice, feigning a stomachache. She wanted to go out anyway. My aunt and mom encouraged me to go with her, just for safety, so I went. But it hadn't done any good. Claudia still fell through the ice. I still hadn't been able to save her. She had still drowned.

When we got to my aunt's cabin in the woods, I was amazed at the scenery. Her cabin and the surrounding forest of pine trees was covered with snow, looking like a winter wonderland. Snow and ice were everywhere. Icicles hung along the edges of the cabin's roof with a string of colorful Christmas lights hanging above them. Smoke came out of the chimney and interior lights shone through the windows. A Christmas wreath was on the door, with a spruce garland covering the top and sides of it. A plastic Santa with reindeer and sleigh were positioned in front of the cabin, with other assorted

Christmas decorations hung on the walls along the front of the cabin wall. There was a real snowman right next to the porch steps, and lit candy canes lined the entire outside of the porch.

We got out of the car and trudged through the snow to the trunk. It popped open and we retrieved our suitcases. Mom removed the bag containing Christmas presents and sighed as she looked down at them. She looked at me and her smile seemed forced. "First Christmas with your aunt in two years."

I nodded. "I think she will like that."

Mom nodded then grabbed hold of the bag containing our gifts with more determination. She slammed the trunk door shut and grabbed her suitcase from the ground.

As I turned to follow behind her, I could have sworn I saw something out of the corner of my eye, next to a nearby tree. But when I turned to get a better look, there was only the tree and snow. Shrugging, I followed behind my mother, catching up to her at the porch.

Seeing Aunt Lizette again, after two years of not seeing her, was almost a shock. She looked so different from the person I remembered.

"When did you get the perm?" I asked.

Smiling, she touched her brown hair. "Like it? I got it a year ago and it just feels right."

"It does look good," my mom agreed, nodding.

Not only did Aunt Lizette look different, but her house was different too. Aside from her Christmas decorations, she had brand new furniture in her small living room, a new dinette set in the kitchen, and even a new bed for her bedroom.

After putting our suitcases away, I noticed the door to Claudia's room was closed. I looked back to see my mom talking with my aunt near the Christmas tree then slowly placed my hand on the doorknob. It didn't turn; I guess my aunt still chose to keep the door locked. I wondered if Claudia's stuff was still in there.

"Juliet, dinner is ready!" my aunt called behind me.

I looked back, gasping as though I was caught. But she and my mom were at the table.

I looked at the door one last time then stepped away before turning to walk to the kitchen.

Dinner was bigger than I expected. My aunt had always been a great cook, and I was happy that at least this had not changed since I last saw her. My eyes feasted on the roasted chicken, mashed potatoes, corn and dinner rolls. It was just as delicious to eat and, afterward, we had peach cobbler for dessert.

Now as we settled in on the couch in front of the roaring fireplace, drinking mugs of hot cider, my mother decided to broach the subject.

"Is that the same tree you had up three years ago, Lizette?"

"Oh, yes," my aunt happily replied. "You'd think that by now that the lights would have died out and the limbs wouldn't stay up, but there they are!" She smiled as she turned her head to look at the tree, admiring it. "I guess artificial trees really do last a long time."

"It is a beautiful tree," my mom agreed, nodding in the direction of it. "But have you ever wanted a real one?"

My aunt shook her head as she looked at my mom. "No. I like this one." She sighed and took a sip from her mug. "Claudia helped me decorate it." She looked at the tree again. "There are some ornaments on there that she made herself."

"Why not keep the ornaments out?" my mother asked, looking at her sister. "You can keep them on your shrine."

My aunt kept a shrine for Claudia in the corner of the room. We had talked about it during dinner; my mom loved the picture my aunt had chosen for it.

My aunt shook her head. "No, I want to keep them on the tree and keep the tree just where it is," she replied as she lovingly looked at her Christmas tree again.

I was glad when my mom changed the subject.

I tried to get comfortable on the couch that night, but it was too lumpy. Lying on my side, I stared at the Christmas tree. I tried to listen for sounds of conversation from my aunt's bedroom, where my mom was bunking tonight, but the whole cabin was quiet. Which was why I wasn't sure I was hearing what I thought I heard.

"Juliet."

I looked around the room. There wasn't anyone there. I could have sworn I heard a voice calling my name. A voice that sounded feminine.

"Juliet."

There it was again!

I slowly stood from the couch, looking around. There was no one there. Both the radio and television set were off.

Then I looked out the window and gasped.

Standing off in the distance near a tree, in the snow, was my cousin, Claudia.

Or, at least, someone who I thought was Claudia.

I hurriedly put on my shoes, threw on my coat, and slowly opened the front door. I stepped out onto the porch, taking a few cautious steps and trying to figure out if I was seeing what I really thought I saw.

The girl looked exactly like my cousin had on that sad Christmas Day three years ago. She wore her white pants, red sweater under a white winter coat, and her pink and red beanie hat over her long blonde hair. On her feet were the same ice skates that her mother had given to her.

"Claudia?" I asked in a whisper, blinking a few times. "Is it really you?"

The girl walked closer. She definitely looked like she could be thirteen.

"Yes, it's really me, Juliet," she said, after coming to a stop a few feet from the porch. "I've missed you."

I smiled. "I've missed you too." I looked back but no one else was at the door or on the porch. I descended the stairs and walked over to hug my cousin. She felt so real!

When we unembraced, she smiled at me. "Please don't feel guilty," she pleaded, grasping my hands. "It wasn't your fault."

"I know," I said, sadly looking down. I shook my head. "I should have tried harder to save you."

"I don't blame you for what happened." I looked up to see my cousin looking back at me with kindness and understanding in her eyes. "And my mom doesn't blame you, either." She shrugged. "It was an accident. The ice was too thin."

Tears came to my eyes. "I should have done more. I'm so sorry."

She nodded. "I forgive you, Juliet. If that's what you need." She smiled. "Merry Christmas."

A rustling sound in the woods made me look away and when I looked back, my cousin was gone. She no longer held my hands. I no longer saw her beautiful smile.

I looked down and cried, wishing she was there again. Wishing I had told her "Merry Christmas" in return.

It wasn't daylight that woke me on Christmas morning but a different kind of light. My eyes opened to see a strong orange light glowing around the Christmas tree. The rest of the room was mostly dark.

I gasped as I sat up, my eyes widening. I stood from the couch, taking it all in.

"It's almost time."

I turned to see my aunt Lizette smiling at me. She stood right next to me. Then she turned to look at the Christmas tree and I did too.

Soon, an image of a person came into view. It was hard to see at first, but after a while, the person's image appeared clearer. Then it came to life. I gasped when I saw that it was Claudia, looking the same way she had on that Christmas Day she had died. The same way she had when I had seen her outside.

The ghostly image of Claudia smiled as she placed a few decorations on the Christmas tree. Decorations that were still there now. Then she turned around to look in the direction of the kitchen.

"Come and look, Mama," she said, and my heart melted at the sound of her voice. "Come and see."

Then her image faded. The orange glow disappeared, and we were back in the dimly-lit living room.

Tears welled in my eyes, and I sniffled. I looked at my aunt, who also had tears in her eyes. She smiled at me. "Isn't it beautiful?" she asked in a soft voice.

I nodded.

We both hugged each other and gently wept. After we regained control of ourselves, I said, "Merry Christmas, Aunt Lizette." I swallowed the lump of tears in my throat.

"Merry Christmas, sweetheart," she replied.

I looked at the tree as I hugged her. Now I knew why my aunt really wanted to keep the tree up all the time. How could she take it down after that? It reminded her of her beautiful daughter. It kept her spirit with her.

"Merry Christmas to Claudia, too," I whispered.

We both sat down on the couch. I stared at my aunt for a long time before I found a voice to speak with. "Does this always happen?"

She nodded. "Every Christmas morning. I saw it on the first Christmas after her death." She looked at the Christmas tree. "I couldn't sleep. I was so depressed. You and your mom slept in my room. I sat next to the tree, just staring at it. That's when I noticed it happening." She looked at me again. "I didn't expect it to happen the next year, but it did. So far, it happens every Christmas morning, at six a.m. The time Claudia woke up that morning."

"Wow! That's amazing!" I studied her. "Is that why you wanted me to sleep on the couch?"

She nodded, smiling.

"Have you told my mom about this?"

She shook her head. "Your mother doesn't believe in ghosts, sweetie. Anyway, if I did tell her, she would chalk it up to wishful thinking. Saying that I just missed Claudia so much that I pretended she was there."

"It might be a good idea to tell her. She wants you to take the tree down."

My aunt nodded. "I know. She told me last night. But that tree is not coming down. Not while it keeps my baby with me, if only for one day."

She fell silent again and she sniffled. She sighed then looked at the tree. I looked at the tree too. Soon I felt her hand holding mine and I squeezed it in response.

"Merry Christmas!"

My eyes slowly opened, and I rubbed out the sleep so I could see clearly. I must have fallen asleep because the room was filled with daylight now. My aunt stood alongside the couch, looking as beautiful and radiant as ever.

"Merry Christmas, Aunt Lizette!" I greeted, standing from the couch to hug her.

"I hope you're hungry!" I heard my mother call from another room. "We made a big breakfast."

I still smiled as my aunt and I moved back from our embrace. "You okay?" I asked, looking at her.

She smiled as she nodded. "I am great. It's so nice to have company over on Christmas morning."

I grinned. "I hope it happens more often."

She gently squeezed my arms. "Me too!"

We walked over to the kitchen table, where my mother had just placed a large dish containing a breakfast casserole. She looked up at me and smiled. "Merry Christmas, Juliet."

I smiled at her. "Merry Christmas, Mom."

We all sat down to eat a hearty breakfast. We all talked, laughed, and had a great time sharing memories. My aunt seemed enthused as she talked about Claudia; I was grateful it didn't make her sad to share memories of her.

After breakfast, we washed the dishes and grabbed a mug of cocoa before heading back to the living room. We sat down to open our gifts and look through our stockings. I noticed there was a gift under the tree for Claudia. Mom noticed it too but didn't say anything. I guess she understood how hard today would be for my aunt and that we should try to make Christmas morning easier for her.

Christmas Day had been great, but the day after Christmas got off to a rocky start.

My mom woke me up early.

"Juliet, I need your help."

I sleepily sat up on the couch, rubbing my eyes. "What's up, Mom?"

"I need you to help me take down this tree."

"What!" I gasped, suddenly sitting up and feeling much more awake now.

"We need to do it before your aunt wakes up," she explained. "Please. It's for the best."

I shook my head. "No, Mom. I'm not taking down that tree. Leave it up." Now that I knew just why the Christmas tree was so special to my aunt, I knew why she kept it up. There was no way I was going to help my mom take it down.

"I told you, it needs to come down," my mother reminded, her voice a little firmer.

"It's Aunt Lizette's Christmas tree, Mom. It's special to her. Please let her leave it up."

My mother's gaze hardened. "Not you, too."

"Diane."

We both looked to see my aunt standing in the entryway to the hall, her opened bedroom door a short distance behind her. She stood wearing her long white nightgown.

"Why won't you let me keep up my tree?" she asked, looking at my mom.

My mother stood and turned to walk towards my aunt, coming to a stop in front of her. "It's not healthy, Lizette." She gripped my aunt's arms. "We've talked about this. The tree is only reminding you that Claudia is gone, and the longer you keep it up, the harder it will be for you to move on with your life."

Instead of anger, my aunt only looked at my mom with love and compassion. "I know Claudia is gone," she said. "I know that every morning that I wake up to her empty bedroom and every night she's not at the dinner table with me. You kept your distance from me for so long that you didn't know what was going on with me. I got better, Diane. I went to therapy. I attended support group meetings and found the courage to say goodbye to my daughter."

"But you keep your house decorated for Christmas all year!" my mother began.

My aunt shook her head. "Not anymore. The last time you saw me, I was a wreck. I couldn't put away the Christmas decorations or the tree because I was grieving the loss of my daughter. I may keep the tree up, but everything else still gets put away."

My mother sighed, stiffening as she dropped her arms to her sides. "I think the tree should come down, too."

My aunt had a very serious expression on her face as she said, "The tree stays up, Diane. I won't budge on that."

"Mom, let her have her tree," I said, knowing it was wrong to interrupt, but I felt I had to say something. "It's not hurting anyone."

My mother turned to give me a firm look. "Stay out of it." She looked at my aunt again. "I just want you to be able to move on with your life, Diane."

My aunt shrugged, smiling. "I am. I have. You don't need to worry about me."

"But you're using the Christmas tree as some kind of crutch," my mom said.

"It's not a crutch." Her smile disappeared. "Diane, you have nothing to worry about. Everything's fine. I'm fine. Really."

My mom sighed again. "I'll believe that when I see it." She walked over to get her coat and scarf from the coat stand. "I'm going to go get coffee and doughnuts." She grabbed her purse and walked out the front door. Soon we heard her Jeep start up outside and drive away.

My aunt sighed and shook her head. She looked at me and smiled. "I'm going to get dressed. Go ahead and use the shower if you need to. I have a bit of work to do today."

"What kind of work?"

"Why, taking down all the lights and decorations, of course," she replied with a surprised look. "Christmas is over, after all."

Nodding, I got up from the couch. "I'll help!"

We had the lights down and the Santa with reindeer put away by the time my mom got back. As my mom carried the box of doughnuts and tray of coffees up to the cabin, she looked at us with surprise. "What have you two been doing?"

"Putting away the Christmas decorations, of course!" my aunt replied with surprise.

"Yeah, Mom," I added. "Christmas is over."

Chuckling, my mom walked up to the porch right around the same time we were taking down the wreath and wall decorations.

"You know, Lizette," she said, getting my aunt's attention as she picked up one of the banners from the wall. "I have been thinking." She sighed. "Juliet is right; the tree really isn't hurting anyone. I'm glad you got therapy. If the tree makes you happy, then that's all that matters."

My aunt's posture relaxed, and she smiled at my mom. "Thank you, Diane. And thank you for your concern about me."

"Yeah, don't get used to it," my mother joked as she went into the cabin.

My aunt chuckled and turned to look out past where the Jeep was parked. I noticed her gaze was fixed on something, so I looked out too and smiled. The ghostly image of Claudia stood by the same tree I had seen her at the other night.

"I don't need to keep the tree up, but it's still nice to have," she said in a soft voice. I wasn't sure if she was talking to me, Claudia, or to herself, so I kept quiet.

I stepped up to her and placed my hand on her shoulder. "Let's go inside and have some breakfast," I suggested.

She nodded, still looking away. Then she looked at me and smiled. "Thank you for being here."

"I'm glad I was," I replied, smiling in return.

We walked into the cabin, and I watched my aunt begin chattering with my mom as she walked to the kitchen. As I turned to shut the front door, I looked out and saw that the ghost of my cousin was gone. Closing the door, I had a feeling we would see her again.

About the Author

Dawn Colclasure is a writer who lives in Oregon with her husband and children. She is the author of three novels as well as various other books and eBooks. Her short stories have appeared in magazines and anthologies.

Her websites are:

dawnsbooks.com and www.dmcwriter.com

Find her on Twitter @dawncolclasure.

Epiphany Star Singers

by
Mary Jo Rabe

Epiphany Star Singers

Karlheinz Nowak rubbed his bloodshot eyes with his stiff, cold fingers and looked at his group of Epiphany star singers. Right. A popular tradition to commemorate following the star of Bethlehem. Always on January sixth, the Feast of the Epiphany, when it was bitterly cold in Germany.

The girls stood in the grimy piles of snow that the snowplow had deposited on the sidewalk. Inversion. The foggy air reeked of burnt wood from the many chimneys in this part of Nova Civitas. Not unpleasant, but also not great for air quality.

Six expectant twelve-year-old faces, five eager and one bored, looked at him. Kids that age didn't mind cold or snow, especially when they were excited about being official Epiphany star singers. Karlheinz, on the other hand, preferred to spend his free time in his warm cabin in the woods where he could stretch his long legs from the soft, cushioned couch to the wood-burning tiled stove.

Yes, even though he was an environmentally conscious forestry manager by profession, he indulged in the use of his wood-burning stove. After all, inhabitants of the Black Forest had warmed their homes with these tiled stoves for centuries, not a problem back when the population of Nova Civitas was about one tenth of what it was now.

Damn. It was starting to snow again, and the wind was picking up. Why had he let himself be conned into running around in the cold on a dark late afternoon when he could be relaxing at home? Easy. Because Tante Agnes, his favorite aunt, had asked him to help out.

Tante Agnes, a short but feisty seventy-year-old with stubbornly curly, thick, white hair, was also the world's best baker. He was always overjoyed to see her drive up to his cabin with her latest pastry. Last week she showed up with a chocolate cream cake and said, "I need you to chaperone a group of Epiphany star singers on January sixth."

"Why me?" Karlheinz asked. "Are there so many singers that you have to find more chaperones?"

"The churches that supervise this activity are amazed and delighted that so many kids want to participate this year," Tante Agnes said. "They have even organized a party for the kids after they return from singing. But each group of five or six has to have an adult chaperone with them when they go out to sing on the Feast of Epiphany."

"I didn't know kids today were that religious," Karlheinz said.

"They aren't," said Tante Agnes. "But that's not important. Kids are much too stressed these days. They have schedules that would burn out an adult. That's why it's good for them to take part in this kind of thing."

"If they're so stressed, why do they need one more thing to do?" Karlheinz asked.

"The rest of their lives involve being judged, whether it's their grades in school or their athletic prowess. Kids from eight to thirteen need activities where they are appreciated, where they see that people enjoy having them around."

Karlheinz looked at the cake. He could almost taste the thick, gooey, chocolate frosting and the moist chocolate layers. Tante Agnes had always been very good to him, and it wouldn't kill him to do her a favor. "All right, I'm in. What does this involve?"

"You have to meet the kids at the ecumenical youth center and then walk with your group," Tante Agnes began. "The kids will ring doorbells, then if someone opens the door, the kids sing specific Epiphany songs and write the letters 20 C+M+B 20 on the lintel above the outside door.

"The people who open the door often give the kids a donation for the project they are singing for, a different one each year. Many of the people even insist on also giving the singers cookies and hot chocolate. Don't worry! You'll all have fun."

That was how he ended up here standing here in the cold with six somewhat patient twelve-year-old girls. Karlheinz caught a glimpse of his reflection in the windows of a car parked half on the snow-covered sidewalk and half on the icy street. His vanity was going to kill him yet.

For walking around town in January, he should have worn his work clothes, the heavy wool cap, the parka guaranteed to keep him warm down to minus forty degrees, thick gloves, and sturdy boots. However, when he wasn't at work, he preferred to be considered well-dressed.

As coincidence would have it, snowflakes on his thick, curly, longish, brown hair created the image he wanted, even when he was just playing chaperone for a group of children star singers. You never know, maybe he would run into someone he wanted to make a good impression on.

Tante Agnes kept insisting that it was time for him to find someone and settle down; after all he was almost forty. Unfortunately, so far, the women he dated lost interest when he showed them his cabin in the woods. For most people it was too "out in nowhere," too quiet, and too isolated.

Yet, as fate would have it, he liked it there. After a strenuous day managing the forest, dealing with city officials, foresters, and customers, he liked to retreat to a refuge of peace and quiet. He had made many improvements to the cabin over the years, adding rooms, modernizing the electricity and plumbing. He thought it was now close to perfect.

Right now, of course, Karlheinz was shivering. The six girls didn't seem to notice the cold. They probably wore sweatshirts and sweatpants under their "Three Kings of the Orient" costumes. His group contained the mathematically correct costumed numbers of two Balthazars, two Melchiors, and two Caspars.

Unlike previous years, this time Tante Agnes made sure that none of the Melchiors among the star singers performed in blackface, to the dismay of naïve traditionalists in villages and small towns who still refused to recognize their unconscious European racism.

Karlheinz didn't want to count the number of times he had heard older people insist, "It's not racist if we laugh; dark skin just looks funny." His two Caspars didn't even ask for blackface cosmetics, so there was hope for the next generation.

"When do we get started?" Daniela asked. She was the most persistent girl in the group, the tallest, the huskiest, and also reputed to be the best singer. Fortunately, four of the others didn't look intimidated by her. Carola, a short girl with straight, brown hair sticking out from under her ski cap, probably the youngest of the girls, seemed to be the outsider of the group.

Tante Agnes had asked him to keep an eye on her. The girl was new in town and lived with her mother in the only cheap section of Nova Civitas, up in the Neuwies Hill region. Tante Agnes, who knew everything that went on in town, had heard that Carola still didn't have any friends and wasn't doing well at school. Carola's mother was a police officer who had to work varying shifts, and so her daughter was often alone at home. The father apparently wasn't in the picture.

"This is the north side of the Saierstrasse," Karlheinz said. "Our route includes the houses all the way from the Edeka grocery store, past the school center, and ending at the St. Gabriel nursing home. Another group will sing in the nursing home."

"Then let's go," Daniela shouted. "People are waiting."

"Watch out for patches of ice," Karlheinz said. "They're easy to miss in the dark."

The girls marched gleefully from house to house, ignoring the possibility of fractures from slipping on the ice. Karlheinz struggled to keep up. At his relatively advanced age, he didn't want to risk the loss of work time that would result if he broke any bones. He had too much he wanted to get done this year.

Every door opened as soon as the girls rang the bells. Karlheinz was no judge of singing, but he thought his group sounded quite pleasant. Daniela indeed had a beautiful voice. The little audiences in each house clapped enthusiastically, donated generously, and often did insist on giving the girls cookies and hot chocolate. Some were even considerate enough to offer Karlheinz a cup of seasonal hot wine punch, which warmed him up so quickly that he didn't even notice how long they were out in the cold.

"Now we just have one house left, Frau Riedel's," Karlheinz said after two hours and consulting his map and list. "Then it's back to the ecumenical youth center for the star singers' party. You girls deserve to celebrate; you've done a great job."

"Yes," Daniela said firmly. "We collected at least two hundred euros for children in Lebanon. Last year we didn't even come close to that, and who knows how much the other groups got."

"The people loved your singing," Karlheinz added. "You are really good. So, let's give Frau Riedel her short concert, and then we can march back."

"I know Frau Riedel," Daniela said, her red face beaming. "She used to walk her dog past the bus stop behind the school center, and I always talked to her while I was waiting for my bus. Her husband died a few years ago, then her dog died last year, and I haven't seen her much since then. She's old, maybe ninety, but she likes to have the Epiphany star singers come and sing. She always gives groups a large donation."

"Then by all means let's go to Frau Riedel," Karlheinz said.

The old woman lived in a modest brick home several meters back from the sidewalk. Daniela marched up to the door and rang the bell. "We're the star singers," she said.

A fragile-looking, scrawny, old woman with wispy, thin, white hair opened the door quickly and looked out. "I'm sorry," she whispered. "But you have to leave. The policewoman will be here soon."

"What?" Karlheinz asked, as he forced himself out of his punch-induced sluggishness and made his way to the door. "Why are police officers coming?" He had never done this chaperone business before, but he suspected he wasn't supposed to let the kids hang around in situations where the police had been called. Obviously, the sensible thing to do would be to get the girls back to the ecumenical youth center immediately.

However, Daniela had other ideas, and he didn't know how the girls would react if he insisted that they leave.

"Why is a policewoman coming, Frau Riedel?" Daniela asked.

"I'm not supposed to tell anyone," the old woman said. "The nice policewoman on the phone said not to. She told me I can't trust anyone right now, because criminals have infiltrated the police force and the banks."

"But you know me," Daniela said. "You know you can trust me. What's going on?"

"The nice policewoman called me several times to warn me about the burglars in my neighborhood," Frau Riedel said. "They are breaking into people's houses and stealing their valuables. She also said some of the people at the bank are stealing the customers' money."

Karlheinz stared at her. He knew what was coming and didn't know what they should do.

"She was very kind," Frau Riedel continued. "The police want to protect my valuables, and so the nice policewoman said I should get my money out of the bank and put all my jewelry with the money in a bag. I did that already. She will pick it up for safe keeping tonight. After she puts my valuables in a safe place, she will watch out for the criminals who try to break into my house. That's why you have to leave."

"Did you call the police and confirm what she said?" Daniela asked.

"No, no," Frau Riedel said anxiously. "The nice policewoman warned me that there are criminals in the police force."

Karlheinz motioned to Carola to walk back to the sidewalk with him. She seemed reluctant but came with him. "Do you have a cell phone with you?" he asked. She nodded.

"Then call your mother and tell her what Frau Riedel just said. Your mother will recognize the scam and will know how the real police want to react."

Carola looked astonished, but she pulled her cell phone out of her pocket and moved away while she talked. When she came back to Karlheinz, she said, "Mama says we should stay here and keep Frau Riedel from giving anyone anything. The police will be here in a few minutes."

Karlheinz walked back to the door. "Frau Riedel," he said. "The policewoman who talked to you must surely know that today is January sixth, the Feast of the Epiphany. She won't be upset to see Epiphany star singers at your door. Why don't you let the girls sing? They sing so well, and they have really been looking forward to singing for you."

The old woman looked confused. "But the nice policewoman said," she began.

"Herr Nowak is right," Daniela said. "The star singers have come to your house every year. I can see the chalk up there on the lintel of your door. We want to sing and write the numbers of the new year next to the C, M, and B."

Frau Riedel seemed less agitated. "All right," she said. "Do you girls know what C, M, and B stand for? It's not Caspar, Melchior, and Balthasar like so many people think."

"I've been taking Latin for two years," Daniela said and laughed. "It stands for *Christus mansionem benedicat*, may Christ bless this house."

"I guess my house could always use a blessing. If the policewoman comes while you're here, I suppose she can wait until you write this blessing on my house," Frau Riedel said. "What songs can you sing for me?"

The girls went through their entire repertoire, "From Door to Door," "We Bring the Blessings," "We Have Seen the Star of Bethlehem," "Come, Follow the Star," and then "Children Help Children."

"That is so sweet," Frau Riedel said. "What are you collecting donations for this year?"

"For children in Lebanon," Daniela said. "That's the charity all the Epiphany star singers want to help."

"Wait just a moment," Frau Riedel said. "I can give you something from all the money I took out of the bank." She turned around and went back into her house.

Karlheinz looked around and was relieved to see a genuine police vehicle drive up the street. However, it drove past Frau Riedel's house and onto the back rows of the nursing home parking lot where it was no longer visible.

Two people got out and walked over to the group of girls. Karlheinz recognized Boris Horn, the chief of police. His picture was in the newspaper fairly often. Carola ran over to the woman whom Karlheinz assumed was her mother. The two of them talked for a few minutes.

Then Carola's mother and the chief of police walked to the door and waited until Frau Riedel returned and gave Daniela twenty euros. Karlheinz saw them talk to Frau Riedel, and then the three of them went back into the house. Carola's mother closed the outside door.

"Can you write the numbers in chalk for us, Herr Nowak?" Daniela asked. "All you have to do is erase the number 19 and write 20 in its place. Frau Riedel has a really high door. I'm even too short to reach up to the top."

"Always glad to help," Karlheinz said as he looked around. He noticed an unmarked car with two police officers drive past the house and onto the nursing home parking lot where it parked next to the marked police vehicle.

"What's going on?" Daniela asked.

"It's a vicious scam," Karlheinz said. "Criminals pick older people out of the telephone book by their old-fashioned names. Then these criminals call the old people and talk them into giving them all their money and valuables."

"The criminals claim that they are the police and that they will take care of the money. It is all well organized, generally by gangs outside the country. A helper picks up the stash and hands it over to other criminals who rush it out of the country, where it disappears forever."

"They tried a variation of this trick on my grandmother," he continued. "They called her and told her I had been in an accident in Russia and needed money for the hospital. They said they had to bring the money to Russia quickly which was why they needed to drive my grandmother to the bank where she could get her savings."

"Fortunately, my aunt Agnes came into the house while my grandmother was still on the phone and put an end to the whole business. Unfortunately, that meant that the crooks didn't get caught and probably cheated some other old person."

"Herr Nowak told me to call my mom, and she talked to her police colleagues," Carola said. "They are going to try to catch the criminals when the woman comes to collect the money and jewelry."

"What happens now?" Daniela asked.

"Mom said the biggest problem will be persuading Frau Riedel that the woman who called is a criminal and not a policewoman," Carola said. "Mom says these people are very persuasive on the phone."

"That's a terrible thing to do," Daniela said. "Taking advantage of these kind, trusting, old people like that."

"That's why Mom decided to become a police officer," Carola said. "She wants to protect people from criminals."

"That's a good thing," Daniela said.

"You know," Karlheinz said. "We really should head back to the star singer party. If the police can persuade Frau Riedel to trust them, they will try to catch the woman who wants to steal from her. As long as our group stands here, with you in your Three Kings costumes, the woman is unlikely to go to the door."

The girls grumbled a little but then did turn around. The sidewalks were especially slippery; the ice was covered with a thin layer of snow. Karlheinz almost fell down several times. His leather shoes were truly worthless for this kind of activity. The sure-footed girls had no problems.

The closer they got to the busy Raufferstrasse, the worse the air quality got. Inversion plus auto exhaust made Karlheinz want to flee to his cabin in the woods where the air was always good. Once they got to the youth center in the Boscostrasse behind the city park, things improved.

The ecumenical youth center was a large room, a good two hundred square meters, somewhat cold, with a pleasant scent of cookies and hot chocolate permeating the air. Plates and mugs stood on tables along the walls. Folding chairs were stacked up around the room, but no one wanted to sit.

All the Epiphany star singers, children between the ages of eight and about thirteen, ran around comparing how much money they had collected. Other volunteer adults, probably also recruited by Tante Agnes, refilled the snacks and drinks on the tables for the kids.

The choir director of the church next door, a middle-aged bald man with a thundering voice, went from group to group and led them in singing one of their favorite songs. Once he determined that all the groups had returned, he asked the kids to reassemble in their groups so that they could report how much each group had managed to collect in donations.

"The groups collected one thousand euros altogether," the choir director proclaimed proudly after each group had reported its amount. "This is a record!"

Daniela moved to the center of the room. "Thank you," she said. "But while we're all here, I want to say that we shouldn't wait another year to visit the people we sang for."

"Epiphany is only once a year," the choir director said, looking confused.

"But lonely old people need visitors more than once a year," Daniela explained patiently. "Otherwise, they can become victims of criminals."

"That's an excellent idea," Tante Agnes said. "Write up some suggestions, and I'll see to it that the youth center organizes such a service that you kids can take part in."

Daniela smiled and said, "Maybe Carola can ask her mother to help us. It would be good to know about the criminals we're up against."

Carola looked astonished but managed to mumble, "Sure, anything I can do to help." Karlheinz saw the other girls in his group start to talk to her.

The singers in the room continued to eat, drink, and talk but gradually started to leave. Daniela and the other five girls told Karlheinz they were walking home together because they were all neighbors. Daniela waved to Carola as they left.

Karlheinz saw how Carola looked at the door apprehensively. He walked over to her and asked, "Do you need a ride home?" He knew that the Neuwies Hill part of town was a good two miles away, uphill, and not well-lit.

Carola shook her head but continued to stare at the door. "Okay," Karlheinz said. "Then I'll wait here with you until your mother comes to pick you up. That's who you're waiting for, isn't it?"

Carola nodded, and Karlheinz sighed to himself. Actually, he had hoped to hurry home once he got his group back to the youth center. He had a long hard day ahead of him tomorrow. A new lumber company wanted to see which trees the city had for sale, and it was generally more efficient to take them on a hike through the woods.

Obviously, Tante Agnes's ideals were starting to rub off on him. Of course he would stay until every girl in his group was safely home, one way or another.

An hour later everyone had left except for Carola and Karlheinz. He pulled out two folding chairs and they sat down. Some of the other adult group leaders also volunteered to stay, but Karlheinz felt he was responsible for his group. Tante Agnes said all he had to do to lock the building was pull the outside door shut when he left. After a while he decided to try to strike up a conversation with Carola.

"How do you like it here in Nova Civitas, Carola?" he asked.

"Fine," she said.

"Well," he said. "Sometimes small towns aren't easy to get used to. But there are a lot of good people in Nova Civitas. I'm sure you'll come to like it here. It looks like Daniela is grateful for your help."

"Yeah," Carola mumbled. "I admire her energy."

That was pretty much the end of the conversation. To her credit, Carola didn't pull out her smart phone and stare at it. Karlheinz really didn't know how to talk to a twelve-year-old girl.

Fortunately, Carola's mother came through the door some ten minutes later and sat with them. She was taller than Carola but had the same slight build and the same straight brown hair that stood on end when she took her hat off. Karlheinz guessed that she was in her late thirties.

"Could you catch the thief?" Karlheinz asked.

"I'm sorry it took so long," she said. "It was very difficult to make Frau Riedel believe that the woman who called her was a member of a gang of thieves. The only thing that finally persuaded her was my boss, Chief Horn. He is the nephew of one of Frau Riedel's friends, and so she gradually decided that she could trust him. We finally got her to listen to us."

"Did the thief ever show up?" Karlheinz asked.

"Yes," Carola's mother said. "That went well. Frau Riedel did what we said. She told the woman to come into the house and help her pack the jewelry. Once the woman was in the living room, we came out of the kitchen and explained just how much jail time she faced if she didn't help us."

"The woman immediately told us where her accomplices were waiting. Chief Horn called the plainclothes colleagues who located the car just one block south of Frau Riedel's house. They were able to arrest both thieves."

"Great," Karlheinz said.

"Well, we did what we could. We caught three small fish, but the masterminds are most likely out of the country."

"Maybe your small fish will tell you something," Karlheinz said.

The woman sighed. "Anyway, thank you so much for staying with Carola. I told her to wait here for me, but I thought I would be here much sooner."

"I'm Karlheinz Nowak," he said.

"Sorry," she said. "I should have introduced myself much sooner. I'm Veronika Dietlicher, and you know my daughter Carola."

"My aunt said you haven't lived here for very long," Karlheinz said. "How do you like it here?"

"I like my colleagues, and the area around Nova Civitas is beautiful, but I hope we can find a better place to live. Our building in the Neuwies Hill part of town is noisy and crowded."

"Housing is hard to find everywhere," Karlheinz said. "Even in Nova Civitas. What kind of place are you looking for?"

Frau Dietlicher sighed. "Sometimes I wish we could live in a cabin in the woods where it is quiet, where Carola and I could relax after a hard day at work and school."

"Really?" Karlheinz asked. "Most people wouldn't like to live like that."

"We're introverts," Frau Dietlicher said. "We enjoy being away from crowds."

"Hmm," Karlheinz said. "Then I'd like to invite the two of you to visit me. I happen to live in a cabin in the woods between here and Faulenfirst. When are you off-duty? My Aunt Agnes will be thrilled to make us a Black Forest cake."

Carola smiled. "Is tomorrow good?" she asked.

Karlheinz nodded. Maybe things were looking up after all. He was sure Tante Agnes would approve.

About the Author

Mary Jo Rabe grew up on a farm in eastern Iowa, got degrees from Michigan State University (German and math) and University of Wisconsin-Milwaukee (library science) where she became a late-blooming science fiction reader and writer. She worked in the library of the chancery office of the Archdiocese of Freiburg, Germany for 41 years, and lives with her husband in Titisee-Neustadt, Germany. She published "Blue Sunset", inspired by *Spoon River Anthology* and *The Martian Chronicles*, electronically and has stories published in *Fiction River, Pulphouse, Penumbric Speculative Fiction, Alien Dimensions, 4 Star Stories, Fabula Argentea, The Lost Librarian's Grave, The Lorelei Signal, A Flight of Dragons, Draw Down the Moon, Dark Horses, Wyldblood Magazine, One-Way-Ticket to Epsilon Eridani, Boundary Shock Quarterly, Blaze Ward Presents*, and other magazines and anthologies.

She indulges in sporadic activity on Facebook:
www.facebook.com/rabemj
Blog: maryjorabe.wordpress.com

The Bravest Dish

by
Steve Ruskin

The Bravest Dish

The boar's head, as I understand,

Is the bravest dish in all the land.

–Traditional English Carol

*I*n the fireplace of the Great Hall of St Visla's College, Cambridge, the fire hissed and popped as it gnawed its way through the Yule log. The fire was the hall's primary source of light and warmth, though it provided comparatively little of either to the cavernous room.

Two rows of dining tables—a dozen in each, all long and wooden and worn smooth by age and use—stretched away into the darkness. Atop every table flickered candles in silver candelabra, feebly providing what illumination the fire could not. Wrapped around the base of each candlestick were garlands of holly, their waxy berries roseate and glowing. All along the tables were silver plates, goblets, and cutlery at precise intervals, one setting for each student and member of the faculty.

High Table, perpendicular to the other tables at one end of the hall, was raised a good three feet above the rest. It was already occupied by the Master of St Visla's, Smithwin Kettletoft (DPhil), and his invited guests: college dons, a visiting provost, and a vice chancellor or two.

The undergraduates, black-robed like all the other scholars on such a formal occasion, had been filing into Hall for the past quarter hour, taking their seats and chatting in hushed voices, occasionally punctuated by jests and laughter. Michaelmas term was over. Tomorrow they would leave Cambridge to begin their Christmas holidays. Tonight, however, was the Feast of St Visla: their college's oldest, and most revered, holiday tradition. Naturally, most of the students were already drunk.

The tables nearest the fireplace were reserved for the rest of the College's faculty: the fellows and tutors, lecturers and readers. These had filled more slowly, the in-college faculty inclined to arrive as late as possible from the Senior Common Room to have time to finish their pre-dinner port, while others rushed in last minute, stamping off the snow, rubbing their hands before the fire, and eyeing with approval the bottles of sherry that had been set out for them.

At the table closest to the fire sat the Toads—the Three Old Ancient Dons. The Toads were as senior as senior faculty could be and had every right to sit at High Table. They instead chose to sit as close to the fire as possible, especially now that winter had arrived.

They were not called the Toads to their faces, of course, but only behind their hunched and crooked backs, as if the three aged gentlemen constituted a single entity, and not a tight trio formed by decades of friendship. It was true, however, that they were nigh inseparable, having been friends and faculty at St Visla's longer than anyone else at the College could remember.

Their nastiest detractors were the other dons, particularly those who coveted any of the Toads' nice suite of college rooms for themselves, and who watched the Toads like hawks for any sign of infirmity that might indicate the imminent shuffling off of a mortal coil or two (or, fingers crossed, all three!), freeing up some prime College real estate for occupancy by the younger members.

Tonight, however—and to the great consternation of their fellows—the Toads looked hale and hearty, their cheeks rosy from the heat of the fire and the warmth of the wine.

The Toads had been in Hall for the past hour, having arrived early in order to get the warmest seats. The Great Hall, like the oldest parts of St Visla's, dated from the fifteenth century. Although other buildings were added to the college over time, the medieval Great Hall had never been insulated, and thus remained inwardly conductive of the winter chill outside. The Toads had arrived so early, in fact, that the stewards, who had only started setting the tables, frowned disapprovingly when they sat down and opened one of the dusty bottles recently retrieved from the cellars. Now, with an hour's head start, the Toads were well into the sherry, their rheumy eyes reflecting the glint of candles as they watched the other tables slowly fill up.

Stefan Hoult-Apsley, Senior Fellow in Ancient Languages, was the youngest of the Three Old Ancient Dons, but still somewhere north of seventy-five. Next to him sat Ira Eggby, Professor of Maths, who had stopped counting in his mid-eighties. Reginald Bunn, Lecturer in Medieval History, sat at the end of their table, closest to the fire. Bunn was frail and thin and well into his nineties; undergrads often snickered that his knowledge of the middle ages came from direct experience.

"So, St Vizzy's Feast comes around again, does it?" said Hoult-Apsley. "Hard to believe another year has come and gone. Here's to the arrival of winter, and to hope that we survive the night. I understand the new soloist has a bit of a speech impediment." He tipped back his glass and drained it.

"Heehee," giggled Eggby. "I hear he's the Master's nephew—soloist by nepotism. Well, *that* ought to make for excellent entertainment. Hope you're ready to run for it, Reggie."

"Egads," replied Bunn morosely, gripping the blackthorn walking stick in his lap. With the damp, cold air niggling his arthritis, he wouldn't be running anywhere. "Let's hope it doesn't come to that. Surely they remember the last time someone buggered the carol, don't they?"

"Don't count on it. None of this lot," Hoult-Apsley gestured at the other fellows settling in around them, "were around then."

"I tried to warn them at the last faculty meeting," said Bunn, staring into the fire. "I told them I've been the carol's soloist for ages now, and that you two have always sung the chorus. I told them they can't just up and change everything all of a sudden! I tried to explain that we are the traditional carol singers for a reason, that we alone know the proper inflections and intonations, and that the carol must be sung *just so*."

Hoult-Apsley frowned. "What did they say to that?"

Bunn looked morose. "The Master patted me on the back and said that I've a good voice *for someone of my age*, but that it was time for *new blood*. Oh, and that I was too slow, what with my cane and all"—he looked dejectedly at his knobby blackthorn—"and that I simply can't move the procession along fast enough."

"Well," Eggby whispered, glancing surreptitiously up at High Table, "the Master has been pushing for all this, this...*reform* since he took the position last term. 'Time for a few changes!' he said. 'Bring some new life into these old traditions!' He has his supporters among the younger faculty. Why, Dean Housley even told me that the carol was just a song and it didn't matter who sung it or how badly it was done, so long as it was got through, and got through *quickly*."

Hoult-Apsley slapped the table and hissed. "Just a song? *Just a song!* Why, if they only—"

Movement from High Table stopped him. Master Kettletoft cleared his throat and rose to speak.

Bunn sighed. "Maybe we should take a seat closer to the door?"

"Won't matter," Eggby said. "They're already closed and anyway, the procession is ready to begin. We're stuck here, I'm afraid."

"Settle in then," Hoult-Apsley said, topping off his friends' sherry. "At least we've good seats to the show if it all goes higgledy-piggledy."

"*If?*" Bunn muttered, clutching his walking stick even tighter.

Master Kettletoft made a *tink-tink-tink* on his sherry glass with a spoon.

"Students and faculty, esteemed fellows, tonight once again we arrive at our annual Feast of St Visla. On this winter solstice, the longest night of the year, when tradition holds that the veil betwixt worlds is at its thinnest, we remember the valor of the founder of our College, Johannes Visla, who, while walking through the Cambridgeshire fens so many centuries ago whilst absorbed in reading his Aristotle, encountered the large and ferocious boar that had long threatened the University. With great presence of mind, Visla subdued and then killed the beast, first by singing to calm it, and then suffocated it to death by stuffing his copy of Aristotle down the yawning beast's throat. Thus, history records that Visla 'choked the Savage with the Sage.'"

Hoult-Apsley leaned between his companions and whispered, "More likely old Vizzy simply bored the boar to death. Aristotle! Now there's a soporific." This elicited a snigger from Eggby, and a look of disapproval from Kettletoft, who glared down his nose at them before continuing.

"But what is oft forgotten, overshadowed—like so many things—by the towering figure of Aristotle, is that Johannes Visla first subdued the boar not with his intellect, but rather with his voice. By all accounts, Visla's voice was that of an angel, with which he sweetly lulled the boar and, when it yawned, asphyxiated it. He brought the boar's head back to Cambridge for all to see, the pages of Aristotle still wedged in the monster's throat. Tonight, as on every winter solstice since, Visla's feat is celebrated by our College. Yes, despite what some of you may think of our recent reforms, we maintain this ancient tradition. We are one of the few colleges of this University still doing so!"

Hoult-Apsley rolled his eyes and coughed, but Kettletoft paid him no mind and, with a smug air, brought his speech to a close.

"We present the boar's head in remembrance of the great deed of Saint Johannes Visla—of course, with the pages of the Greek philosopher replaced with a more palatable substitute. Tonight is sung the traditional Boar's Head carol. And…for the first time in many years, it is to be sung by new voices! Voices of youth, voices that represent the future of St Visla's!"

Amidst tepid cheers and abortive applause, the Master sat down. At the far end of the room, the doors leading to the kitchen swung wide. Every head turned as a small procession emerged.

A pimply undergrad named Snivens was at the front; he was the Master's nephew and the newly appointed soloist. Behind him were two weary-looking cooks, aprons stained and faces damp with perspiration, their raised arms bearing an enormous silver platter. Atop the platter was a roasted boar's head, dressed with herbs, and an orange stuffed in its mouth. Smells of roast meat, bay leaves, citrus, and rosemary wafted through the hall. Behind the cooks were two members of the St Visla Chapel choir, dressed in white robes and carrying flickering torches.

"This should be good!" snickered a seated undergrad from somewhere near the back of the hall, apparently too drunk to realize how loudly he spoke. "I hear the soloist has one doozy of a lisp!"

Another drunk student shushed him almost as loudly as the procession made its way down the center of Great Hall, bearing the platter toward High Table. In the middle of the hall, they paused.

It was time for the carol. Snivens drew in a deep breath…

…and butchered it. His tone was flat, his rhythm off by a royal mile, and he tortured each syllable beyond what any lyric should be forced to endure. Worst of all was the effect of his lisp. The words emerged from his mouth like startled squid: soft at the front, flailing at the back, and dripping with moisture.

> "Thhhe boorth's headth in handth bearth ayyyeee,
> Bethhh-ecked withhh baythhhs and rosth-merrieeeths!
> And ayeee prayth youthh math-thters, beee merrieeethhh…
> Quoddthh ethtes een conviviothhhh!"

Around the room, eyes widened in horror (at High Table) and hilarity (everywhere else). Master Kettletoft's mouth dropped open, and a Vice Chancellor buried his head in his hands. A few considerate undergraduates bit their palms to keep from laughing, while the majority—along with most of the faculty—howled outright.

The Master stood unsteadily, quavering at the travesty the ceremony was threatening to become. He gestured wildly at the two singers with the torches, who were among the most accomplished members of the College's student choir, and they hurriedly launched into the chorus.

> *"Caput apri defero,*
> *Redens laudes Domino!"*

To which the assembled fellows and students—most of whom had tears streaming down their cheeks—did their best to answer with the English refrain.

> "The boar's head I offer,
> Giving praises to the Lord!"

Through all this, the Three Old Ancient Dons remained calm…barely.

"What's that Latin bit mean again?" Eggby asked, masking his growing nervousness. "*Quod estes in convivio?*"

"*As many as are in the feast,*" Bunn replied, his eyes focused on the silver platter.

"I bet most of 'em wished they weren't in the feast now!" giggled Hoult-Apsley. "Soon they might *be* the—"

"Wait," Bunn interrupted, squinting as if trying to discern something in the gloom. "Do you see…?"

At that moment, an undergrad sitting near the platter stood up and pointed at the boar's head. "I—I saw it move!"

"Dear me," said Eggby softly.

Bunn raised his blackthorn cane off his lap, keeping one hand firmly around the middle.

The laughter and singing subsided as everyone in the hall froze, watching the boar's head. Even the flames of the Yule log seemed to pause mid-flicker.

The boar's head—still steaming from the kitchen ovens—looked delicious. It was cooked a pleasing golden-brown, and gravy trickled slowly down the folds of its crisped skin. Fragrant bay leaves and rosemary sprigs had been placed artfully around the platter, adding to the mouth-watering aroma.

But then the head's upper lip—which up to that point had been draped over the orange stuffed in its mouth—twitched once.

Then it twitched again.

The entire snout curled into a snarl.

"*Vivit!*" exclaimed Hoult-Apsley, a little too gleefully and far too loudly. "It *lives!*"

Master Kettletoft, peering over his spectacles at the platter held by the nervous cooks, stared for a long moment. When nothing further happened, he said, "Nonsense. It's only cooling."

Everyone sighed with relief, nudging and elbowing and nodding, and resumed chatting and snickering.

"Good show, Snivens!" someone called out. "Let's see how you do with the second verse!"

"Can't be any worse than the first!" yelled another.

"Hear, hear!" came a chorus of voices, and the undergrads thumped the tables to chants of "Second verse! Second verse!"

Snivens looked as if he might bolt. But one of the choir members had come around and placed a hand on his shoulder, while the other whispered soothingly in his ear.

It was then that the orange, which moments before had been wedged between the boar's tusks, slowly rolled across the front of the platter and down onto the top of Snivens's ceremonial cap, where it landed with a soft *plumpf.*

All eyes went once more to the platter. A deep growl, like distant thunder, came from the boar's mouth.

Then its eyes flew open.

Snivens yelped and fled down the long aisle between the tables. The orange rolled off his cap and disappeared. The two choirboys flung their torches aside and pursued Snivens, while the cooks ran back to the kitchen, leaving the silver dish to clatter to the ground. Sprigs of rosemary and bay skittered across the floor.

Kettletoft screamed and pointed to where the procession had stood. Although the cooks were gone and the silver platter lay upside down on the floor, the boar's head remained suspended in midair, red eyes wide, tusks gleaming. Stiff hairs bristled from its half-severed neck like tiny black spears.

Its ears waggled, as if listening for…something.

"It's…it's floating!" shrieked a panicked provost.

The Great Hall erupted into chaos.

"Here we go again," said Bunn.

Down by the fire, the Three Old Ancient Dons kept their seats. They were the only ones.

As the boar's head floated in the middle of the Great Hall, eyes darting and lips twitching, the entire assembly of scholars scrambled over, under, and around each other in a desperate attempt to flee the room. But when they reached any of the hall's doors, they found them shut tight—no amount of tugging would open them.

The boar's head began bobbing back and forth and up and down. Its tongue came up and licked its snout, moistening its dilating nostrils. It snuffled a few times and inhaled a deep breath—although with what lungs was anybody's guess.

Then it emitted an eldritch bellow and launched itself at the nearest undergrad, a portly lad named Jenkins. Its tusks tore into Jenkins' robes and flipped the young scholar head over heels onto a table, scattering cutlery and candles.

This caused everyone—except for the Toads—to claw each other even more aggressively as they made to put more distance, or at least a few of their colleagues, between themselves and the boar's head.

"Did it float that high in the air last time?" said Eggby, peering at the hovering head. "I seem to recall it being lower to the ground."

"I dare say you're right," replied Hoult-Apsley. "Bunn?"

"Hmmm?" said Bunn absently. His blackthorn stick was on top of the table now, and his knuckles were white where he gripped it.

"It could be *us* who are lower now," suggested Eggby. "You know, age and whatnot."

"Indeed," nodded Hoult-Apsley.

The boar's head circled the hall, and by all appearances was having a jolly time of it. It snapped and snarled at terrified clusters of St Visla's finest intellects, now pushing and shoving each other like schoolboys in a rugby scrum. Now and then, one poor soul would make a break for it, seeking safety elsewhere, and the beast would bray exuberantly as it lunged after them with the wild abandon of a predator on the hunt.

"It's as we feared." Eggby took a sip of sherry. "Reminds me of that one Feast of St Visla right before the war. *That* boar's head gave old Professor Abbs an apoplexy."

"It was after the war," corrected Hoult-Apsley. "And Abbs had a heart attack. Sure of it."

"*I'm* quite sure it was before the war," said Eggby defensively. "And an apoplexy."

"*After*, Eggby. Heart attack."

Bunn interrupted. "It was before. And Abbs had a seizure. That's when we three decided..." At that moment the boar's head roared past their table, and Bunn took a swipe at it with his cane. "...to take charge of all this."

"If you say so," said Hoult-Apsley. "I was sure Abbs had a coronary. Disembodied boar's heads'll have that effect on a man. Especially when that man shows up for a feast expecting to *eat*, not *be eaten*."

They watched as one enterprising undergrad scrambled up onto a side table in an effort to reach one of the high transom windows that opened in summer to cool the hall. When the climber realized the window was also shut tight, he tried—and failed—to smash it, whereupon he lost his balance and splashed into a punchbowl.

"Lot of damage at that feast, too, as I recall," said Eggby, watching the punch-drenched lad roll out of the bowl and sprint for the far side of the hall. The boar's head bobbed along in gleeful pursuit. "Poor old Abbs notwithstanding."

"Indeed," agreed Bunn. "After that mess, we didn't have a proper dinner in here for months while they made repairs. Missed the Holy Week ham. That was a shame. And that's a hock, not a head, mind you. Lesson to be had, there. A hovering hock would never cause *this* kind of mayhem. Never let a swine head run amok, I've always said. You'll wind up paying for it out of the general fund."

As if to make his point, there was a tremendous crash as the boar's head slammed into a cabinet of crystal glassware, toppling it.

"See?" Bunn exclaimed, shaking his blackthorn. "That's a pretty penny, and no mistaking it. This is what happens when you mess with tradition! Either do it right or don't do it at all. Where'd they find that soloist anyway?"

"He's the Master's nephew," said Eggby. "I said that already."

"He did," said Hoult-Apsley, refilling his companions' sherry glasses yet again. His hand shook, and he splashed a little on the table.

Bunn sighed and took a sip.

Like a dog herding sheep, the boar's head had driven one hapless junior fellow out of the safety of his group and was chasing him around an overturned table. It was clearly toying with the panicked man; each time the scholar thought he might escape, the beast sped up and nipped at his heels, causing him to shriek and redouble his efforts. This went on for a few rounds until the boar's head seemed to grow tired of the game, at which point it surged forward with a frightening growl and gave the hysterical man a bite in his plump calf. The fellow tripped and collapsed into a thrashing heap.

"Go away, go away, go away!" he howled, flailing his arms.

Hoult-Apsley kicked his legs up, laughing. "Isn't that Dr. Birdwell, the new Reader in astrophysics? As I recall, he seconded the Master's motion to replace Bunn with Snivens as Feast soloist. Wonder how they like their new blood now."

They watched as Birdwell scrambled on top of the pastry table, sobbing as he tried to hide himself behind a pile of cream buns.

Hoult-Apsley wiped a tear from his eye. "Ooh, this is fun. How much longer should we let it go on?"

As the boar's head scanned the Hall, deciding whom to harry next, Bunn frowned at the robe-covered arses jutting unceremoniously from under High Table and sighed. "I suppose they've learned their lesson. Upending tradition, indeed. Best we put a stop to this before it gets out of hand."

At that point, however, the Great Hall could hardly be said to be in hand. Undergrads wept and called for their mums. So did some of the faculty. Senior fellows fought one another for a spot close to the exits, while Master Kettletoft cowered under High Table, now and then popping out to yell orders at his bickering faculty.

"Come," said Bunn, rising slowly by aid of his walking stick. "Let us save these fools from themselves, for tradition's sake. It is Yuletide, after all."

At that point the boar's head was rooting beneath High Table, trying to dislodge the Master and his cohort as if they were a cache of buried truffles.

As one, the Toads hobbled past overturned tables, torn tablecloths, and discarded dinnerware until they reached the middle of the room.

"Ready?" said Hoult-Apsley.

Bunn nodded and tapped the tip of his blackthorn on the floor three times. The sound was much louder than one would have expected from such a diminutive man's cane. But the room went suddenly silent as the sound echoed through the Great Hall. Even the boar's head stopped snuffling and turned toward them.

Bunn closed his eyes and cleared his throat, while Eggby and Hoult-Apsley bent down and picked the silver platter off the floor.

"It's…it's the Toads!" someone gasped.

With a ferocious bellow, the boar's head flung itself at them, closing the distance terrifyingly fast.

And then Bunn began to sing.

His voice was the sound of mulled wine, of moonlight on the river Cam, of a candle in a dark winter window—warm, clear, and bright.

> "The boar's head in hand bear I,
> Bedeck'd with bays and rosemary.
> And I pray you, my masters, be merry
> *Quod estes in convivio.*"

The boar's head slowed its charge and, a few feet from the Toads, stopped and bowed, closing its eyes. Its nostrils contracted slowly, emitting a gentle, lung-less sigh.

Eggby and Hoult-Apsley sang the chorus, their deep, resonant voices belying their age.

> *"Caput apri defero,*
> *Redens laudes Domino!"*

Then they tilted the platter toward the hovering head, while Bunn sang the second verse.

> "The boar's head, as I understand,
> Is the bravest dish in all the land,
> When thus bedeck'd with a gay garland.
> Let us *servire cantico."*

The head, seemingly hypnotized, settled gently onto the platter as if it were laying down for a nap in a forest bower.

Eggby and Hoult-Apsley repeated the chorus while Bunn bent slowly and gathered trampled bay leaves and rosemary sprigs. He sprinkled them around the boar's head, which now rested quietly—eyes half-closed, their red glow fading.

Then Bunn sang the third and final verse.

> "Our steward hath provided this
> In honor of the King of Bliss;
> Which on this day to be served is
> *In Vislasi atrio."*

Eggby and Hoult-Apsley raised the dish over their heads as all three of them sang the chorus together one final time.

> *"Caput apri defero,*
> *Redens laudes Domino!"*

Around the hall, faces watched anxiously. The boar's head lay unmoving, its eyes mere slits of ruddy light, like the glow of dying embers.

Eggby looked at Bunn nervously.

The eyes had not fully closed.

"It's not working," hissed Hoult-Apsley.

"But the carol's been sung!" said Eggby.

Bunn furrowed his brow. "We sang it properly…" he trailed off. Then, after a moment, he said, "The orange!"

Eggby and Hoult-Apsley looked frantically around them but didn't move, afraid to disturb the platter. Slowly, painfully, Bunn got down on his hands and knees to peer under nearby tables.

There was a low growl, and one of the boar's eyes reopened.

"Hurry!" Eggby hissed. "It's coming round!"

"Found it!" Bunn stretched his arm beneath a table. "I…can't…reach…it…"

The boar's other eye opened.

Bunn used his walking stick, pushing it as far as he could ahead of him.

"Almost… Almost… I have it!" He pulled the stick, rolling the orange toward him.

The lips on the boar's head twitched, and it emitted a second, longer growl.

"Hurry!" Eggby said.

Bunn tried to push himself up on his feet, but collapsed. "My knees!"

"Throw it to me, Reggie," said Hoult-Apsley. "Quickly now, there's a fine fellow."

Bunn tossed the orange at his friend. The throw was short, but his aim was true, and the fruit rolled to a stop at Hoult-Apsley's feet.

"Steady now, Eggby," Hoult-Apsley said, and together they bent their legs, keeping the platter level.

With a free hand, Hoult-Apsley felt around the floor until his fingers touched the orange's round, textured skin.

"Got it!"

Too late, they felt the platter lighten as the boar's head lifted itself back into the air and howled triumphantly.

"Look out!" yelled Bunn, still on his knees.

"This may not be Aristotle," said Hoult-Apsley, "but you can stuff it nevertheless!" And with that, he reached up and slammed the orange directly into the boar's open maw.

The head floated there for a few seconds, a look of surprise in its wide red eyes, as the Great Hall held its collective breath.

Then the boar's eyelids fluttered, and with each successive blink, the head dropped lower until it settled once more onto the platter.

Then its eyes closed completely.

For a few moments longer, the Great Hall was silent. And then, with an audible series of clicks, all the doors swung open.

In less than a minute, the hall had cleared out: undergrads, faculty, fellows, dons, deans, vice chancellors, and Master Kettletoft himself disappearing into the wintery night without stopping to gather their coats.

Only the Three Old Ancient Dons remained.

Bunn struggled to stand while his friends carefully set the platter on a nearby table.

"Well," said Hoult-Apsley, looking around at the destruction that had been the Feast of St Visla. "Just goes to show you the importance of having a good soloist who knows the proper way to sing the carol. As if just *anyone* can do it."

They gathered their overcoats in the Senior Common Room and prepared to head off to a pub. Dinner was ruined, and they were hungry.

"So passes another Feast of St Vizzy," muttered Bunn, wrapping his scarf around his head until only his eyes were visible.

"Makes you wonder if it's a tradition worth keeping around at all," said Hoult-Apsley. "If they aren't going to use a decent soloist, maybe they ought to just sod the whole thing."

Bunn and Eggby nodded in agreement.

"You know," said Eggby, tugging on a woolen cap. "I've always wondered why the words of the carol vary from college to college. For example, over at Queens' they sing that the boar's head is the '*rarest* dish in all the land,' while here at St Visla's our version of the carol calls it the '*bravest*.' Rum thing."

"Well," said Hoult-Apsley, "I understand Queens' College almost never serves the boar's head anymore. I suspect they've had one too many feasts end up as ours did tonight. No wonder they've made the dish a rarity."

"Humpfh," added Bunn. The folds of his scarf did nothing to filter the vitriol from his words. "These days, with each new master and provost trying to out-do one another with their *revamping* and *revising* and *reorganizing*, one has to be not only brave but also completely daft to serve it."

Hoult-Apsley chuckled and opened a small side door. They stepped out to the bracing chill of North Court. Above them snowflakes spiraled down between the jumble of mismatched towers—Gothic, Tudor and Victorian—that made up the skyline of St Visla's.

"I seem to recall," said Eggby, "that the last time Feast of St Visla ended this way, the three of us spent the rest of the night at the Green Dragon, calming our nerves with a half-dozen pints apiece. What say we head there again, for tradition's sake? You lot up for a few rounds?"

"I still say it was after the war," said Hoult-Apsley. "No matter. Hie, the Green Dragon! For tradition's sake."

Together they crossed North Court, Hoult-Apsley and Eggby supporting Bunn as they navigated the icy cobbles.

When they'd passed through the porter's lodge and left St Visla's behind them, Bunn muttered, almost to himself, "I suppose some traditions *are* worth keeping."

Though the words were muffled by his scarf, his friends heard him just fine, and smiled.

About the Author

Steve Ruskin writes science fiction with a streak of rebellion, and thrillers with a hint of magic. He is also an award-winning historian, with a PhD in History of Science. He's been a professor, a mountain bike guide, and a number of things in between.

What Are the Chances

by
Yvonne Lang

What Are the Chances

Susie smiled as she inhaled the glorious scent of freshly baked cookies. They had turned a lovely golden colour with the chocolate chips looking slightly gooey, but they hadn't melted and run. She'd timed it to perfection and things were going her way. She'd put a lot of pressure on herself to ensure this Christmas was special. Quite an ask when funds were still tight.

Still, her Christmas miracle was something you couldn't put a price on. The fortuitous change in circumstances made everything better. She was walking taller these days, not dragged down by life and carrying worry as if it were a physical burden. She had caught herself humming earlier as she set the mince pies out to cool and started on the Christmas cookies. It had only been a matter of months ago that she stopped crying every night once the kids were in bed and Ed had retreated to his workshop—his way of coping. Unlike her reaction which was to lie awake plagued by worries, what ifs, and calculating the odds that never seemed to land in their favour. Even ones that no longer mattered such as the odds of contracting leukaemia at that age, with no family history, the odds of not one family member being a bone marrow match. Tiny. Almost impossible that none of them did.

Still, Susie could go back to work soon, and although the extra money would relieve a lot of the pressure, that wasn't the reason she was so delighted to be returning. Rather, the thing that allowed her to return after her enforced break was also the source of her lifted spirits: Leo was in recovery. A recovery she was tracking and calculating and looked as if he were on track to be able to live an almost normal life. She and Ed had spent a lot of time eyeball-deep in numbers these past few tumultuous years. She was just grateful they were finally starting to be on their side.

Susie could hear *Home Alone* playing away on the TV even though she doubted anyone was watching it. Still, despite so much TV being played recently, as they isolated to protect Leo's immune system and no-one had the capacity for anything with concentration, there was a different vibe to it now. The TV was on because the children wanted it on, not because there was nothing else to do and they needed a distraction. And Christmas films were fun.

Susie ventured out of her cosy kitchen to check on her family and bask in the warm feeling of their happiness. Katie, Becky, and Leo were sat on a cluttered lounge floor in festive pyjamas and dressing gowns that, despite being new, already had splodges of chocolate and remnants of silly string and glitter—which was usually banned these days on the children's new eco-principles. Trapped inside meant all three children had gotten interested in nature, particularly bird watching, and passionate about the environment. It was why they were having a vegetarian Christmas this year. Susie didn't care. She'd happily have Christmas lunch sat on the floor, consisting of just sprouts if it meant her children were happy and healthy.

Her children certainly looked content now, huddled round a board game as they built their train routes across Europe. Celebrating as they picked the correct coloured cards or grumbling good naturedly if a sibling claimed a rail they wanted.

Leo didn't look any different to his sisters. At that instant, there was no indication of the traumatic few years he'd had. He wasn't bouncing around as much as either of his sisters, but that may be to do with the fact that Baxter, their chocolate Labrador, had his head planted on Leo's leg. Baxter had stuck by Leo's side throughout his leukaemia battle, offering wordless comfort and reassurance. It had been his doggy sixth sense and continued fuss that made Susie and Ed take Leo to the doctors in the first place and not presume it was a bug.

Google hadn't given a clear answer about the chances of a dog detecting cancer, but Susie knew she trusted her doggy diagnostician one hundred percent. It was also why he still got turkey for Christmas and their meagre Christmas fund had covered some doggy Christmas gifts. The entire family was celebrating being together this Christmas.

Baxter raised his head and the children paused playing as Ed called out from a wobbly position on a precariously placed set of steps.

"What are you doing?" Susie exclaimed as she rushed over, dodging scattered board games.

"Hanging up some of the paper chains and wreaths the kids made," Ed answered as he regained his balance then twisted to get some more Sellotape.

"Let me help, I'm not having you breaking your ankle and us spending an evening in A&E. I've had quite enough of hospitals thank you!" Susie admonished.

Ed offered a sheepish grin,

"I didn't want to disturb anyone when everyone's having so much fun."

"I assure you, your clumsy self falling off a ladder would most certainly disturb us, you daft thing."

Susie couldn't help but smile as she cleared a floor space for the steps to stand safely and held onto them.

Susie loved her husband. Apparently, a sick child could break a lot of marriages—Susie knew the chances of divorce with a seriously ill child were over 70% no matter which study you looked at. It had only strengthened her and Ed's bond though, as they united to do all they could to save Leo and support their two girls.

Even after all these years Susie marvelled that her husband could fix engines, repair anything electrical, and craft such wonderful pieces of art from wood, and still be so clumsy. He almost had a permanent bruise on his hip from walking into door handles, the kitchen counter and tables. It was as if he saved all of his energy, focus and coordination for his work or fixing duties. He was a master at wood-whittling and carving. As well as an accurate eye and steady hand with a paintbrush. Which made it even more baffling that he couldn't see their table.

The decoration he was hanging now had his Christmas carved figurines strung at various intervals. They had plenty to spare. When the children were in bed, and the horror of the trials they had faced as well as the new challenges ahead started to crowd his and Susie's heads and sink their negative tentacles into their tired brains, Ed retreated to his workshop. A task that occupied his mind and a situation where he was in control and had all the answers. He'd made some beautiful toys for the children's ward where Leo was treated, most notably a train set that snaked its way round the playroom.

Then a match had been found on the bone marrow register—the chances of a match with a stranger low and nothing came with guarantees, but things finally seemed to be falling in their favour—and Leo had a likely bright future. If all went well Leo would likely be well enough to enjoy Christmas. Ed went a bit Christmas-mad then—carving bauble after bauble, soldier and nutcracker figurines galore, and even tabletop nativity scenes. They'd sold some at the local post office—the pieces were exquisite and everyone in the village knew of their family's struggles so had bought generously. It had funded their Christmas shopping.

Susie's eyes came to rest on a carved angel figurine, close to a foot high. Ed had added some lines of colour, such as a gold rim for a halo and a hint of pink for a heart but mainly left it in its natural wooden colour. The beauty came from the carving. Ed had crafted such a beautiful look of contemplation, a Mona Lisa smile, and such details on the feathers. He had made it after they found out a donor had matched Leo. The angel had been carved in honour of their guardian angel.

The whole process was anonymous, so they didn't have a name of the person whose generous act had saved Leo. Ed wondered about asking the hospital to forward the sculpture, but they were worried it may be seen as having religious connotations and accidentally offend. So, the angel stayed pride of place on their mantelpiece, crowded by Christmas cards, standing as a reminder of stranger's lifesaving generosity and kindness. Feeling herself tear up with gratitude once more, so relieved at how different things were from this time last year, Susie forced herself back into the very happy present. She was going to savour and enjoy every moment, even the washing up.

"Kids, can you tidy away the games you're not currently playing with please? I'm worried about you losing pieces, and I've forgotten what my carpet looks like. Get it tidied and you can each have a warm cookie before dinner."

The current game was abandoned as the children became a whirlwind of tidying, Baxter bounding along for the energetic activity even if not helping.

"When are we leaving for the carols round the tree?" Katie called as she shoved games out of sight onto the top shelf. She stood head and shoulders above her siblings but still looked so young in her lilac dressing gown and bunny slippers.

Susie held her breath as she gripped the steps Ed was still up. She was hoping they had forgotten.

"What time does it start?" Ed called, not taking his eyes from the home-made tinsel bunting as he hung another piece.

Susie wished he hadn't engaged. She'd created such a Christmassy home—the tree was so crammed with baubles you couldn't really make out any greenery. It looked like a mass of gravity-defying, levitating baubles. About a third of which were Ed's creations that he had let the children decorate. Arts and crafts had been a good hobby for Leo when he was in recovery—stimulating but not strenuous.

She'd let them blare out Christmas music as she baked, the TV had been on for hours. They'd gorged on sweet treats, lounged around playing games in their pyjamas, and they still wanted to go out.

To where crowds and germs abounded. They wanted to leave the safety of their home—where no-one with a bug or a cough lurked, and surfaces were cleaner than an operating table.

"Best be setting off around now then," Ed replied, oblivious to the anxiety radiating off Susie.

"We don't want to be rushing, and we want a good spot. Best go get changed. You're not going out in your pjs," Ed continued.

"Ok, Dad!" The children chorused as one as they thundered upstairs.

How could her petite children, in slippers nonetheless, create such a racket?

"Do you think this is a good idea?" she whispered to Ed as the children left earshot and he descended.

Her husband seemed surprised to see the worry etched on her face.

"It's a small outing, not far, outside, doesn't go on too long. We can't keep them in here and dig a moat. The doctors' say it's safe for Leo to start mixing, and this is a low-risk activity that will bring them joy. We're going all out for this Christmas, remember? And it's a reasonable request from them that means a lot. I think it would be good to go."

"Mum, do you know where my reindeer jumper is?" Becky bellowed down.

Susie nodded to Ed and knew he was right. Even if there was an uncomfortable lump in the pit of her stomach.

"I'll come help you look!" she called back.

The village square was decorated beautifully. The tree stood over fifteen feet tall and was draped in twinkling lights as well as oversized, giant spherical baubles. They were multi-coloured with the fairy lights reflecting off their shiny surface like mini disco balls. There were also

Ed's carved figurines hanging round the tree—the village decorating committee had insisted on paying handsomely for his work. Their community had been so supportive. Susie was glad they came.

Everyone said hello without making too much of a fuss over Leo. Those with red-tipped noses and a possible cold stayed away. Becky had left them before the carollers started, in order to help some school friends put the finishing touches to a giant snowman. Her gloves were now sopping wet. Susie could see them dripping from here even in dim light. She'd packed spares though. She was determined not to fret and to enjoy the event.

Ed had taken Leo to try some roasted chestnuts, but from the face Leo was pulling as the glow of the fire illuminated him, Susie didn't think he was enjoying his first taste. Baxter was nosing around, seeing if it was something he could help finish off, but his snort suggested they didn't appeal to him either. Susie saw Ed dig out his wallet again, to purchase a skewer of marshmallows instead, but Tom who was manning the food cart waved the money away as he handed over a stick dotted with pink and white treats.

Susie was going to have to make sure no matter how tired they were tonight that everyone gave their teeth a thorough brushing. Bad oral hygiene increased the chances of all sorts of other health issues, not just tooth and mouth related, such as heart disease. Some studies even showed it increased your chances of dementia or kidney disease and arthritis. Another worrying set of facts she had in her head after going off down internet rabbit holes when researching Leo's health and treatment options.

Katie reappeared at her side, her gloved hands crammed full. She was clasping three cookie lollipops, five electronic candles and had a sheaf of papers pinned to her side by her squeezed-in elbow. Susie took some of the candles.

"What's all this?" she asked her daughter.

"It's a candlelight service, we have to go the whole hog. And now that Leo has his appetite back again, I figured we may as well indulge and properly enjoy tonight. They gave them all to me half price as well. Everyone seems to be happy to see us out tonight. Oh, and these are lyric sheets since there's no way we'll know all the words, and we can't have tonight ruined by Dad belting out his version full blast."

Susie took the papers and glanced over the song titles, struggling to rifle through with her wool encased fingers. All familiar titles but she hadn't realised how few of the words she knew.

"Thanks Katie. You've been a wonderful daughter and a magnificent big sister during this."

"Don't get all soppy on me, Mum. What else would I do? I'm just glad it's behind us. Thank goodness for that donor, eh?"

Susie gave her eldest an awkward hug through their bulky coats and full hands and let the subject drop. She knew, from support groups she and Ed had attended online, that the chances of such terrible news, feelings of helplessness, and their parents having less time for them, meant a lot of siblings of very sick young people went off the rails. A likelihood her family had avoided.

The church chimed seven and the crowds began to move as the singers assembled. Electric candles were switched on and the first carol was announced as 'Away in a Manger.' Becky ran back, closely followed by Ed, Leo and Baxter.

There was a small collective gasp before the first note was sung, as snow began to fall. Tiny white flakes glided down from the dark sky, twirling lazily past the golden Christmas lights strung along the main street. All you could hear for a brief few moments was the crackle of the fires that snacks had been roasted on. The wood smoke mingled with the scent of mulled wine as all the electric candles hung in the air amongst expectant faces like tiny golden fireflies hovering. Then the singing began.

Susie lost herself in the music and the atmosphere. She had never felt so Christmassy. The joy was giving her a warm glow. Or maybe it was her extra thick socks and the fact they were huddled together like penguins. Leo was out front, surrounded by family and the villagers giving him a bit more space than anyone else. Except a man she didn't recognise that Baxter seemed to be taking an interest in.

Maybe he was just enjoying having someone new to smell. She hoped he didn't annoy the gentleman. You never knew how a stranger was with dogs. Although the man seemed happy enough and Baxter's thick chocolate tail was wagging, creating a mini blizzard of flakes around his rear end.

There was a pause in singing as volunteers came round with wine, hot chocolate and mince pies. As the crowd dispersed slightly to stock up on refreshments, Susie realised it probably wasn't the man Baxter was so interested in—the stranger had a golden retriever with him.

"Hello there," the man said down to Baxter. "I presume he's OK with other dogs?" he asked Ed, who was closer.

"Absolutely fine. Baxter's a big, friendly softy," Ed assured him.

The man smiled back from beneath his flat cap that had a little layer of snow on it.

"Lovely. This is Gordon. I only adopted him a month ago, but he seems to love everyone and everything."

"Can I pet him?" Leo asked.

"Of course you can, young man."

Leo tugged off his gloves to pat Gordon, who was delighted with the extra attention.

"Are you new to the area?" Susie asked.

"I live nearby, over in Todminton, but it's my first Christmas as a widower, so I wanted to get out and not wallow. Make new memories, instead of being in the usual place with too many memories. Also wasn't sure how people would act around me. All kind but a bit awkward, or over-the-top fussing. You know how villages are. Everyone knows everyone's business. I adopted Gordon to get me out of the house, and they say dogs are a great conversation starter. Which he's proven now!"

Susie nodded, not sure whether to offer condolences or whether that would create the fuss he was trying to avoid tonight. Then Baxter started barking excitedly, sticking his nose into the man's hip before spinning round to face Leo and yap at him.

"Baxter, what has gotten into you?" Susie asked as Ed moved to pull their dog back.

"Do you have something in your pocket?" Leo asked the man.

The man shook his head, sending some snow falling from his cap,

"A tad sore in my hip so I don't keep anything in that pocket at the moment, to avoid risking bumping it. Just recovering from a minor op."

"I've had a lot of surgeries and hospital procedures recently. It sucks, doesn't it?" Leo volunteered, sharing an amount that shocked Susie.

"Yes, it does, young man."

"My name's Leo. You should get ginger biscuits. They're easy to eat when you're queasy, and settle you down."

"Thanks for the tip, Leo. I'm Malcom. Are you getting better now?"

Leo nodded, the bobble on his knitted hat wobbling all over and shedding snowflakes. Baxter was pulling at his collar, tail a blur of wagging as he strained to get away from Ed and between Leo and Malcom. People were starting to move back into position for the next songs, the crowd shifting like a murmuration of starlings. Leo ignored it all.

"I am. I had a bone marrow transplant, and it will be my first healthy Christmas in four years. Are you getting better now?"

"Leo!" Susie hissed. "We don't ask people prying questions about their health!"

"I was being polite!" Leo insisted.

Susie looked to Malcom who was still smiling, though something had shifted in his smile.

"I'm so sorry. He's just excited about his recovery. He doesn't usually ask such rude questions."

"It wasn't rude, Mum!" Leo protested.

"No trouble at all," Malcom assured her. "I wasn't ill though. I had a surgery to be a bone marrow donor to help a struggling family out, make a difference after I lost my May. Relieve my grief by preventing others suffering a bereavement. After I recovered, I then tried adopting Gordon here to help—not sure which step was more drastic!" He chuckled.

Everything froze. Susie was aware of snow falling but the crowds chatter became a background hum. The lights seemed to dim.

"Baxter thinks he can smell you on Leo. He thinks you're connected," Becky announced.

What were the chances of bumping into the anonymous donor who had saved their child's life?

"Do you mind me asking when your op was?" Ed asked.

Susie was glad he had as she desperately wanted to know but was frozen to the spot, numb with shock.

"Around four months ago," Malcom replied, a look of understanding passing between them.

It wasn't definite, but the odds meant it was highly likely. The chances of it just being a coincidence were minute. They had found their guardian angel. Ed looked at Susie and she broke from her trance to nod.

"Malcom, I hope this is not too forward, but do you have any plans for Christmas day?"

He shook his head,

"I was just going to have a walk with Gordon and a quiet lunch."

"We would be honoured if you joined us for lunch. My husband has a carving to offer you as well. He's the artist who did the wooden decorations all around us."

"Well, that is very generous of you. If you're sure? I wouldn't want to impose?"

"It would be our pleasure after what you have given us, or if not us, a family like ours."

Susie didn't know what the chances were of accidentally meeting the man who had saved your son's life. She did know, however, that the chances of letting him go without thanking him profusely and letting him see the results of his kindness were zero.

About the Author

Yvonne was a librarian for 15 years before moving to children's publishing—but she loves writing for adults. Her work has featured in a range of publications from magazines, to ezines and anthologies. She has achieved success in a few genres but is best known for her horror and weird fiction—but she promises she is a delight and can pass as quite average in real life.

She resides in Yorkshire with her partner and a cat who does not respect personal space. This furry intrusion has improved her typing though. www.yvonnelang.co.uk

Lost Ornaments

by
Ronnie Seagren

Lost Ornaments

A flash of bright yellow darted across the grass. Distracted, Tim missed an easy pop fly. The softball took an odd hop into the weeds beyond the outfield, and while he searched for it, he heard cheers as two runs scored. Just when he was about to give up, a ray of late afternoon sunlight slipped through scattered clouds to glance off the white orb, turning it for a moment to silver, like a Christmas ornament lost in a tuft of grass. He scooped it up and turned to throw the ball to the infield. His dad was watching from the bleachers with a scowl. He shook his head and returned to reading his newspaper.

Walking across the park after the game, all his dad said was, "You have to pay attention, kid. You don't see Reggie Jackson chasing butterflies. Mark my words, the Yankees will take the Series this year." He tapped Tim's head with the folded newspaper. "Yep, '77 will be their year."

"But I hit a double, Dad. Did you see that?"

His father frowned. "I don't know, Tim. Maybe you're not old enough to play Little League yet. You're only six."

"But I want to play!" Tim blurted out. It was the only time they did something together, even if his dad didn't pay him much attention. "I could get better if you'd teach me. Can we play catch when we get home?"

"Not now. I have to rake the leaves and wash the car before dinner," his father responded and increased his pace so that Tim had to run to catch up. Tim was silent, kicking at pebbles on the sidewalk, until a bit of fluff wafted past.

"Hey!" Tim dropped his baseball mitt and dashed after it. As he leaped off the curb, a green station wagon swerved past, horn blaring.

"Timothy!" his dad yelled. He grabbed Tim by the collar of his blue jacket and jerked him back to the sidewalk, just as Tim's hand closed around his quarry.

"What are you doing?" Dad yelled, gripping Tim by the arms. The car had startled Tim, but Dad's anger scared him even more. "You know better than that! You could've been killed."

"I saw a fairy, Dad!" Tim explained. "See, I caught her." He opened his hand, but the fairy had escaped, leaving behind only the wispy bell of her skirt.

Tim's dad released a sharp laugh whetted with scorn. "Tim, that's just a milkweed seed. There's no such thing as fairies."

"But Andy's grandpa says—"

"Jack Herbert's as crazy as his old man. They should be locked up together," his dad responded harshly. "It's all nonsense and make-believe."

"But he says fairies live in the forest. And elves and—"

"You're almost seven, Tim, old enough to know better. Only little kids believe in fairies."

"Did you believe in fairies when you were little?"

"No," his dad replied quickly. "They weren't real," he added, sounding both bitter and sad. "It was just pretend," he muttered as he scooped up the boy's mitt. "Come on. I don't have time for fairies and foolishness." He strode down the sidewalk with steps too big for Tim to match. Without turning, he tossed his voice over his shoulder. "And no TV for you tonight."

"That's not fair! The car wasn't even that close." Tim argued, feeling betrayed as much by his dad's disbelief as his anger.

"Don't get smart with me."

"You don't understand!" Tim yelled, voice gone shrill and body stiff, and he couldn't help it. "You don't care!" Tim ran back into the park.

His dad's voice chased after him. "Timothy David Grant, come back here *now!*"

Tim paused and turned, for no one ever called him by his full name. But he hurt, deep in his tummy, and that made him angry. "You never believe anything I say," he yelled with all his six-year-old might. "I'll show you! I'll find a fairy and bring it back."

His dad started across the lawn toward him. Tim turned again and ran into the trees at the park's edge. He wasn't allowed in the forest alone, but he was certain his father would follow. However, when Tim finally stopped and turned around, his dad wasn't there. Tim frowned.

"Hey, Dad, where are you?" he called. The only answer was the rustle of something in the bushes. Tim started back the way he had come, but the trail twisted sidewise and circled around to where he'd begun. Tim looked back, looked ahead, but nothing seemed familiar. The trees towered so far above him, Tim couldn't see their tops, even when he tilted his head back until he almost fell over. They swayed in the wind, creaking and sighing and telling tales. Ferns, almost as tall as he, whispered in voices like rustled paper. *I should stay here,* he thought. That's what he was supposed to do if he ever got lost. Dad would find him.

But Dad didn't come. "Where are you?" Tim called. A butterfly, all orange and black, flitted past him and paused in the middle of the trail.

"Are you a fairy?" Tim asked, stooping down for a better look. It fluttered away, stopping again just a few feet down the trail. *This way. Follow me!* it seemed to say. But every time Tim caught up, the butterfly flitted ahead. Then it darted up and over a fallen log, leaving him alone.

Tim looked around at the tall redwoods and deep shadows. "Where are you, Dad? Why don't you come find me?" He looked up at the patches of sky showing through the trees.

"Don't you care, Dad?"

Still shaking with the fear that had bred his anger, Pete Grant watched his son run across the park. With an impatient grunt, he started after the boy. Park yielded to forest, tended lawn and flower beds and concrete walks blending into trees and native plants and trails paved with pine duff. Pete glimpsed a patch of blue weaving among the hemlock and cedars, and that lured him on until it disappeared among the bracken ferns lining the trail.

After another quarter mile or so, he paused to get his bearings. Tim would never have gone this far alone. Pete backtracked and tried another trail. An hour later, he stopped. It would be getting dark soon and the coastal fog was already sliding down through the valleys to meander through the forest. It was time to get help.

"Tim!" he called, and "Timothy!" once more, reluctant to give up too soon. The boy might be close, hiding or waiting.

The forest fell to utter, secretive silence. Pete headed back toward the park, still peering into bushes and behind trees, turning to walk backward, pausing to listen.

"He's probably already home," he muttered, already plotting a suitable punishment for running away.

Tim was tired and hungry, and still nothing looked familiar. A ground squirrel scolded him, then dashed under a fallen log as dark wings glided overhead. Sunlight faded until all was dark upon black. Soon, though, the moon cast slivers of light between the trees, leaving thick puddles of dark where creatures might lurk. Ogres, maybe.

Tim shuddered, wishing that the fairies would find him. They take care of lost children, Andy's grandpa had told him, though sometimes, they played tricks.

A light appeared, not so far away. A streetlamp, Tim thought, or maybe a house. He hurried toward it, but it bobbed ahead of him. "Maybe that's Dad with a flashlight," he told the trees, and he ran to catch up.

Moonlight silvered the trail as the light lured him on and brought him to a small clearing, the grass autumn yellow and flowers faded and drowsy. A pine tree stood alone in the center, no bigger than the trees Dad brought home for Christmas. Tim stopped at the edge, for it was a quiet place lit by mellow starlight.

"You shouldn't be here."

A girl stood next to the tree, hardly as tall as Tim's shoulder. She wore a yellow dress. Leaves gone scarlet and gold were braided into pale blonde hair. Her eyes were the deepest green he'd ever seen. She held the ball of light he had followed through the forest. "But then, I shouldn't either," she added with a wink and giggle. "This is an Alfaen place."

"I'm looking for fairies," Tim replied with the certainty that he would find one. "My dad says they're not real, but—" Tim stopped abruptly, his breath caught in his throat, eyes so wide his eyebrows pushed against his scalp. In a whisper hoarse with wonder, he asked, "Are you a fairy?"

The girl giggled, studying him with tilted head and whimsical smile. "If you believe so. It's an old name, gone wrong in the repeating. People forget." She had an odd accent, soft and lilting. "You can call me Elli."

"I'm Tim," the boy responded.

A glint of mischief colored Elli's eyes as she spoke. "You're wise to keep your true name secret. There's power in names, you know. But did I not hear your father call you Timothy?"

"You know my dad?" Tim asked.

"We used to play games when he was a boy."

Tim was pretty sure that couldn't be, for his dad hadn't been a boy for a long time. Still, he asked, "Can you take me to him? I got lost, and I—"

Elli set a finger on her lower lip, head cocked to one side. "Later, perhaps. After the festival. You want to stay for the festival, don't you, Timothy?"

Tim found himself nodding, though all he really wanted was to go home.

"Come with me, Timothy," Elli commanded. Tim obeyed, following her into the clearing. Setting her light upon the branches of the little pine tree, Elli led him to a place where the grass grew in a ring of dark, rich green. They took to their stomachs in the shallow depression at its center, heads raised to peek over the grass. "The circle is a sanctuary," Elli whispered. "None will disturb you here. But be still."

Other children came, too, and set their own glowing lights upon the little tree until it looked like a Christmas tree all lit up. They glanced sideways at Tim and Elli, whispered to one another behind their hands, then danced back into the forest.

Now Tim heard singing—a magical sound, he thought, like the stars must make floating across the sky. A line of people threaded among the trees, clad in long shirts and dresses of gold and red and orange, and cloaks like butterfly wings. They carried baskets woven of sweetgrass and filled with fruit and nuts and flowers. Tim and Elli watched the procession circle the clearing.

"What's happening?" Tim asked in a wary whisper.

"'Tis the full of the moon in the season of turning, when night equals day and the world tips toward winter. We celebrate the reaping and gather seed for next year's planting."

"What kind—"

"Shh! You'll get us both in trouble."

As the fat, round moon drifted high above the trees, turning the autumn grass to silver, the people set their baskets beneath the little pine tree, then festooned the surrounding trees and bushes with garlands of autumn leaves and dried flowers bound by mist and sparkles. When the moon had reached its midnight zenith, they danced around the meadow, stepping so lightly they seemed to float.

A woman glanced at Tim. She nodded at Elli and waved one hand to draw a symbol of light that drifted into a glittery dust settling on the little circle of grass. Tim blinked, and blinked again, his head bobbing. The ground within the circle was soft, the grass sweet. He settled into its warm comfort, and Elli wove a drift of leaves over him like a blanket. The rest was dreaming.

"See, Dad," Tim murmured in his sleep. "I told you fairies were real."

It's my fault, Pete told the trees, begging them to release his son. Every day he berated himself for his failure. If he hadn't yelled at Tim, if he hadn't laughed— *Why didn't I go after him right away?* But he'd believed Tim would come home once the boy was over his tantrum. *I shouldn't have given up so soon.*

People often lost their way, Pete kept telling himself. They would turn up days, weeks, even months later, dazed and confused and with no accounting for where they'd been. But if the forest was callous, it was also capricious, and sometimes kind. So, Pete searched diligently with his neighbors and friends, while his wife stayed home so the house would not be empty if Tim should return. Meg never blamed him aloud, but her gaze kept asking, *How could you lose our boy?*

"More likely the Folk have him," Old Jack Herbert told him. "He'll come home when they're done with him."

Pete threatened to punch the old man out, yelling, "It's your fault he ran off, you and your crazy stories." For a while, that soothed his own sense of guilt.

The police eyed Pete as a suspect, of course, and often followed him into the forest. *And if I come home with Tim's body?* Pete asked himself. *What then?*

After a fruitless month, when Sheriff Grayson declared the certainty that Tim could not be alive, others gradually dropped out of the search. Beyond all hope of finding the boy alive, Pete kept searching, doggedly checking every hollow and burrow, any place small enough to conceal a boy.

Fathers don't quit, he told himself.

As the holidays approached and Pete watched other families gathering together, the more he longed for Tim and the more he searched, spending his days methodically tramping along every trail and track. He became increasingly obsessed with the feeling that time was running short. *If not now, never,* sang the brittle wind.

Now it was near Christmas, the season of waiting. Anticipation adorned the town, but Pete ignored the lights and the trees and the presents. A forlorn little tree slouched in the living room, barren of presents and hope. The only gift Pete wanted was his boy. "Come home, Tim, and I'll play ball every day," he whispered in prayer. "Please, come home.

"Come to the church," Meg said on Christmas Day with her flat, grief-battered voice, eyes worn out of tears, shadowed with grief. She was on her knees searching under the tree.

"I can't," Pete responded. "I have a feeling—"

"You always have a feeling," she said with a wistful sigh as she pushed herself out from under the tree. She paused to gather her breath and brush pine needles and memories from her skirt. "I've lost another ornament," she murmured as she tried to stand. "So many lost." Pete reached out to help her up, but she waved him back. "Maybe it's time to let go."

Her bleak words echoed the thoughts he could never force through the thick place in his throat, past tears swallowed and words prayed and the binding of his own guilt.

"I can't," he responded with a forlorn shudder. If he gave up now, then he had truly killed his son, just as the police suspected.

"But it's Christmas Day."

"And a full moon. What better day for a miracle?" Pete argued, certain he'd find the boy, a lie he told himself every time he went out to the woods. He pulled a flashlight from a kitchen drawer and checked its charge. "One more night. I promise. If I can't find him on Christmas Day, he's not meant to be found."

"You'll get lost, yourself," she chided, bitter despair with an edge of anger. She'd never blamed him, not aloud. "I couldn't bear to lose you both."

Pete shook his head, turned and walked out the door.

"I'll have hot cocoa waiting for you," she called in what had become a custom each time he went out, an expression of faith.

He paused to offer a thin smile and a thinner hope. "Make enough for two."

By now, Pete knew the forest intimately, every path and every tree and rock. Until now, his search had been dogged and systematic, yet it seemed the trails led him astray, diverting him from the one spot where Tim might be. This last day, though, and with no other days to come, Pete abandoned himself to impulse and whimsy. "Show me the way," he shouted at the trees, daring them to deny his quest.

The forest was hushed with winter silence. No sound but the crunch of dry grass beneath his boots. Snow drifted in hollows and the lee of the great trees, printed with the tracks of deer and rabbits, but no size-six shoes. Pete hiked through the day until the sun slipped away, just four days past the solstice. Pete felt cheated. *I'm not ready to give up just yet,* he told the fleeing light. He pulled out the flashlight, but its feeble beam soon faded.

"No!" he yelled at the darkening sky. "I need more time!" Desperation clotted in his gut as raw cold seeped through his parka to chill his bones. Tim might be just around that curve, just past that outcrop, waiting to be found. How could he risk missing him? This last day, he would search until his breath froze and his feet faltered. Until the last stroke of midnight. He fell to his knees, weeping as he never had, tears soaking the frozen soil, melting the ice.

"Let me find him," he said aloud, praying to the night, the trees, to whoever would listen. "Please! Let me find him!"

Beyond the trees, the moon rose—the Long Night moon, in ancient folklore. A single beam pierced the trees to cast a path of silver, a trail he was certain had not been there before. The narrow trace led through the dried remnants of summer's bounty.

"That way, then," Pete decided. It was as good as any other. He pushed through barren brush and waded through frost-dried bracken. Ahead, a light flared like a promise, bobbing among the trees. Pete followed after, for where else could he go?

A child, a girl smaller than Tim, waited for him at a curve in the trail, clad in a dark green cloak over a dress of yellow, with eyes like green gems. A circlet of pine and holly adorned hair fair as wheat.

"Hello, Pete."

"Who are you? How do you know my name?"

"Don't you remember?" She turned to skip down the trail, leading Pete deeper into the forest. "We played together when you were smaller." Memories surfaced like bubbles in water—running through the forest, playing at games, and telling tales. The sort of adventures every boy plays at. And a girl with hair as pale as moonlight, laughing and dancing and leading him on merry chases.

"Elli?" he asked. But that couldn't be; she would be so much older by now, grown to an adult. "What are you doing here?"

"Are you ready to take Tim home?" she asked. "I've watched you searching. It's time now to find him."

"You know where he is?" Pete knelt before the child, eyes level with hers. "Why didn't you tell me?"

"You weren't ready yet. You didn't love him enough."

"But I do!" Pete protested. "I love my son!"

"Ah, but you didn't know it before."

"I—" Pete left his mouth open, words lost to him. He reached for her. "Please, Elli. Take me to him."

She studied him with a cocked gaze that seemed to read his soul and scan his heart. She nodded solemnly. "Follow me, then."

As she led him through the forest, the moon rose higher, its light illuminating a small clearing. More shadows moved among the trees, a procession of folk, each bearing a globe of light, silver and blue and purple to match their velvet cloaks. They danced around the open space and set their lights upon the small pine tree at its center, frosted branches hung with clusters of colored bubbles and garlands of delicate crystals, more festive than any Christmas tree.

"What is this?" Pete asked in hushed wonder.

"Have you forgotten? This is the winter moon, the time when the sun returns and night ebbs."

Vague memories floated just shy of awareness, but Pete swept them from his mind. Only one thing mattered right now.

"Where's Tim? You promised."

Elli brought him to a circle of grass, still green, and settled her own light there like an ornament fallen from the tree. She waved her hand, sweeping aside a coverlet of leaves brown and dry. At first, Pete saw only barren earth, but then he discerned the shaping of an arm, a shoulder draped in blue nylon. Tousled hair and boyish face. Pete knelt, hands hovering over Tim, afraid to touch him, afraid to find his son dead and frozen. How could he be otherwise?

"Tim? Timothy?" With a soft shudder, Tim sighed and shifted to his side. Pete scooped his son from his earthy bed, took him into his arms.

"Tim," he whispered. "Tim, wake up," he said louder. The boy's eyelids flickered, blinking once, twice. "It's Dad, Tim. Wake up. It's time to go home." The boy opened his eyes and peered at Pete's face.

"Dad?" he said. "I was lost, Dad, but the fairies took care of me. I told you fairies are real." He pushed himself up, though not out of Pete's embrace.

Pete held his son close. "I've been looking for you. Every day, I searched." Tears stung his cheeks as he whispered a litany of *I'm sorry*s and *I missed you*s.

"I wished for you, Dad, and the fairies brought you," Tim said. "I heard you coming." He scrunched his face in a dubious frown. "But I was asleep. I was just dreaming."

Fairies or angels, Pete wondered. Or were they the same? He held his own Christmas wish, here in his arms, a lost ornament found. Pete laughed, a great, joyous song that bubbled up from his innermost core. He helped Tim to stand. "Let's go home, Son. Your mother's waiting. She'll have hot cocoa ready."

"But the fairies—" Tim whispered.

They were gone now, except for Elli, waiting to show them the way.

About the Author

Ronnie Seagren is a story teller, and her own story began in Colorado, segues to California for her school years, then back to Colorado. Its cast of characters includes husband Frank, three sons, and seven grandchildren (so far). Plans to celebrate their fiftieth wedding anniversary standing in the moon's shadow in South America succumbed to Covid in 2020.

Ronnie began creating stories in sixth grade and, smitten by the original *Star Trek*, turned to science fiction in high school. The landscape is often as much a character in her stories as people, and as a Colorado State Park volunteer, she enjoys telling visitors tales of rattlesnakes, mountain lions, and rocks. The sequel to her novel, *Seventh Daughter*, is currently under construction.

"Lost Ornaments" is her latest, part of a collection of tales about a small town on the edge of a forest where people frequently encounter the "real behind the myth"—folk just slightly out of sync with our reality. It was inspired by the music and images of the Trans Siberian Orchestra concerts.

The Elf Who Got Fired

by
Gretchen A Keefer

The Elf Who Got Fired

*I*t was the month before Christmas, the days were full of deadlines. All hands, including the seasonal workers, were singing merrily, happy to be helping with the important work. Bramble enjoyed the presence of the seasonal help. Many were old-timers, back from retirement for the last big push. They had a variety of stories to share—some of which could be true.

Piet, for example, insisted his great-grandfather had accompanied the original mortal St. Nicholas on his rounds to provide dowries for poor girls. Bramble wondered at that. Piet would have to be really old, even for an Elf. Other short-term helpers were new at the job, gaining experience and an excellent addition to their resumes. Bramble received huge satisfaction in mentoring and correcting them. The experience really boosted his self-esteem.

The workspace was light and pleasant. Large windows filled the room with sunlight, even during snow days. The walls were painted a calming cream so as not to conflict with the bright colors of the toys. Each Elf had the appropriate work attire and a comfortable stool to perch on while working on the line. The noise was kept to a safe limit, even in the construction areas. Conversation was cheerful, light-hearted and friendly. Bramble considered himself truly blessed to work in this ideal environment.

He was a bit concerned about Crocus, a young Elf just getting started at Santa's workshop. He chatted a lot, which wasn't so bad really, except he didn't know how to keep his hands as busy as his mouth. Bramble had shown him it was possible to talk and box toys at the same time. However, Crocus's chatting was not what Bramble really worried about. Crocus spent a lot of time with an older Elf, Carson. Generally, the Elves were kind and tolerant of one another and always spoke well of each other. They all adhered to the maxim, "If you can't say something good about someone, say nothing." Carson was different. His opinions bothered most of the other Elves, so they stayed away from him if possible. Which is probably why Crocus spent more time with him—there was no competition for Carson's attention.

And that is what bothered Bramble. Carson could pour his off-beat opinions into Crocus's ears and head without any buffering from other views. Recently in his chattering, Crocus had said, "Carson says it really doesn't matter how neatly we paint the toys. The children don't care, and their parents won't look." Bramble had immediately told Crocus that Carson was mistaken, and Crocus should do the best work possible.

One afternoon, a couple of weeks earlier, when the boxing Elves came back from a break, they were full of news about the latest reading on the Belief-O-Meter. The numbers were lower than last year, and everyone was troubled by the news. Belief in the world, in general, had been in decline for a couple of generations. This was the worst year anyone could remember. Crocus was quick to announce "Carson says the Belief-O-Meter doesn't matter. It's all a bunch of…"

Bramble interrupted Crocus. "Carson is definitely wrong about that," he chided Crocus firmly. "You had best not listen to Carson."

Crocus's eyes widened in surprise. Bramble had not spoken so strongly to him before. In mute appeal, Crocus looked at Piet for support.

"Bramble is right, Crocus. The Belief-O-Meter is extremely important. Without belief, Santa and his helpers cannot do their jobs."

Crocus looked concerned. He asked, "What does it mean to believe? I mean, I think I do, of course, but what does it really mean?"

Piet smiled at the young Elf. "To believe is to know without having visible certainty. You know, you feel the truth of an idea, even if you cannot explain or prove it. Belief is the foundation of Santa's success in encouraging kindness among the people in the world."

Crocus relaxed. "Then I really do believe. But I don't understand what would happen if the people in the world didn't believe. If parents buy toys anyway, what does it matter if Santa can't deliver everywhere?"

Piet handed Crocus a box, indicating he should keep packing toys even while they were discussing this important topic. "Belief makes the reindeer fly." Piet smiled at the young Elf. "Not all parents can buy toys or gifts for their children," Piet explained. "What Santa and his helpers, like Pere Noel, Das Christkindle, and others, bring is hope. No matter if the children call the gift bringer Sinter Klaas, Ded Moroz, or Father Christmas, no matter what their personal circumstances may be, the children know that someone loves them enough to bring a gift. That provides hope for them, hope that will help them survive the troubles in their lives."

Bramble added, "It's our job to spread hope throughout the world. Without hope we see a lot of blackness. If the world becomes too black, Santa cannot travel."

Everyone had stopped working to listen. Concern and, in some cases fear, filled their faces.

Bramble clapped his hands. "That's enough speculation about bad news. Belief is still in the world. Back to work. Josh, please start a song for us."

In the future, everyone would remember exactly where they were that afternoon when lives were changed. There was an overall feeling of cheer throughout the workshop. The Belief-O-Meter was holding steady. The Elves were wrapping up many important tasks. Just a few toys needed to be finished, and the fudge packaged. The sleigh had been cleaned, polished and stocked. The reindeer had been in training and were at peak form.

Bramble, Piet, Crocus, and Josh were boxing toddler train sets, sturdy blocks on wheels painted in bright primary colors. The line moved quickly. Josh liked to joke that the Elves had taught Henry Ford how efficiently an assembly line could construct anything, including a car. There might have been some truth in Josh's story; Mr. Ford got the idea from somewhere.

Anyway, all the Elves were cheerfully working hard, anticipating relaxing with marshmallow-decked hot chocolate after their shift, when it happened. The line abruptly halted. Everything came to a dead stop, the colorful blocks standing in silence on the motionless belt.

Stillness filled the room. Before chatter could begin again, a buzz sped along the line, whispers from one Elf to another. The whispers did not explain why the line had suddenly halted, why work was being left undone during these deadline-filled weeks before the Holidays. The explanation that arrived soon after the surprise stoppage shocked even the most experienced Elves into awed whispers and stares. Carson had been fired.

Bramble, Josh, and Crocus looked at Piet. Bramble asked, "Could an Elf even be fired?"

"Of course," the old Elf replied, "but that rarely happens, and NEVER before Christmas."

"Everyone has to meet certain standards before they are even hired," Crocus said.

"I know those standards," Josh added. "I worked for a gnome in Alaska once with those same standards."

All the Elves knew the standards—hard working, honesty, kindness, a willingness to share, and, most importantly, believing.

Bramble asked what all the others were thinking. "What could Carson have done to warrant such drastic action?"

The succeeding waves of whispers provided a little more information to the Elves at the end of the line. Apparently, it wasn't Santa himself who had sacked Carson, but Bobber, the second head Elf and shift lead. Bobber was notoriously difficult to work with, and one could easily cross him. However, he generally only shouted at an offender or sent one off to a less appealing job, like cleaning the reindeer stalls. No one had ever known Bobber to actually FIRE an Elf, most certainly not during such a rush time.

"But what did he DO?" Crocus whispered nervously. Crocus had once painted a batch of model planes the wrong color and Bobber had sent him to polish the sleigh. To be fired, Carson must have done something worse.

"Maybe Carson stole Bobber's lunch."

"Or smashed his favorite cookies."

"Could he have mislabeled a package?"

The buzzing conversations grew louder as the Elves offered suggestions about Carson's offense. Soon the sounds of hundreds of talking Elves rivaled the noise in the construction shop where the blocks for the train assembly line were cut and shaped. This was a serious event.

It looked like there would be no more work done on this shift. Elves all along the line were chattering, speculating and worrying about the incident. It was serious to fire an Elf. Bramble wondered what was happening to their pleasant, well-ordered lives. Josh broached the possibility of seeing the pink slips of firing in their own pay checks.

"No," Piet reassured him. "We are on a contract. We will leave when our work contract is over. Carson and Bobber's actions won't affect us."

Josh was only slightly reassured. Tension was high as rumors raged about. There was a danger the work stoppage would spread to other departments. That would definitely ruin the fudge.

Suddenly the noise abated, quiet settled on the train assembly line. The big man, Santa himself, stood in their midst. Finally, they would know the truth.

"I understand you have heard about Carson. You are, of course, worried and have many questions." Santa paused and murmurs floated through the crowd. He continued, reassuring all the assembled Elves that their jobs were secure and Bobber had not gone off his rocker.

"You see," Santa said, "Bobber was justified in his prompt action. He was following a standing order set down long ago. Based on something Carson said to several coworkers, Bobber had reasonable cause to fire Carson immediately. I approved his prompt action." More murmurs arose among the now confused Elves. They had never seen Santa so serious.

Santa looked around gravely. Then in a gentle voice ringing with compassion for the banished Elf, Santa explained, "Carson broke the most important rule in Elfdom. His statements may have caused a shadow on our ability to do the work we do. He did not believe." Unable to say more, Santa left.

Two fudge workers exchanged glances with their coworkers. They all wanted to hear the explanation, but they could not leave the fudge. It was at a critical stage in the cooking.

Bobber tried to calm the troubled staff. "Santa is concerned that Carson's disbelief will spread and cause more trouble here in the workshop, as well as in the world. Our purpose is to help the people in the world, not make their lives more difficult. The Holidays are meant to be a time of peace, love, and hope, a respite from the trials of daily life for the beleaguered people of the world. They work hard in difficult conditions all the time. They struggle with family relationships. They fret over the decisions their leaders make, which affect them and over which they have no control. The people need every bit of hope we can provide. Parents who cannot provide that bit of hope and joy for their children know that Santa will come through. As long as they believe. When belief falters, despair rises and quickly takes its place. Desperate people behave badly, leading to more trouble in the world."

The majority of the Elves had enough experience to understand what Bobber was saying. They nodded their heads in agreement and turned back to their tasks. Gradually the work resumed. Everyone relaxed, confident that their lives were as secure as before. The level of joy in the workshop rose again.

Feeling positive now about his position, Crocus picked up a box and carefully inserted the correct toy. He hummed softly as he worked, remembering to keep his hands busy. "I believe. I do, I do. Here's some hope for Tommy. Here's some hope for Morgan. Here's some more hope for Dieter. Hope for Ling Mu, Hope for Nkruma. Hope for…"

About the Author

After teaching English to adult learners for a long time, Gretchen Keefer started writing short fiction for fun. Her stories are family friendly and, hopefully, entertaining and/or thought-provoking.

She has been published in *Chicken Soup for the Soul – The Magic of Christmas, Rain Magazine,* CommuterLit.com, Academyoftheheartandmind@wordpress.com, and some local anthologies.

She can be contacted at gkeefer46@gmail.com.

I'm Sorry, Christmas Tree
by
James Rogers

I'm Sorry, Christmas Tree

*I*t was already dark when I got out of the local man's car. I thanked him for the lift as I closed the passenger door and he drove off with a wave.

Home from college for Christmas, and with the exams behind me, I stood on the footpath in the middle of the town, looking up and down Main Street. At one end of the street, at the top of the hill, stood the church. The tall belfry, crowned with four pointed pillars at the corners, was easily visible in the orange glow of the streetlights, but the rest of the building was blocked by the giant Christmas tree just inside the gates, the red bulbs shaking in the wind. Down at the bottom of the town, by the river, stood the statue of O'Carolan, the blind harpist. Above him stretched the branches of a cherry blossom, their shapes traced out by a string of white bulbs. Just to the right of O'Carolan sat a lighted timber structure, housing the Virgin Mary, Joseph and the usual collection of animals.

From the top to the bottom of the town, perched outside a second-floor window of every house, was a fir tree bedecked with multicoloured lights. If you visited the town at any other time of the year you might ponder the purpose of the metal bracket sticking out of every building. Only in December would their function become apparent.

For years there had been much talk about collecting money and arranging to have lights strung across the street at Christmas. But talk was all it ever amounted to. Then one year, some local lads came up with the idea of mounting a tree outside of each house. They provided the bracket, the string of lights, the tree and the installation service. I remember that first year being surprised that everyone joined in, and, within days, the town was aglow with Christmas. In Ireland in the 1980s, there was very little spare money; the economy was on its knees and there was huge national unemployment. And so, the spontaneous spending on what could be deemed superfluous decoration was an unexpected but welcome development. Perhaps the fact that the entrepreneurs were local was the reason for the universal acceptance.

Standing on the footpath a few years later, I didn't think the decorations were overdone. Even when times are hard, some things are worth it. Anyway, it didn't cost an arm and a leg.

Well, that seemed to be the general opinion—except for one businessman. I smiled as I made my way across the street to Gilmartin's Grocery & Newsagents, the only naked establishment in town. "Some things never change," I said to myself.

I walked through the door and into the small, narrow shop. The counter ran the whole way down the right side of the long room, shelves to the ceiling packed with sugar and tea and salt and all the non-perishables. On the left side, just inside the door, was a stand with newspapers and magazines, then shelves of light hardware and cleaning solutions. At the very back of the shop were the fridges with dairy and meat products and, to the left, one with Coca-Cola written across the top in shiny plastic. I wasn't surprised to see that one wasn't switched on.

Hanging from the ceiling were old fashioned crepe paper decorations, the kind my mother used years earlier. She would always get the stuff from the attic on the first Monday in December, hating to see others decorating earlier. "Diluting Christmas," she would complain. My brother and I loved to play with the delicate paper, delighting in the way the flat sheets would expand into beautiful, coloured globes and streamers. Inevitably, we'd tear some and get an earful. "Get out of my sight and don't come back till I'm done!"

Most people had now moved onto the plastic replacements and the nodding reindeer and Santa popping out of a chimney and so on, but Uncle Jack, my mother's eldest brother, continued to use paper. In January it would all be packed neatly and safely into boxes, to be used again.

The man himself was standing at the cash register, halfway down the counter. He was tall and thin, with surprisingly dark hair, considering he was in his late sixties. "Ah, you made it. Any trouble getting a lift?" He was pushing tobacco into his pipe with his thumb, a straight pipe with a dark timber bowl and a vulcanite stem; the same one he'd had for as long as I could remember. I've heard it said smoking a pipe is not nearly as bad for one's health as smoking cigarettes. While this claim is hotly contested, in Jack's case I felt it was true; he seemed to spend most of his time trying to light it.

"No. There's always someone from town at the station."

"I'd have gone out for you myself, only I'm stuck here on my own."

"Where's Theresa?" I asked, referring to the woman who helped run the place.

"She went home early. Tomorrow will be a long day. She's bringing in her young one, Lily, to help out. And I suppose you'll give a hand too."

"Of course I will." Working in my uncle's shop on Christmas Eve was something I always looked forward to. It would, of course, be very busy with everyone stocking up on milk and butter and bread and the likes for the days ahead when most places would be closed. We probably wouldn't shut the door till ten. But people tended to be very jovial, wishing each other Happy Christmas and having a bit of a joke and a laugh.

In the big shopping centres with the massive crowds, it would be uncomfortable and tiring, but in small shops in small towns, it was good fun. Anyway, I always tried to avoid the mad rush during the last few days, and I had all my presents bought the week before. I enjoyed going around from one shop to another, when they weren't yet crowded but were still in full swing, with the trees and the lights and the silly catchy Christmas classics in the air. And I simply liked buying things, even if I wasn't buying them for myself: not a good habit for one surviving on a college grant, but it was only once a year.

"No tree, Jack?" I'd gone inside the counter to help myself to some chocolate.

"Seven pounds, he wanted."

"But he'd have put it up for you too."

"How long does it take to put up a tree? And me with most of the work done, making sure all the bulbs are in order. Anyway, you can give me a hand with that in the morning. We'll need to do it bright and early, so as to be back to help out Theresa and the young one."

"Out to the forest again?"

"Why not? Now go in there and make a pot of tea. And then you can come back out here and give me a break."

"Ok. Let me drop this upstairs," I said, indicating the large canvas bag on my shoulder. As usual on the 23rd of December, I would stay the night with Jack; there was no point going out home and then back in for the morning. And Jack enjoyed the company, even though as a bachelor, he also enjoyed his freedom.

The following morning, after a quick breakfast of tea and toast, we got into Jack's car. I'd had a good sleep, badly needed after the late nights celebrating the end of exams. The day was cold but dry, and for that I was thankful, as Jack would be determined to negotiate the ditches and brambles and barbed wire that separated the road from the fir tree forest.

The sun was just making its appearance when we got out of the car on the narrow lane. I knew the early start had more to do with Jack's desire to carry out the plunder unseen than it had with getting back to town to help Theresa.

My feet were quickly freezing inside the flimsy Adidas, whereas my companion wore heavy socks inside heavy boots. But it could have been worse; at least the ground was hard, the frost crackling as we walked. Jack was much more used to outdoor activities than his nephew, even though I was the one who grew up in the countryside.

He had quite a large garden, unusual for one living in a town, and it was the finest for miles about. I loved to spend time there in the summer, walking about the immaculate lawns as Jack told me all about the different types of trees and shrubs and what they were called, even though I could never remember one from another. He would try to get me involved, to teach me, but everything I put in the ground died. I'd help him nonetheless, carrying the can on those odd times in the West of Ireland when there wouldn't be enough rain and Jack would water the plants. I'd just begun learning biology at school, and I would inform the master gardener that there was no point in pouring the water over the leaves as the plants drew it through the roots only. "But some of it goes in through the leaves," he would respond, and I would vehemently argue the opposite. It was only years later I realised the quiet laugh he was having at my expense.

After some time walking with bent backs amongst the trees, Jack saw what he was after. Even in the shadows of the tall slender trees, I could see it was a beautiful sapling, a lighter shade of green than the older trees about it. We stood together admiring it, saying nothing for a few moments. Eventually Jack spoke. "It's bent at the bottom," he said, pointing with the yellow Bushman saw. "You see?"

"Yeah." But I couldn't. It looked perfectly fine to me.

"Bent at the bottom. They'll cut it down anyway."

Neither of us said anything for a moment. In the distance I could hear the rattling sound of a tractor. Jack stooped towards the tree, then straightened up again. We looked at it some more. "Yeah, they'll cut it down anyway," he said. Then he bent to it quickly and started sawing. "I'm sorry, Christmas tree," he said. As I took hold of the tree near the top, I almost laughed. Then he said it again, as the blade made it through. "I'm sorry, Christmas tree."

Without too much difficulty, we threw the tree into the boot of the car and headed back to town, Jack with the unlit pipe in his mouth. Once again, he informed me the tree would have been cut down anyway. I felt obliged to agree.

When we got back to the shop, I went to the garden shed to fetch the ladder, bringing it through the house to prop it next to the bracket.

"You weren't arrested," Theresa laughed, standing outside watching her daughter help Jack drape the bulbs about the tree. I looked at her, smiling and shaking my head. The plump woman then walked inside to get ready for the busy day.

With me at the top of the ladder and Jack handing up the tree and Lily taking the plug through the window, the job was done in no time. Jack and I stood looking up, him striking a match and applying it to the bowl, only to have it extinguished by the wind. We waited a few moments for the lights to come on.

"Lily," Jack shouted only a few seconds after they did. "Lily!" As I was taking down the ladder, he took it from me and said, "Go upstairs and tell that girl plug it out. A score of twenty-Watt bulbs eat a sight of electricity."

So, with the town's decorations finally complete, we got ready for the rush. And it came, hard and fast. There were times when customers were finding it difficult to move about the narrow space, but all went well, and we didn't run out of any stock, except for milk at about four o' clock. Lily had to nip into the back to give the dairy suppliers a call and so the milkman arrived and stocked us up again. He wanted to turn on the Coke fridge and put some packs of milk in there too, but Jack vetoed the move. "Put them outside the back door. On a day like this, that's as good as any fridge."

When you're busy, the time flies, and before we knew it the rush was over. Ten o'clock was approaching and many people were on their way to midnight mass. There hadn't actually been a midnight mass in the town for a number of years, not since the Pope had decided going to mass the day before would suffice, yet the ten o'clock mass on Christmas Eve would always be called midnight mass.

Theresa and Lily had left about an hour earlier to go home and get ready with the rest of their family and head for the church. Jack and I would go in the morning with my family. Not that I was religious, but it pleased my parents to see me go. Besides, I enjoyed it; I had so many wonderful memories of going to the church on Christmas morning, only hours after opening Santa's presents. I loved the choir's renditions of the Christmas hymns, and the crib in the corner with Jesus now placed in the manger, and the advent wreath with the four candles lit.

For me as a child, the advent wreath was a special delight as it counted down the four Sundays before the big day. When the pink candle was finally lit, I would be bouncing about, capable of no thoughts that didn't involve Santa and his elves, the firm belief that they were completing their preparations for the huge journey paramount in my mind. I would drive my mother crazy with technical questions like, "How can he visit every house in the world in one night?" or "How does he pay for the toys?" (Even I could see the toys weren't made in Santa's workshop.) My mother would patiently invent answers like, "Because he's magic, and he can slow time," and, "He takes the toys from shops and leaves the money on the counter."

Finally, Jack and I were alone in the shop, him behind the counter sucking the pipe, the flame from the match being repeatedly dragged into the bowl. I was leafing through one of the magazines on the stand by the door when it opened and a man in jeans, jacket and big boots walked in. "Jack Gilmartin?"

"That's me," Jack answered.

"Where'd you get that tree?" the man asked, nodding towards the front of the house.

"Why do you want to know?"

The man reached inside his pocket and pulled out some identification. I could see a logo with a tree on it. "Forestry Commission. We believe you stole that tree."

There was a long pause. I could see Jack was rattled. This encounter was something he knew could happen, but like me, he never really expected it. The uncomfortable silence was broken by the squeak of the door as a few local men walked in.

"In fact," the Forestry man continued, "we know you stole it."

"And how would you prove such an accusation?" Jack asked. He was probably wondering if our early morning escapades had been caught on film. Here's one for candid camera: what happened next? The old fella went to jail.

"We've been monitoring you. It's come to our attention that you've been doing the same for quite a few years. So, you have two choices. You can deny all and go to court and we'll prove you wrong. Or you can give us your garden."

"What?" Jack and I both said together.

"You can hand over your garden to us and we'll plant trees, therefore somewhat making up for the destruction you've caused. We'd have the place until the trees mature, which would be about thirty years."

"Thirty years! I'll be gone before them."

"Well, I know it would be a shame to ruin such a beautiful garden. I had a lot of good fun there in my youth."

"Ruin it you'll not. We'll go to court."

A moment later, that last statement from the Forestry man registered with Jack while I was wondering why the locals were smiling so much. It would be unlike them to take pleasure in Jack's predicament.

"What do you mean by that?" Jack asked.

The Forestry man started laughing. "Ah Jack," he said. "I can't believe you don't know me. You used to let me play for hours in your garden."

"He's Robert Humphries' son," one of the locals explained. "Paul." I'd heard the name, but the family had moved away when I was young, the bank manager-father transferred to another branch.

"You're an awful man," Jack sighed. "I might have had a heart attack. And you lot only came in to enjoy the show," he said to the men who were now laughing and leaving, heading back to Clancy's pub across the street.

"Close up and come over," they said. "Clancy'll be dying to hear this one."

Then Paul walked over to the counter to shake Jack's hand. "Sorry about that," he said, smiling. "They put me up to it."

"They didn't have to try too hard, I'd say. How's your father doing?"

"Good. He's enjoying his retirement."

Jack turned off the lights and we headed for the door. "What brings you about here on Christmas Eve? Shouldn't you be at home with your family."

"I should indeed. It's a long story, but I ended up staying in this part of the country much later than expected. So rather than go driving home at this time of night, I decided to book into the hotel and then pop down to Clancy's for a few drinks. Nice to be amongst people I know."

With the shop all locked up, which involved nothing more than pulling the door behind us, we walked into Clancy's. There was a big cheer from the men who were now back at the bar and their pints. Clancy himself was laughing and rubbing his hands. I ordered a pint and Jack, who didn't drink, had an orange juice. Paul paid for them, feeling he ought to, I suppose.

"I can't believe you didn't recognise him," Clancy said. "I knew him as soon as he walked in. And I had heard something about him working for the Forestry, and with seeing you putting up the tree this morning, well I couldn't resist. Anyway, it serves you right; if you'd buy a tree like the rest of us you wouldn't have been caught out."

"And I suppose the tax man knows all about those rooms you're renting out upstairs," Jack spoke around the pipe, to loud cheers. Yet another match flared and was applied to the unwilling appendage.

After a while the bar started to fill up with people coming down from mass and before long it was a struggle to get through the crowd to the toilets. But Jack and I only stayed for a few drinks, as we wanted to get out to my house before midnight. So, we said goodbye to all and wished Paul a safe journey home in the morning. We nipped into the shop to throw our bags in the car and were out the road to the house in minutes.

Along the way, I noticed most homes had a tree standing inside a window, the multicoloured fairy lights, some flashing, plainly visible from the road. I imagined all the children snug in bed and the parents putting the finishing touches to the presents. In a matter of hours, the little ones would be up, waking those tired parents who would have to forget their fatigue and feign wonder and astonishment at the collection of delights that had appeared in the night.

Jack of course would be staying with us. He had a big hello for my parents and brother when we entered the kitchen, heavily laden plastic bags in his hands. My father was getting the turkey ready, whatever that involves, while my mother was peeling a big pot of potatoes; the last thing you want on Christmas Day is to run out of potatoes.

"Well, young fella," Jack said to my brother as he removed the gift-wrapped items from the bags and placed them under the tree. "You were off fraternising with the enemy again today." He was referring to my brother's weekend and holiday job in the local supermarket. "You have no shame. Taking food out of your poor Uncle's mouth."

"At least they pay me," my brother replied. "You have that poor idiot working for nothing," he finished with a nod at me.

"Doesn't he get the run of his jaws." Despite the many years, Jack still managed to come out with sayings my brother and I had never heard before. We both looked inquisitively to our father who, laughing, explained it meant I got fed. Which of course was true. And in fairness, Jack looked after us both throughout the year with extra pocket money.

I also placed my presents in a random arrangement beneath the tree that stood in the corner of the living room, the lights reflecting off the tinsel and glass balls we'd had in the house for years. The tree's roots together with damp soil were wrapped in black plastic. My father always got one with roots as he liked to plant it after Christmas along the fence behind the house. Some of them survived and matured, others didn't.

A short while later my parents were finished in the kitchen, and we all sat about the fire in the living room. With central heating, there was no real need for the open fire, but the room would be less cosy without it. To sit and watch the dancing flames was very relaxing, almost hypnotic. On the television George C. Scott was mostly ignored as he played out Dickens's wonderful addition to Christmas.

My brother and I had a few bottles of beer while my father had a whiskey and my mother took to the port. Jack stuck to the tea with two sugars. We had pleasant, pointless and meandering conversations, and lots of teasing of the young lads by the two older men. More than one sentence started with, "in our day…"

It was all so warm, comfortable, and predictable. Jack even got the pipe lit.

About the Author

Originally from Ireland, James Rogers lives in New York and is a teacher at the United Nations International School. His short fiction has appeared in a number of literary magazines, including *The First Line*, *The Galway Review* and *Inscape*. His debut novel, *Flight of the Eternal Emperor*, is set for publication on 24th November 2023. jameswrogers.com

HO! HO! HO!

by
Fran Scannell

HO! HO! HO!

"Ho, ho, ho, my little friend. Come and tell Santa what he can bring you for Christmas."

Melanie was shy with strangers. She looked at her mom who was standing in line at the entrance to Santa's workshop. Mom nodded to her. With small steps, Melanie moved between Santa's legs, and leaned against the calf-high, black shiny boot on his right leg. He lifted her. She sat squirming on his thigh.

Santa winked at her mom across the open space and then asked, "What's your name, my little one?"

"Melanie...Melanie Walker, but everybody calls me Mel."

"And how old are you?"

"I'm six-and-a-half, almost seven."

"Well, Mel, you sure are wearing pretty slacks, and your big brown eyes are sparkling. That rhinestone tiara makes you look like a little princess."

Melanie grinned and leaned a little more into Santa.

"Did you really come from the North Pole?" she asked.

"Yes, that's where I live with my elves and reindeer."

"Then how did you get here? I didn't see any reindeers out front or on the roof."

"Well, when there's no snow, I have to take the Polar Express down from the North Pole. It's nighttime so nobody sees my little train traveling on the tracks."

"Where are your elves? Did they come, too?"

"No, they had to stay to take care of the reindeer. You know, Rudolph, Donner, Blitzen, and all the rest. My, my, you're just full of questions," Santa said as he looked over at the line of children with their moms, waiting for their lap time with Ole Saint Nick. "Do you want to tell me what you want for Christmas, Mel?"

Melanie fidgeted as she looked at her mom and then directly into Santa's eyes.

"Tires," she said.

"Fires?" repeated Santa raising his brows.

"No, tires."

"Wires?" sounded Santa, trying to make sense of what the little tyke was telling him.

"I told you, tires," Melanie said, raising her voice.

"Oh, a choir," affirmed Santa.

"No! No! I said TIRES!"

"Tires! Now what would a pretty little girl like you want with tires? Maybe for your bicycle, huh?"

"No. I don't want nothin'. They're for my mom. Mom says that when it snows, she won't be able to get to work 'cause the car has bald tires. She says she needs to work so me and Jimmy can have food on the table and a place to live."

Santa looked at Mel's mom, who was attractive and appeared to be about thirtyish, smiling a proud mother's loving smile, and then he looked back at Mel. He was at a loss for words.

"I didn't tell Mom what I was asking for, 'cause I want it to be a Christmas surprise. Me and Jimmy's been good all year so please bring Mom new tires. She's been wanting them ever since summer."

Santa tugged on his long white beard not knowing how to respond to the unselfish request. "Well little one, Santa will see what he can do. Ho, ho, ho! Run along now, my little angel, so Santa can hear what the other kids want for Christmas."

"Mom brought me here today 'cause Saturday's her day off, and I said I never seen you before and had something to tell you, but I didn't tell her what. I don't think she believes in you, but I do and so does my little brother, Jimmy. He's five. He's with Nana now, until we get home, 'cause he has a bad cold." As Melanie slid down from Santa's leg, she emphasized, "We live at 405 Oakbrook Street. Please don't forget us. You can leave them on the porch. We don't have a chimney." Then she hopped, skipped, and jumped across the workshop to her mom's hand, feeling assured she and Santa had a secret pact and a special bond.

John ho-ho-hoed it with kids along the way through the department store to one of its dressing rooms after his four-hour stint as Santa. He'd loved playing Santa over the last few years because it put him in the Christmas spirit since he now lived alone and had no one with whom to celebrate.

John retired about five years ago from being an actuary for an insurance company. He had a small pension, some savings, and supplemented his income by doing odd, fun jobs like playing Santa. He was comfortable but not well-off. For exercise and a small stipend, John had a dog-walking service for his working neighbors in his apartment building. He also filled in as a substitute teacher at a district grade school and high school when needed. John's gigs were for small change that gave him spending money for things he ordinarily wouldn't buy for himself: a TV subscription, internet connection, cell phone service, accoutrements for his vintage 1957 Ford Thunderbird convertible, and touring Broadway plays when they came to the Arts Center. A good seat was expensive.

John's wife had died seven years ago of a brain aneurism, when she tripped on their bathroom mat and hit her head on the tub. They had been married for forty-five years. No kids, just the two of them. They got along famously and were a perfect complement to each other's creative interests—John, with his penchant for art-house movies and the live theater, and she with her vegetable garden and volunteer work at the botanic gardens.

Today's session with the kids was disturbing. He couldn't get little Mel out of his mind as he removed his boots, trousers, stomach padding, white beard and wig, and a knit Santa's cap with a tassel. He folded his red outfit and returned everything to the Human Resource Department. It was Saturday. There was only one more Saturday to go before Christmas day on Sunday. *That little kid wants nothing for herself. Just for her mom to be able to put a roof over their heads and food on the table. She and her younger brother are probably spending their days with their nana while the mom works at a low-paying job.*

John walked to the parking lot and hopped into his red vintage T-bird with the continental tire assembly on the rear bumper. He planned to head home and watch a movie on Netflix after dinner. It was a little after four o'clock and still daylight. As he hit the main road from the mall, he was still saddened about Melanie's request and wondered where 405 Oakbrook Street was.

What the hell. Won't hurt to check the place out. John knew his way around town, but this street was foreign to him. Once he gave Siri the address, he knew why. It was the poorer section of town. He had no reason to ever go there.

John exited the highway and eased into the somewhat impoverished community, turning left on Oakbrook, a narrow street with a few small potholes. Both sides were sparsely lined with barren, leafless trees, self-prepped for winter. He noted how old the single-story houses were; nevertheless, the residents seemed to take pride in their humble abodes, keeping them in order with no peeling paint, clean and orderly sidewalks, and uncluttered lawns with few fallen leaves.

There it was: 405—a small, brown-shingled duplex with an iron railing leading up to and dividing the miniscule, wooden porch into halves. Each unit had its own entrance from its portico. *Rather non-descript*, John thought as he pulled up adjacent to a well-used, 2001 white Plymouth Neon next to the streetlight.

He could see the tires were bald. *Yes, Melanie and her mom are right. Those tires will never make it through even a light dusting of snow. With today's inflation, she's probably looking at maybe…six hundred dollars, minimum, for four all seasons. That kid is cute, and her mom is probably a hard worker. Wish I really were Santa.*

John pulled away from the duplex and continued his roundabout trip home after taking his curiosity tour. Home was an apartment with underground parking, which he'd moved into just after his retirement. He'd gotten rid of belongings he and his wife had accumulated over the years, and then sold their single-family home. He now lived the life of an aging, somewhat lonely but involved, senior citizen.

John tried to watch an episode of *Unsolved Mysteries* after he fixed his baked chicken pot pie frozen dinner, washed down with a glass of red wine, followed by vanilla ice cream for dessert. *This plot is escaping me. Lack of concentration*, he thought. *Can't seem to get little Mel out of my mind.* Realizing it was impossible to concentrate on the murder mystery, he finally turned off the TV and went to bed.

John slept intermittently and woke up with a restless-night's sleep-deprived yawn on Sunday, remembering it was his day to do volunteer work at the local animal shelter. It promised to be a slow day—no adoptions on Sundays, so all he had to do was feed, brush, and play with the cats and dogs. It gave him time to interact with a few other volunteers, and mentally prepare for Monday, when he'd agreed to substitute teach across town at elementary school PS 19 and again on the following Friday before Christmas.

John liked the duty because he enjoyed working with the young kids. But tomorrow would be a challenge because he'd been assigned a class of second graders. *Short attention spans, fidgety, and loud. Not like the sixth and seventh graders. I can give those kids math tips and work out number problems with them.* He loved bringing his actuarial skills into the classroom, especially when he was assigned to high school students. *Maybe we'll read some stories. We could solve some simple math problems and have a spelling bee—one side of the room against the other. Should be fun.*

John pulled his shift at the animal shelter having gotten his warm-fuzzies for the day. He didn't know why, but on the way home, he made a slight detour to drive by Mel's place once again. The old Plymouth was still parked out front. He shook his head at Mel's mom's plight and hoped the next snowstorm was far off, giving her time to come up with the hundreds needed for new tires. *Wish I could help her… Need my savings to last as long as I do. Hmmm, wonder what could I do without?*

John stopped at his neighborhood's fast-food chain for a quick bite to eat followed by a shower at home and a change of clothes for a trip to the Arts Center to see the touring Broadway musical *Cats*.

A perfect way to top off a day of working with abandoned animals. The musical will give voice to some of the furry felines I was playing with. Don't know how humans can make a commitment to animals to love and protect them and then turnaround and give them up for adoption. Maybe Cats *will show me they can make it on their own, without human intervention.*

Monday came bright and early. John was in the classroom by 7:30, waiting for the eight o'clock troops. He had the day planned for his second graders, ending with the rollicking spelling bee. The little ones came filing in wide-eyed, bushy-tailed, and boisterous. They became somewhat subdued when they saw Mrs. Monahan was not sitting at her desk to greet them as usual. John nodded his hello

221

to each as the youngsters took their seats. Then, as if on cue, a familiar face with a large smile and big brown eyes walked through the door and took her assigned seat in the front row. It was Mel.

John was taken aback for a moment and then realized she had no idea who he was because of his Santa disguise at the department store. *This kid's been haunting me ever since Saturday, and now she shows up again right in front of me.*

To ease the tension of a new face in their familiar classroom, he introduced himself as John Jaster, their substitute teacher for the day. John asked each child to state his or her name and how each got to school that morning. The longer he could keep them engaged, the more relaxed they would be in his presence. Most came by school bus, a few rode their bikes on this cold morning while some were dropped off by a parent.

When it was Mel's turn, she said, "My mom brought me on her way to work. She's a waitress at Tally-ho and serves breakfast and lunch and then picks me up after school on her way home. Sometimes she brings the cook's leftovers home for us to have for supper. It's really good and it's free."

True to form, Mel gave him more information than he needed to know. But her effusive personality was heartwarming and endearing, like a tail-wagging puppy showing its affection by lapping your hand. In the cafeteria, he noticed she qualified for the reduced-cost lunch program. She sat with her friends, laughing and talking up a storm. Mel looked to be the alpha female in the group.

The rest of his day he spent trying to keep the kids quiet, entertained, and engaged. The math games were a struggle. No one was too interested in solving some of the easier puzzles, but the spelling bee was a hit—one side of the room against the other. If you misspelled a word, you sat down. Last person standing from each team faced off. John brought a bag of saltwater taffies for the winning team and suggested they share with their worthy opponents. They did, and all chomped on the chewy delights.

The school day ended at 2:30 p.m. At the sound of the bell, all the children said, "Goodbye, Mister Jaster" as they scrambled out the door. John began to gather his materials and put them into his book bag—Mel was still seated. She informed him her mother did not get off from work until 2:30 and asked if she could hang around inside the classroom with him until her mother came because it was cold outside.

At 3:15 her mother still hadn't shown. John was a little worried, as was Mel. She said, "Mom's never late cause we have to pick up Jimmy from Nana's on our way home."

They walked down the hall to the school's office to see if her mom had called in. The receptionist said there was no message. It was getting late, and the school was preparing to close. John had been on the roster as a substitute teacher for the last five years, so the administration knew him well. He bumped into Tom, the principal, and mentioned he would be happy to drop Mel off at her home since it was on his way. John knew this was a highly irregular suggestion—a young female student alone with a teacher in his car off school property.

The principal said, "John, wait a minute. We'll try her mom's cell phone that we have on record." There was only a recorded message to leave a number. Tom looked into Mel's file and noticed an emergency contact number for her grandmother. He tried that number but there was no answer there either. At Mel's suggestion, he tried the Tally-ho, who informed him Mel's' mother had left there around two o'clock because of an emergency call she'd received.

The situation was getting dire, and they were running out of options. Since the school was locking up for the day, Tom agreed to John dropping Mel off at her home with the stipulation John call him when the mother and daughter were reunited. They traded personal mobile numbers.

Mel and John hopped into his old T-Bird. "Cool car," noted Mel, as they headed first to Nana's house, which was only a few blocks from Mel's, to see why the phone call had gone unanswered.

The inside was dark, and all the doors locked. The only option was to drive to Mel's home with the hope her mom had returned. When they pulled up in front of her house, it looked deserted with no lights on. Mel's mom's car wasn't there. Mel informed John she didn't have a key to get in. He left her in the warmth of his front seat while he tried the doorbell. No one home. Mel and John sat in the car worrying about her mom, hoping the emergency was not serious.

Mel, being the loquacious young lady that she was, proceeded to tell him her life story, all six-and-a-half years of it.

Two years after Jimmy was born, Melanie's father died in a hit-and-run car accident. The police never caught the perpetrator. Her father, a city worker, had no life insurance, so her mom and the two kids were left to fend for themselves, with nothing more than meager Social Security benefits.

Mel's nana lived in the neighborhood and had volunteered to babysit four-year-old Mel and her baby brother while their mother worked to try to support the family. The three left their rental unit and moved into Nana's small, two-bedroom bungalow until her daughter could get established with a job and develop a credit and work history. Two years later, the threesome was able to move out of the overcrowded house and rent the duplex they were now living in.

They were happy, even though they were living paycheck-to-paycheck. Mom had purchased a run-down Plymouth, which had a "million miles" on it, according to Mel, and hoped for the best.

As Mel chronicled the family's history, the white Plymouth pulled up behind them. It was her mom. She opened the passenger's door and hefted Jimmy from the seat as Mel and John came to her aid. Jimmy was in a cast from his right wrist to his elbow, his arm in a sling. She put Jimmy down and hugged Mel saying, "Jimmy fell and broke his arm at Nana's. I've been in the emergency room at the hospital with him. When I could finally call the school, they told me that your teacher was bringing you home. I got here as fast as I could after I dropped Nana off. I'm so sorry I left you alone, but I knew you were in good hands." She looked at John and said, "Won't you come in for a minute so I can settle down and thank you properly with a cup of tea for all your troubles?"

Mel jumped up from kneeling while kissing Jimmy and asking him if it hurt. She grabbed John's hand and began pulling him toward the house. "Come on, Mister Jaster, Mom makes really good tea."

"Well, if you insist. I guess I have no choice," John replied, winking at Mel's mom.

"My name's Gloria, Gloria Walker," she said as the four of them entered the living room through the front door. They shook hands as John watched her eyes to see if she recognized him as Santa Claus. No response. She pointed to one of the upholstered chairs for him to sit in as she took the other chair.

The room was sparsely furnished but clean and comfortable. The small sofa and coffee table, next to an end table with a lamp, faced the two cushioned chairs situated on a throw rug.

"I want to thank you, Mister Jaster, for all the trouble you went through today. I wasn't thinking too clearly after I got the emergency call from my mom. I rushed to her place to take Jimmy to the emergency room."

"Happy to help out in a bind. Please call me John."

"Mel, put the kettle on so we can all have tea together," Gloria instructed. "Jimmy, you lie on the sofa and rest. You've had a tough day, my little guy."

When Mel left the room, John said, "Your daughter is quite the little chatterbox, Gloria, and she knows her way around the classroom. Won our spelling bee today."

"Yes, sometimes I can't keep up with her—questions, questions, and more questions. I'll be right back with the tea. Make yourself comfortable. Jimmy, tell Mister Jaster how you fell and broke your arm."

Gloria and Mel returned with the kettle and teacups with tea bags. Gloria apologized for not having any tidbits to go with the hot refreshment, saying that the accident was all so sudden. They passed the time with idle chitchat. Mel poured each of them a second cup as she lingered in the room, listening to the conversation. Jimmy nodded off on the sofa.

Gloria inquired about John's home life. He mentioned he'd been a widower for the last seven years and lived alone in an apartment on the other side of town. She said she could sympathize with him, having lost her husband a few years ago. "Thank God, I have my kids. Wish I could spend more time with them."

Jimmy awoke and they listened to Jimmy tell Mel how he was walking home with Nana from his half-day at kindergarten when he tripped over a raised portion in the sidewalk.

"Jimmy, Nana told me you were skipping and not looking where you were going."

"Well, I was hopping over those sidewalk spaces. Nana said, 'Step on a crack; break the old man's back.' Nana walks too slow."

As John finished his last sip and rose to leave, he mentioned to Mel that he would be seeing her again in a couple days, because they wanted him back again at school on Friday.

At the door, Gloria said, "John, I can't thank you enough for taking care of Mel today. You weren't obligated to do that. Since you're going to be in the neighborhood again, stop by after you're done at school so you can have a proper tea party with us. I'll include some homemade cinnamon rolls this time."

"No, you don't have to do that," John said. "You don't owe me anything."

"It's no problem. I think Mel likes having you here, and Jimmy appreciates a grown man's attention."

"You've hit on my weakness. I can't resist cinnamon rolls," John confessed. "Since I'm coming over, you won't have to pick up Mel. I'll bring her here with me after class. The principal's given me permission today so Friday won't be a problem."

As John walked to his car, he dwelled on the plight of the Walkers. *They're barely scraping by,* he thought, *and now it's only a matter of time until the snow falls. Wish I could do something about the tires... A bit beyond my budget. Perhaps I can forego... Maybe the T-Bird's new canvas top I've been saving for.*

The second graders were well behaved on Friday. They enjoyed taking turns reading aloud individually from the one storybook on hand, *School Is Where I Am,* studying phonics, working out some easy math problems John gave them, and practicing penmanship. The day passed quickly.

Mel couldn't wait to tell him about her little secret on the drive home. She confessed her highly-classified, for-his-ears-only, confidential request to Santa. Mel was exuberant describing how excited her mom would be when she saw her new tires on the front porch.

She keeps bringing me back to my stint as Santa and those tires. Thank God tomorrow is my last day at the department store. My Santa impersonation will be done for the year, and I won't have to listen to the kids with their heart-wrenching stories. She'll never let me forget the power of Saint Nick to bring joy to children, if only in their dreams. Why couldn't she have wished for a book or new shoes for herself? But tires?

The two of them pulled up to the duplex, and as Mel got out, Gloria came to the front door. She was distressed.

"I have another minor emergency, John," she said. "I hope you know something about automobiles. I'm sorry, but could you take a look at my car. It overheated a bit on my way home from work today. Saturday is my day off. If you find what's wrong, I'll know where to take it and see about getting it fixed tomorrow. I'm sorry I'm such a pest."

John lifted the hood. While inspecting the radiator for a leak, he felt a drip from the underside of the radiator hose—an easy fix but one that required immediate attention. He explained the situation to Gloria and offered to take her car home with him that night after he filled the radiator with water.

He told her he would park it overnight in his heated garage's parking space and take it to his repair shop in the morning, since it was close to the department store where Mel met Santa. He said he could do some Christmas shopping (not wanting her to know he was the department store's Santa) and bring it back to her late in the afternoon. He would call her if it turned out to be anything more serious.

John offered to leave his car for her to use in case of an emergency, knowing she did not have to drive to work in the morning and would probably have no need for it. Gloria, relieved, accepted his offer, thanking him profusely, and then from out of nowhere she said, "Tomorrow's Christmas Eve, John. No one should spend the night before Christmas alone. I insist that, when you bring my car back tomorrow afternoon, you stay for Christmas Eve dinner."

Christmas Eve alone was doubly lonely. John wasn't looking forward to entertaining himself that evening, so he said, "Gloria, you're a wonderful person. You know how to reach into an old man's soul—food and companionship will do it every time. Of course, I will attend your delightful dinner. I'll come with bells on."

"Don't expect too much," she said. "It's only dinner from Tally-ho, you know. They give us portions from the chef's Christmas specials to bring home if we want. The chef's a really good cook."

They sipped their tea and munched on Gloria's homemade cinnamon rolls, which the kids called sticky buns. The little ones made plans for decorating the small, artificial four-foot Christmas tree after teatime. When their cups were empty, Gloria and John traded car keys and phone numbers at the door. He went out hoping he would make it home before the recently added fluid drained.

Saturday morning, before his eleven to three o'clock stint as Santa, John took the old Plymouth to Terry of Terry's Tune-ups, his independent mechanic. Terry agreed with John that it was only the hose that needed to be replaced but noted the tires were shot.

"It'll never make it with even a little bit of snow on the road," he warned.

"I know! I know," John responded. "I'm doing this lady and her kids a favor by bringing her car in. I'll pick up the tab for the new hose. She needs this junker to get to work—no work, no money, no food. Maybe it won't snow this year—ha!"

"Not much sense replacing the hose if you can't take it out on the road," Terry scolded.

"It'll get her by until the first snowstorm, which I hope is later than sooner. Maybe she'll have enough cash by then to replace the four. I gotta walk over to the mall to play Santa. I'll pick up the car before five."

"We close at four today, Santa. It's Christmas Eve, remember?"

"I'll be here with a sack over my back." And with a ho-ho-ho, he parted his company.

At the department store, the kids were excited and jumpy on his lap. It was almost Christmas. Their anticipation was palpable, and the parents were stressed with last minute shopping.

When his shift was over, John changed into his street clothes and walked through the mall, picking up gifts for Mel and Jimmy: a unicorn puzzle for Mel, a Door Pong set for Jimmy. Then he headed to Terry's. He was supposed to be at the Walkers by six for the Christmas Eve thank-you dinner. This would be the first Christmas Eve he hadn't been alone since his wife died.

Walking to Terry's, John mused on the many kids he had seen over the weeks since Thanksgiving, wondering if their wishes would come true, even partially. He assumed, since their parents brought them to see him, those kids would realize at least some of their hearts' desires. He was concerned about the disappointment little Mel would feel when there were no tires on the porch, and if it would squelch her belief in Santa Claus.

John thought, *We all need something to hold sacred and special, be it religion for adult worshippers, or spiritual transcendence for atheists, or the potential for mankind's goodness for humanitarians, or Santa Claus for kids. After all, hope is the pillar of most beliefs and that which makes us uniquely human. It springs eternal because hope promises a life ever after for some.*

When he arrived at Terry's, there Terry was, under the lift with the Plymouth on it. John immediately noticed it had a set of newer-looking tires.

"What's going on, Terry?" he asked. I didn't order these."

"Yeah, but it's Christmas," Terry said, wiping his hands on a rag, "and I had this used set of four that've been laying around here for God knows how long. They were the right size. It's Christmas, you know, so why not?"

"Terry, you're the man!" John knew there was a good reason why he always came to Terry's for his repairs—he had a small garage but a big heart. "Tell me how much I owe you, and we'll settle up."

"Pay me for the hose and my labor. No charge for the tires," he said standing next to one of the wheels. "They're on the house. A working woman with kids needs transportation. She should be able to get at least two winters out of these guys," he predicted while patting the tire on the wheel next to him. "Besides they were taking up space."

Terry lowered the lift, and John paid him for the hose and his labor and gave him the $100 gift card that was a bonus from the department store for his month-long, reliable Santa service. "See, Santa takes care of boys and girls who are good," John said.

Terry thanked him, and off John went to deliver a very special Christmas present.

John parked the Plymouth adjacent to the streetlight behind his T-Bird and walked up to the door. Christmas music sounded from inside. The door opened with Mel and Jimmy in their green and red Christmas jammies, grinning from ear to ear when they saw he had a gift-wrapped package in each hand. The warmth of the home, the glow from the table lamp, the aroma of a baked turkey, and the seasonal sound of music infused John with the holiday spirit.

The kids yelled, "Nana, look what Santa left at Mister Jaster's for us," as they entered the living room. Nana was seated on one of the cushioned chairs, and Gloria was on the other. They all nodded to each other as the kids placed their wrapped gifts under the small, decorated tree. John sat on the sofa and the two youngsters sat on either side of him.

"Welcome," said Gloria, "and a very Merry Christmas. This is my mom, Angela. She watches Jimmy while I'm at work. I invited her over for supper so we could all be together. Hope you don't mind, but I drove your car four blocks to pick her up."

Angela said, "Pleased to meet you, John. Gloria told me about you and how you brought Mel home from school and that you just got Gloria's car repaired. Hope it wasn't too much trouble."

"No trouble at all. Happy to help out," John answered.

"Let me know how much I owe you for my repair, John."

"No charge. Merry Christmas, Gloria. Santa came a day early for you. Sorry I couldn't gift-wrap your radiator hose. You've invited me to this wonderful Christmas Eve dinner. It was the least I could do."

Mel chimed in with, "Jimmy got his arm out of the sling. Mom called the doctor, and he said it was okay, so now he can play like always but with his arm in a cast."

"You wanna see me catch a ball with just my good arm?" offered Jimmy.

"Later," Mom said. "First, let's all have a sip of that special-occasion sherry I've been saving forever." She poured from the just-opened bottle, and they all toasted the evening, the kids sipping their chocolate milk through straws stuck in their make-believe wine glasses.

"I brought some leftover turkey with stuffing home from Tally-ho yesterday, along with mashed potatoes and cranberry sauce. Hope you don't mind re-heats, John. It'll all be good with the creamy green bean casserole Mom fixed, and her apple pie for dessert. Let's get started.

"Kids, you need to be in bed by eight, so you're asleep when Santa comes. He only shows up when children are nestled in their beds, and the stockings are hung on the stairs with care. Shall we?"

They all rose and seated themselves in what passed for a small dining room on the way to the kitchen. The meal was marvelous. Gloria talked about her experiences with diners at the Tally-ho, and John told about his days with the animals at the shelter. Of course, Mel dominated much of the conversation recounting her experiences at school and her plans to become a nurse when she got older. They toasted their deceased spouses with "I'll Be Home for Christmas" playing on the old turntable in the living room. John and Gloria knew that they were with them in spirit. Then came the homemade, warm apple pie Nana made with fresh apples and spices.

"An old family recipe," she mentioned, "with some of my own secret fixins."

It was nearing eight by the time they finished their feast. The kids were getting drowsy after their big dinner. John offered to help with the dishes and said he would drop Nana off at her place. It was almost nine by the time they finished cleanup and the kids finally got to bed.

Gloria said, "John, I can't thank you enough for all you've done for my family. You've been a lifesaver over the past week."

"No problem," he said. "I'm happy to help out. It has been my pleasure, really. The truth is you've done as much for me as I have for you. You've made my Christmas: the kids, your mom, your hospitality, and the scrumptious food."

"And you didn't have to do gifts for the kids. You're a good man. Your wife was very lucky," she said as she gave him a big hug that felt genuine and meaningful and heartfelt. He returned the embrace.

John took his jacket from the hook by the front door and realized her car keys were still in his side pocket. They traded keys and wished one another a very Merry Christmas. Gloria helped Nana with her coat. A gust of cold air hit them as John opened the front door and saw snow had started to fall.

"Looks like a white Christmas," John noted.

"Yes, it will be beautiful. Just like the song," Gloria said with a bit of a frown on her face.

John knew what she was thinking: bald tires and snow, a bad combo. "Santa's coming! Be happy!" he shouted as he helped Nana down the steps and heard the door close behind them. Nana held him tightly as they walked down the slippery pavement.

He made sure she was tucked away comfortably in his T-bird and then pulled a big, brown paper bag from the Plymouth's trunk and walked to the front fender on the passenger's side. Nana was dozing when John hopped in behind the wheel of the T-Bird to drop her off.

On his way home, John was saddened by the thought that he wouldn't be present to see the family's reaction to Santa's surprise, especially Mel's.

On Christmas morning, Mel and Jimmy sprung up early to unwrap their meager gifts next to the small tree in the living room, one each from John and their mom, and knitted scarves from Nana. When Mom came in, still in her robe, Mel and her brother were engrossed with their gifts from her: Jimmy with a two-foot-long hook and ladder fire truck and Mel with a medical kit for kids.

When Mel saw her, she quit taking Jimmy's temperature and listening to his heart with the make-believe stethoscope. She knew the time had come. Breathing rapidly, she hurried to the front window and held the drapery aside so she could peer onto the porch.

It was still snowing. The porch was barren. Nothing. No tires. Not even tracks from Santa in the snow.

Tears welled in her eyes. She was about to release the curtain when, through her blurred vision, she saw the faint, red outline of something on their parked car's front wheel. She rubbed her eyes to clear them as best she could and looked again.

There it was under their streetlight—a big, red-ribbon bow on the front wheel of the Plymouth. Mel knew what it meant immediately: her Christmas wish had come true.

She ran to her mom, who was kneeling with Jimmy. Pulling them by their hands, Mel said, "Come see what Santa left outside!"

"What? What are you talking about, hon?"

"Come outside, please. Santa's been there."

"We're in our pj's, and so are you."

"I'll get our boots and coats out of the closet! Come on! We gotta see what Santa left!" Mel said in a high-pitched, excited voice.

They bundled up and walked onto the porch. At the top of the steps, all three stood in awe as they stared at the big, thick, red ribbon. It adhered to the hubcap of the front wheel, which appeared to have a newer tire. Gloria saw there was a newer one on the back, also.

"What the—? My God, who could've done this?" Gloria gasped, choking up.

"It was Santa. I told him the day you took me to see him we needed new tires. He came with his elves and put them on. See! I told you there was a Santa," she squealed, jumping up and down with delight.

Gloria gathered herself, wrapping the kids around her to keep them warm, said, "Yes, you were right, Mel. All you have to do is have faith, believe, and good things happen. Now let's get inside before we all freeze to death. I have an important phone call to make to find out if Santa left us a granddad at Mister Jaster's home."

About the Author

I have recently returned to creative writing after spending forty-five years as a Creative Director for two advertising agencies, one of which was my own. Having written and produced a few hundred radio commercials and close to a hundred TV spots, as well as a few corporate films, numerous annual reports, outdoor advertising and so forth, it is now time to put my creative juices to the real test during my retirement—literary fiction.

Traveling my career path, I had a one-act play, *All My Heavy-hearted Heroes,* which I wrote, produced, and directed while in graduate school getting my Masters in Mass Communication, shown on Rocky Mountain PBS. Later, in the evenings, I was also an adjunct professor at Metropolitan State University in Denver, Colorado, teaching Advertising/Marketing 301 two nights a week for six years.

Over the last two years, I have written four-literary fiction novellas as well as a few short stories. I am a member of the Rocky Mountain Fiction Writers organization.

I can be reached at: FScannell@comcast.net

Yule Boys

by
Richard Pulfer

Yule Boys

Kris Kringle laid out his sales pitch to the leprechaun. Kringle had a lot of other names, not the least of which was Santa Claus, but this leprechaun only had one name—Puck—and he wasn't interested in playing.

"Look, Puck, if you help me, I can help. Take you off the Naughty List. Get more than a lump of coal for Christmas," Kringle said as he leaned back in his chair. "Just tell me where the sleigh is."

Kringle's famous sleigh was stolen right out from under his big white beard a month ago. Now, forty-eight hours before Christmas, he and his partner were chasing down every lead across the Seasons. They'd drilled everyone from the Easter Bunny to the Thanksgiving Turkey, but none knew about the sled's whereabouts—none except Puck. The leprechaun was holding out on them, and the big man in red knew it.

"I know my rights, Kringle!" Puck's nasally voice crooned. "You haven't charged me, so you ain't got nothing on me save coal in me stocking. And I can tell what you can do with that coal!"

"I'm sorry to hear that, Mr. Puck. I guess you're staying on the Naughty List," Kringle said in a calm voice.

"You think I'm scared of a few elves?" Puck chuckled.

"Actually, I gave the elves the night off. Now if you'll excuse me," Kringle said, before giving a jolly smile to Puck. "I'm going to get me some of Mrs. Claus's famous hot cocoa. You want any?"

Puck started to say something about Mrs. Claus, but Kringle hurried out of the room before he could finish. Kringle's countenance was replaced by a silhouette as jagged as a thistle bush. Puck's small face grew even smaller, his eyes widening as cloven feet clacked across the polished floor.

"You… You're…you're real?" Puck stammered.

Most mythics knew the land of Christmas for the garish lights which shined brightly year-round. They knew it for the diminutive, endlessly cheerful elfish folk who constituted most of its population. They knew it for its most popular citizen, the jolly, white-bearded Sheriff Kringle.

"Don't you know, Puck?" the creature bellowed. "Everything in the Seasons is real. Even me. Even—"

"K-k-k-k…" Puck was having trouble with his name. Puck took in his beastly visage, from his sharp, curved ebony horns to his rich coat of dark fur. The creature smiled a jagged, fanged grin at Puck as he laid his darkened iron chain on the table in front of him.

"Krampus," Puck finally said. His voice was barely a whisper.

Technically, Krampus's job description was punishing guilty children, but once Kringle started up his massive operation in the North Pole, misbehaving kids were seldom an issue. That left Krampus in the office, handling the monotonous task of moving names between the Naughty and Nice lists. Once Santa's sleigh had been stolen, it meant all hands were on deck, and that included Krampus.

This left Puck, who apparently just watched while the whole thing had gone down. He wasn't really concerned about reporting it then. It was different when an eight-foot-tall goat-monster from the shadows of Christmas Past asked the questions.

"Now," Krampus said as he stretched his cloven feet and leaned back in the chair. There weren't too many chairs in the Christmas Precinct that could fit him. But he didn't need to relax. Instead, he just needed for Puck to see the ratio of leprechaun to, well, whatever the heck Krampus was.

"I didn't take it! And that's the truth!" Puck exclaimed. "So, I'll be on my way!"

"And after you saw the sled get carted away by parties unknown, you did your civic duty and alerted my brother it had been stolen," Krampus said as his hooves clicked against the leprechaun's chair. Puck shuddered from the impact.

"Look, I just saw it fly away," Puck said in a quick tone oddly devoid of his accent. "And I don't know where it went or who took it, so this conversation is over!"

"And you didn't think to tell anyone?" Krampus raised a furry eyebrow.

"Not my holiday, pal," Puck said, mustering some confidence this time. "Not my problem."

He leapt down from his chair like a child stepping off a barber stool. Puck made his way to the door, but Krampus stood up, blocking his exit.

"I got nothing you want," he said. "So, this interview is over."

"Oh, I don't know about that," Krampus said with a crooked grin. "I used to punish the guilty back in the day. It was misbehaving kids, but then the Santa thing started, and no one needed a Krampus. So now I punish the guilty mythics…those legends derelict in their origins. And lately, I've been feeling a bit rusty."

Krampus whipped his chain against the ground so hard a link broke and bounced off the wall with a metallic clang. Krampus grimaced. He'd been meaning to have that chain fixed, but now it was too late. This is what he got for using the same chain for six hundred years without a single coat of Armor-All. Instead, he pulled out a long burlap sack from his person.

"Most of my offenders don't fit in the sack," he said as he caressed the corroded metal of his chain. He appraised the Leprechaun with a cock of his goat-like head. "But you… I think you will fit just fine."

Krampus prepared to drop the sack over the leprechaun. With such short legs, Puck didn't have a chance of escaping, especially in such a small room. Krampus was almost an inch away from him when Puck squealed.

"Okay! Okay! I'll talk! Freaks stole Santa's sled, like the ones from the Hallows!" he said. He held the sack where it was.

"What kind of freaks?" Krampus asked with distaste. He was never a big fan of that word.

"Monsters!" Puck exclaimed. "Monsters did it!"

Monsters. There weren't too many in the land of Christmastide, well, other than Krampus. Mostly the citizenry consisted of elves, a few sentient reindeer, a couple Yetis, and one particularly grumpy polar bear. There were a few older legends, but they mostly kept to themselves. In Krampus's experience, however, every holiday had its monsters.

He had to cut Puck loose. There weren't any charges he could hold him on, and he really doubted the leprechaun knew anything else. Besides, painful experience had taught him there's nothing worse than an angry, slightly inebriated leprechaun in an enclosed space.

Krampus narrowed his eyes as he saw a massive troll walk side by side with Kringle towards the desk. He wouldn't be walking her out unless she was being released as well.

This can't bode well.

To call Gryla a troll was unfair, especially when she towered two feet above Kringle, and one foot above Krampus. Most trolls were short and squat, but Gryla was tall and built like a locomotive, with eyes as red as burning coal embers. Her jagged teeth could crush a piece of coal into a diamond in seconds. Gryla wasn't just a really tall, scary-looking troll...she was the mother of all trolls.

Literally.

"And I simply must get a seven-forty-seven turbine for Christmas," she said. "It's simply the only way to dry my hair."

Kringle shot his brother a look that said *save me.* So, of course, Krampus just laughed and stayed put. It wasn't uncommon for anyone in conversation with Kringle to make less than indirect references to their Christmas list. Whether they actually got what they were asking for was another matter.

"I would think, Miss Gryla..." Kringle began.

"Please, just Gryla," she said with a razor-blade smile. Krampus couldn't tell if his happily-married brother was flustered or panicking.

"I would think if you've been good all year...then the small matter of an airplane engine isn't too much of an imposition," Kringle stammered.

"But not just any plane. It has to be from a 747," Gryla says. "I have a lot of hair, and I've found the power of those engines can dry it especially well."

"Of course," Kringle said, making a motion towards the desk, where a wary elf sat, waiting, or perhaps dreading, to process Gryla.

"And I have been good. I really haven't eaten a naughty child in ages. They tend to be high in sugar nowadays and I've been trying to lose weight." Gryla leaned in closer and said in a much softer voice, "One has to maintain her girlish figure somehow."

Kringle shuddered, but he passed it off as his usual eccentric, nervous energy. "Well, I must get to work... Christmas won't happen by itself!" Kringle said, patting Gryla's massive, clawed hand. "I have presents to wrap!"

"Especially ones shaped like airplane engines," Gryla laughed. Or at least, Kringle hoped it was a laugh.

"Err…right," Kringle said as he tore himself from Gryla's grip. "Krampus, do you have those…things I asked you for?"

"Well, I wouldn't want to interrupt," Krampus smirked.

"That's not funny," Kringle growled under his breath.

"Till we meet again, Nicholas!" Gryla waved cheerfully.

Krampus met his brother's gaze. Kringle's eyes were rolling.

"Don't be rude, Nicholas," Krampus teased. "Wouldn't want to put you on the naughty list."

"Must you leave so soon?" Kringle turned to the departing giantess.

"Oh, I hate to, but I must. I have a family reunion to prepare for!" Gryla said, and she was out the door before Kringle could say "Merry Christmas to all and to all a good night."

"Did Puck talk?" he said.

"Eventually," Krampus said.

"And?" Kringle raised a white eyebrow.

"He said it was monsters," Krampus said with some hesitance.

"Freaks," Kringle spat. "So, they were from the Hallows."

Halloween was Kringle's favorite punching bag. There had always been a deep rivalry between the two holidays, and yeah, it had led to more than a few pranks on either side. But with Kringle, it went beyond rivalry. Halloween was the ideological opposite to Christmas, or at least that's what Kringle thought.

Krampus wasn't so sure. He liked the Hallows. It was hard working in the office. His freakish appearance tended to unnerve the elves. And the reindeer. And just about everyone else. In the Hallows, however, Krampus could walk about the ghosts, ghouls, and goblins without so much as a second glance. That's why Krampus spent most of his vacation time at the Hallows.

"I knew they'd try something again, the animals," Kringle said. "This is their way of stopping Christmas before it even starts: with my sled."

"For what purpose? Halloween has been over for almost two months," Krampus said.

"Halloween has no purpose other than chaos," Kringle snarled. "Pure, sugar-fed chaos."

"Maybe it was Gryla…" Krampus started.

Kringle cut him off. "She has an alibi—a family reunion with six of her kin."

"Maybe she's lying?" Krampus shrugged.

"The facts don't lie, Krampus," Kringle said as he turned away. "Well, if I can't have my holiday, neither can they."

Krampus didn't like the sound of that.

"This is madness," Krampus said as he watched Kringle finish pushing the roadblock into place. The squad car's flashing red and green lights pierced the darkness of the bridge. If the sleigh wasn't found soon, Santa would be delivering presents in the back of a Kia Sol. It got really good gas mileage—but it couldn't travel across the world in a single night.

"Madness?" Kringle raised his voice. "This is Christmas!"

Halloween celebrated the time in the world when the veil between the mythic world and the mortal world was at its thinnest, allowing plenty of traffic to the mortal coil. Or at least, until Kringle erected a roadblock to keep that from happening.

"This isn't going to stop Halloween," Krampus said.

"No, but it will hurt, just like it will hurt when stores start carrying Christmas decorations three months instead of two," he said.

"Some stores already do that," Krampus groaned.

"They started this, Krampus, not me," Kringle said, for the fortieth time.

"Yeah, and it didn't make the crazy any less crazy the first time you said it," Krampus replied. Kringle opened the door to his squad car and reached for the radio.

"They can stop this any time by simply returning the sled," Kringle said.

"Assuming they even have it," Krampus groaned.

"Why are you so sure they don't?" Kringle shot back.

"Because if they had it, they wouldn't have hidden it," Krampus said. "They would use it."

"But they have used it. Quite a lot already," Kringle said.

"Then why isn't every country in the world after Santa yet?" Krampus asked. He had fond memories of what happened the last time someone made off with Santa's things.

"Because, in true Halloween fashion, none of the things they stole made the headlines. They don't make sense," he said. "Industrial air conditioners. Freezers. There was even a break-in on a jetliner the other day, one that was thankfully already grounded."

Krampus froze in place, so still only the tiny hairs on his coat blew in the December wind. The change was not unnoticed by his brother.

"What is it?" he asked.

"They do make sense," Krampus said. "If you were in the market for a 747 turbine."

Not many mythical creatures still dwelled within caves nowadays. Elves typically preferred studio apartments. Even trolls made their homes in townhouses, a far cry from their bridge-sheltered roots.

But some creatures still held out in caves like the one Kringle and Krampus found themselves in.

Icy stalactites descended from the roof of the mountainous cavern like a monster's fangs. Even Krampus, in his dense coat of fur, shivered from the cold wind which blew down the chiseled, rocky corridor. The occupant who lived here must have been hardened by such a lonely, bitter existence. It wouldn't be such a stretch for such a creature to lash out against the world—and namely Christmas—by stealing Kringle's sleigh.

The snow crunched beneath Krampus's hooves. Kringle shot him a nervous glare. Kringle had more experience sneaking into places and leaving gifts. Krampus, on the other hand, wasn't known much for his subtlety when he barged into a child's bedroom to terrify them. But despite Kringle's obvious experience, he still had one obvious disadvantage—the jingle bells which hung at his voluminous waist.

"Why are you wearing bells on a stealth mission?" Krampus growled as he watched Kringle try not to ring his bells with every step.

"I was in a rush. I took everything I had. You never know, right?" he said.

Kringle's eyes shot forward, and Krampus turned to see their quarry slumbering in the shadows. The corridor had led to a massive circular opening where a large, misshapen form snored on a plush bed beside a Christmas tree. Or at least, it appeared to be a Christmas tree. Typically, Christmas trees were evergreens, not a giant sequoia that was ripped from the ground, roots and all, with strings of lights haphazardly strung over the tree bark. A single present, equally wrapped in a rushed manner, stood by the tree.

A Boeing-747-turbine-shaped present.

"Looks like we got our thief," Krampus said. Kringle was quiet.

"Oh, come on," Krampus said. "We caught her sleeping by the darn thing. It has to be her."

Gryla gave a fitful toss-and-turn in her bed. After several terrifying moments, she resumed her snoring. Krampus breathed a sigh of relief.

"We better call this in before she wakes," Krampus said.

"Why would she wrap it?" Kringle said suddenly.

"What?" Krampus hissed.

"Why would she wrap it? She already has it. Why wouldn't she be using it to dry her hair?" Kringle asked.

"Look, no one wants to wake up to no presents on Christmas," Krampus shrugged.

"It seems like an awful lot of trouble to go through," Kringle said, his eyes still fixed on the present.

"No, it just seems like an awful a lot of trouble to admit you. Are. Wrong," Krampus said, breathing every word.

"Well, go on, cuff her in irons," Kringle said with a sarcastic flair. "That's your job, isn't it, Krampus?"

Snow lightly crunched beneath his heavy hoof. Then Kringle's hand clasped against his hand. Krampus turned back to him, not eager to proceed with trying to wake a sleeping giant troll.

"Wait," Kringle said. "Didn't she say she was meeting her sons for dinner? All six of them."

"So?" Krampus shrugged.

"Gryla has thirteen sons," Kringle said with pale urgency.

The realization hit Krampus a split-second later, and two seconds too late.

There were over two dozen red orbs burning in the darkness like pinkish flares, with every flare belonging to the eyes of an angry troll. Though they were only half the size of Gryla, they still dwarfed Kringle and Krampus by at least a couple feet. Rage seethed in their eyes.

"Protect the sled! Protect the gift!" their leader's voice cut through the darkness with rage evident despite its whisper.

"Well, at least we know who really took the sled," Kringle, ever the optimist, said, as the dark shapes of the trolls descended upon them. The trolls had stolen the turbine to give to their mother. Now those same trolls regarded Krampus and Kringle with murderous intent.

The trolls circled them like ravenous wolves. While they were as ferocious as wolves, they weren't as quick or as agile. They were still trolls—large and misshapen. They had plenty of drawbacks for the two brothers to take advantage of.

Both Krampus and Kringle had heard of this lot before—the Yule Boys they were called. They used to cause a lot of trouble before Christmas. That started to die down in the latter half of the century. According to their mom, they had parted ways to find fill-in jobs in other holidays.

But not this year.

This year, the Yule Boys were back in town.

And they were hungry.

One troll lunged at Krampus, grinning from ear to ear with a razor blade smile as he opened his mouth to take a bite. Krampus ducked and swooped his chains under the large troll with wooden legs glistening in the moonlight shining through the cave's interiors. Peg legs were good for pirates, but not for brawls. With one tug of his chain, the troll went toppling over.

Krampus turned to see Kringle twisting his shoulders back and forth, dodging blows from a troll who wielded pot covers like bracers, trying to strike Kringle in the face. In response, Kringle laid the troll down with one well-placed blow from his black-gloved fist. The troll sounded like a kitten hitting a pillow as he fell into a pile of deep snow.

Unfortunately, Krampus had made a near-fatal mistake—turning his back, giving a troll an opportunity to strike. Krampus realized his mistake, turning as fast as he could, knowing there was no way he could do so in time to raise a defense.

A whirling whistling sound cut past his face as one of Kringle's bells sang towards the floor, towards the bed holding Gryla. A nearby troll dived to prevent his mother from waking, giving a panicked yelp as he caught the bell before it bounced off the bed. Krampus took advantage of the troll's downed position and elbowed him in the neck, taking him down as well.

Krampus saw Kringle smirking. They had another advantage. These trolls didn't want to wake up their mother. Krampus had a feeling they were just as afraid of her as he was. Which gave them yet another opening to exploit.

The troll known as Spoon-Licker brought his long wooden utensil down on Krampus's head. In response, Krampus grabbed a nearby pot cover and raised it as a shield. Spoon-Licker froze before he could make another strike, knowing all the racket one blow would make. Krampus took advantage of his indecision, pummeling him in the face with his chain-wrapped hand. Spoon-Licker sank back in the snow, unconscious.

Krampus gave a brief look to Kringle to see him standing by an unconscious troll. The victory was short-lived, however, as another troll had leapt out from under his mother's bed and onto Kringle's back—but every kid on the Naughty List knows, you just don't try to bum-rush Santa. Kringle threw his whole body forward in a lunge hook that sent the unfortunate troll sliding over Kringle's shoulder and onto the ground, making him easy pickings for Kringle's left jab.

Another troll blindsided Krampus. He sidestepped the troll, only to find yet another troll descending from the rafters towards Krampus. Hard hooves skidded along the icy floor, providing him with another means of dealing with his attackers. He simply lowered his chains to the floor in the troll's path. The troll saw his plan, or at least he thought he did, so he took a hard right.

Surprisingly none of this awoke Gryla. Ahead of Krampus, Kringle had jabbed a troll in the eyes, leaving the gawking troll to stumble about blindly. He was in the process of jamming one of the candles up another troll's massive nose with a throng of unconscious trolls at his feet. But one troll remained—Meat Hook—with the aptly-named Yule Boy drawing back his carved metal hook towards Kringle's neck.

Krampus thrust forward, dropping his hand in a long arc as he launched his rusted metal chain forward. It wrapped around Meat Hook's metallic arm. The surprised-looking troll started to fall backwards, and Krampus gave the chain another sharp jerk to complete the motion. Then the unthinkable happened.

The chain broke apart as a rusty clanging sound cut through the shadows.

And in that instance, Gryla's eyes snapped open.

"What is the meaning of this?" Gryla's eyes darted from Kringle and Krampus to her sons, many of whom were scattered on the ground in prone positions, and then back to Kringle and Krampus once more.

Kringle started to open his mouth, but Krampus shot him a look. The jig was up. There was no way Gryla was going to let them haul her sons away. Either way, they still needed to explain themselves.

"Merry Christmas!" one troll, Candle-Stealer, said. He was nervously munching on the candle that had been stuck up his brother's nose.

"Christmas isn't until tomorrow," Gryla said with a suspicious tone. "It's Christmas Eve."

"Unless it's Christmas Early," Krampus said. "It's like Christmas Eve, except, you know, early."

Gryla's wide face remained blank, unsure what to think of such a thing. Krampus nudged Kringle in the ribs.

"Yes! It's Christmas Early! It's a new tradition, very popular with the kids these days," he said.

"I haunt the dreams of children," Gryla said. "And I know nothing of Christmas Early."

"But Santa just said so," Krampus protested. "And Santa never lies."

"We just wanted to surprise you, Mother!" Meat Hook said, still wearing half of Krampus's chain around his arm.

There was no way they could keep up this line of inquiry. Thankfully Gryla's eyes scanned past them, falling upon the gargantuan tree and equally over-sized present. Her eyes lit up as she looked back to her fallen sons.

"For me?" she said in a tone of genuine surprise.

"Yes!" the trolls beamed in unison. Their collective voices sounded like plastic scraping ice off a windshield. Krampus felt Kringle lean in close as Gryla's claws ripped the paper to shreds, revealing the turbine beneath. She cooed and shrieked at the present with glee.

"How are we going to get that away from her?" Kringle asked.

"You want to take it from her?" Krampus hissed beneath my breath.

"Well, it's not hers…" Kringle began.

"She didn't steal it. It was given to her," Krampus said.

Kringle narrowed his eyes. "That is extremely flawed logic," he said.

"I'm not arguing logic with the man who travels around the world giving gifts to children in a single night," Krampus said. "Unless you have a way to take it from her."

Kringle's silence conceded that last point. Krampus's victory was short-lived as he felt Gryla's appraising eyes on him. Soon all eyes in the cave turned to the two of them.

"And what brings such distinguished guests to my humble home?" Gryla inquired, with drool from her parted lips. They had to think fast. Telling her about the sled would only trigger her rage—at both her sons and Kringle and Krampus. But without such pretense, they were trespassing, and even mythical figures feared to trespass in a troll's lair.

"We come to give gifts, as one does on Christmas!" Kringle spoke up.

"And what has jolly old Saint Nicholas brought me!" Gryla's eyes lighted up expectedly.

"Ummm…" Krampus saw Kringle fidget for a bit. He then produced a small orb in his hands—a bell.

"This is a special bell!" he announced to Gryla, and all assembled around him. "As it once hung on my belt."

Another cooing sound escaped from Gryla's lips as the bell rattled when it fell into her massive paws. She held it into the light, transfixed by its beauty. She turned back to Kringle.

"I shall treasure this gift always," she said, but she looked forlorn for a moment. "If only I had something to hold it with."

Kringle and Krampus looked around. Krampus continued to do so futilely, until Krampus realized Kringle's eyes had fallen on him, or rather, something on him.

His chain.

"You have got to be kidding me," Krampus growled.

"It's broken anyway," Kringle whispered.

"I've had this chain for six hundred years," Krampus protested.

"I've had that bell for eight hundred years. And you know what I've had even longer?" Kringle said. "My skin!"

"Yeah, well, you could stand to lose a little more than that," Krampus said. "Mr. Bowl Full of Jelly."

"Give. It!" Kringle urged.

Krampus dislodged the chain from his shoulder and proceeded to unwrap it from his body. Then he laid the rusted old chain into Gryla's waiting paws. Her eyes lit up immediately as she wrapped the old, brown-laced chain around the bells and hung it on a stalactite. "This is the best Christmas Early ever!" she bellowed.

They left Gryla's after the longest and most awkward bout of Christmas carols ever. It turns out singing on key was one more thing that trolls weren't good at. But after an hour and a half, they left the cheerful Gryla's house, with all thirteen of her sons in tow. Truthfully, the Yule Boys were just as anxious to get out of that cave as Krampus and Kringle were. They seemed all too eager to accept their punishment for taking Santa's sleigh, even as they were huddled together in the tight quarters once reserved for short, slender elves.

"I'm just saying," Krampus said as he looked over his shoulder to the trolls in the back seat of the sled. "We could have left them."

"No one is that cruel. Not even you," Kringle said. Krampus huffed in response. "Besides, I have a use for them. There's been a shortage of coal to put in stockings lately."

"Yeah, well, you can let me off here," Krampus said as the lights of Christmastide came into view. "I know the drill."

Santa got the glory of Christmas—the smiles of children plus all the cookies and milk he could swallow. All Krampus got was the paperwork.

"We made a good team," Kringle said after Krampus stepped off the sled as it hovered above the precinct.

"We usually do, when the occasion calls for it," Krampus said. "Merry Christmas, Kringle."

"Merry Christmas, Krampus," he said with that infectious twinkle in his eye.

Krampus turned and headed back into the precinct, feeling the familiar gust of wind as the sled lifted into the air and resumed supersonic speeds even when carrying thirteen trolls and one particularly large man. Krampus pushed through the doors, where he expected to find a large stack of paperwork.

Instead, Krampus found a large box wrapped in a red bow with green wrapping paper. Krampus raised an eyebrow as he noticed the card atop it. He picked up the card with clawed hand and opened it.

Dear Krampus,

I was wrong about the Hallows, but you were also wrong about that chain of yours. Let's both start the New Year's on a new foot.

Signed Kringle.

Krampus found himself grinning ear to ear. Santa could be a pain in the hooves sometimes, but every now and then he could amaze. It was good to see the magic of Christmas was still intact.

Krampus shredded the wrapping paper into specks of brightly colored foil. He gasped at what lay within. It was a shimmering, steel chain, brand new from the factory by the looks of it. Krampus picked up the chain and slung it over his shoulder.

"Merry Christmas, Kringle," Krampus said to no one in particular. Though he had no doubt Kringle could hear him, wherever he was.

Krampus scanned the room for paperwork, but it seemed his brother, in his gift-giving zeal, had done all the work for the evening. It was a pity, because Krampus wanted to take this chain for a test drive.

"Now where did that Naughty List go?" Krampus grinned as he descended into the office, his new chain clacking against his cloven hooves.

About the Author

Richard Pulfer works at a small library in northern Illinois. He has been published in *Futurescapes: Blue Sky Cities*, *Call of the Wyld*, *Insurgence: A Fae Rebellion* and *The Rockford Review*. He enjoys comic books, reading, writing and avoiding long pants at all costs.

Old Traditions

by
Eve Morton

Old Traditions

*C*hristmas was five days away when Chester realized the woman across the street was pregnant. Very pregnant. Her belly hung out of her purple coat as she went to get her mail, and she had that waddle to her walk that all pregnant women got nearing the end. Chester had never had kids himself, and his wife, now ex, never wanted any, but he'd been around enough pregnant women in his family. And this woman was about to pop. He waited on the balls of his feet as she made it over the ice and freshly fallen snow and into her door once again. Then he only shook his head.

"There go my observation skills." Chester was a retired police officer, now working as a security guard. He should have seen this change in his neighbor, whose name evaded him in the early morning hour as he sipped his coffee, but he didn't. And if not for this chance observation, made because he was still on his night shift schedule though he was on holidays, he wasn't sure if he would have.

Chester didn't exactly speak to his neighbors on a regular basis; working nights put him on a different schedule than everyone else around him, family included. He only sometimes spoke to his ex-wife, though that was happening more and more through his lawyers, and he had a lot of other stuff going on. Bank loans, that thing with his car's engine. Stuff like that, on top of Christmas, which was going to be a solo event this year. He blamed all of these items, as inconsequential as some of them were, for completely missing the fact that the woman he sometimes spotted on her morning runs when he came back from work was pregnant.

And he'd done *nothing*.

"But should I do something?" Chester asked his sister, Maureen, over the phone when the image of the woman waddling in her ill-fitting purple coat had not left his mind. "I mean, it's the holidays. She's nine months pregnant. If I don't do something, I fear God may actually strike me down."

Maureen let out a low, smoker's chuckle, though she'd quit with him seven years earlier. "What do you think you can do? She clearly has her own place. There is room at the inn, so to speak."

"I don't know. Give her baby clothing?"

"You don't know the gender. And everyone's weird about that now. You hear about that genderless kid in Toronto?" Maureen went on a tangent, not waiting for him to respond, and so Chester went to the window again. Hours had passed, and so had a nap he attempted to take in the afternoon, but he hadn't seen the woman since. Melissa, Melody, something like that. He wondered if it would be too forceful to use his former police cred to look up her name. Probably. Yes. That was too much, like this genderless kid, and the sheer idea of raising a genderless kid in this world, was a bit too much.

"Anyway," Maureen said, "I think you're doing a fine job. You don't need to be a man on a white horse anymore, especially not since you're still paying for your wife to ride that horse every Saturday."

Chester would have told Maureen to stop teasing his ex-wife, Lydia, except that she wasn't teasing, but speaking literally. They'd owned horses together, a perk of not having kids themselves meant they had money and time for such extravagance, and now she was the one who got to keep them. He shifted the subject instead. "When you were pregnant, what was the one thing you wanted, you know, near the end?"

"Someone to get the baby out of me."

"Other than that. I don't think I can provide that luxury."

"You could. Bring her pineapple and spicy foods, or scare her. There's lots of folk wisdom on how to get that baby going. Like stimulating the nipples for hours on end." Maureen laughed. Chester just coughed. She sighed and told him to relax. "How old is this lady? You never told me. And you never said if she had a husband or not. I assumed she did, but then again, I'm regressive according to my daughter, who thinks genderless baby-making is a fantastic idea."

"She's young," Chester said. If he'd had his own kids, right around the age when everyone on the force was having them, he guessed this woman would be their age. "Maybe a few years older than Krista. And I don't think she has a husband."

"Wife?" Maureen asked. "Can't be too careful, you know."

"I've seen no one at that house for months, actually." Chester thought back, realizing he'd been missing the woman for her morning runs—which made sense now, considering the huge belly.

She'd probably been going until she could not stand it, until she started to show, and then he'd not given her a second thought. Like he should be doing now, and like Maureen was telling him to do.

"She's not your responsibility. She's her own woman, doing her own thing. She probably has a plan, has a family of her own, and she clearly has a house. In a nice neighborhood like yours. She's not hurting for anything."

"I know." But Chester hesitated. He was not convinced. The first time he'd seen this woman and waved to her on the start of one of those runs, she'd startled as if he'd jumped from a car. She stared at him like a doe, like a woman in a house he'd once raided, who stood in the center of the storm and simply screamed at the commotion. There was something haunted about this woman. Something that made him check off a box in his mind every morning when he saw her—*ah, that lady, good, all is right with the world*—and now he felt as if he had failed. He was involved, no matter what Maureen said. They were neighbors.

"Do you know?" Maureen caught his hesitancy. "Because this is not *Rear Window*, Chet. Not even *Love Actually*, okay? Just be careful. You used to be a cop, but she can still call those cops if you get too close, catch my drift? Don't be a dirty old man."

"I know. I'm not. And I'll be good just in case."

"Good. Now…" Maureen went off and spoke about Christmas plans. Though he'd declined to visit any of his other siblings this year, not wanting to travel or do anything of the sort, he now longed for someone to fill up his empty house. He hadn't even bothered with a tree, and still didn't want to deal with pine needles everywhere, but he missed the lights. He had bought presents and mailed them, so even they did not grace his house. Looking around, Chester couldn't believe it was almost Christmas at all.

Did that woman have a tree? he wondered aimlessly as Maureen continued to talk. *A family she was going to visit? Someone to welcome the baby into the world?*

Chester peered outside. Still nothing in front of her place, no movement at all. A car was in the driveway, a rusted Mazda that was always there. He vowed to keep an eye on her—but from afar. As long as he didn't impose himself, what was the harm in making sure a young woman wasn't alone on Christmas Eve? It was only four days away. If anything changed, well, then Chester could accept it.

But not a moment before then. Only after the holidays would his mission, however strange, be complete.

By the time Christmas Eve rolled around, Chester had done a couple festive things. Bought hot chocolate and eggnog, only to remember that eggnog was the richest drink in the entire world. You simply needed to add bourbon or brandy to it in order to temper the strong sips. He'd also bought a small cactus. It wasn't a Christmas tree, but it was green and had a red flower, so it fit in the Christmas color motif, and it would keep long beyond the standard timeline of a tree. He put on the radio, which now blasted mostly holiday music, and even the most recent stuff done by artists he'd never heard of wasn't too bad. Maureen and his other sister Julia had called and chatted with him over Skype, and they would call again and open gifts online on the actual day. It had snowed, too, and though the light dusting on the ground was probably not going to stay, Chester appreciated it.

He still looked out the window, hoping to spot the woman again, but there was no sign of her. The car was still there; the lights were sometimes on, sometimes off in the upstairs rooms, giving the impression of life, but that was it. Chester hated that he felt like a spy, worse than Jimmy Stewart because he did not have a broken leg as an excuse. Only a police officer and security guard's instinct, no work to attend to now that he was on holidays, and a creeping suspicion that if he didn't do something soon, some kind of vengeance from an angry God would strike him down.

So, when someone knocked on his door, just as the sun set on Christmas Eve, he was shocked and delighted, if not a little frightened, to see the woman on the other side. Her dark hair had been pulled behind her in a ponytail. Her face was made-up, as if she were about to go out somewhere, though her outfit was covered by that oversized purple coat.

"Hello," she said, and smiled awkwardly. "I'm sorry to bother you, but I think you're the only one home on the block."

"It's no trouble," Chester said, a bit too quickly. She was not done with her introductions, and now seemed flummoxed by starting again. "Would you like to come in?" he offered. "I don't want you to be cold."

"Sure, thanks. I was just wondering if—"

"I'm Chester, by the way." He stuck out his hand, and with a sigh, she shook it. Her fingers were cold. "Let me get you a drink...?"

"Lisa," she said.

Damn. Chester's guesses had been way off for her name. He ushered Lisa into the kitchen, insisted that she sit down and that he take her coat, and gave her a mug full of hot cocoa. "This is all very nice," she said. "Thank you very much. But I was wondering if I could ask you for some bourbon."

"Bourbon?"

"It's not for me." She gestured to her stomach—as if he had not already noticed the belly in her fancy, but somewhat dated red dress—and added, "Don't worry. It's for someone else."

She was lying. Chester could see it the way he saw it in petty criminals who were not good at bending the truth just yet. She may not be the one drinking bourbon—he did believe that in her voice—but she wasn't getting it for someone else. Not really. Not true.

Yet, he was compelled to give her whatever she asked for. "You know, you're in luck. I just got some bourbon for eggnog, and it turns out I don't like either one. Do you want both?"

"Yes, that would be lovely. Thank you so much."

Chester grabbed both items from his kitchen, the bourbon from the top of the fridge and the eggnog from inside the door. Since the eggnog carton had been opened, he emptied the remainder into a thermos for her. Then he went into the parlor where he'd also laid out some Christmas bags he didn't send to his sisters and their kids, and added it all together with a bow. "Here you go."

"Oh, this is too kind."

"Not for a pregnant woman on Christmas."

She smiled, but it seemed pained. Chester gestured for her to sit down again, so they could keep talking, but she shook her head. "I should get going. Thank you again for this. All of it. It's been quite nice."

"Okay. If you're sure..." Chester waited. There was something more in her voice, something more in her body language he wanted to parse out. When she said nothing, did nothing, and Chester's own impatience at the mystery before him was too much, he offered to walk her to her house.

"It's just across the street," she said, utterly defeated. Chester grabbed his coat, returned hers to her shoulders, and soon he was holding the door as they both set out into the mild night. Lisa wrapped her coat around herself tightly. She narrowed her focus, turning inwards, becoming quieter and quieter as the salt crunched under their boots.

"Here you are," Chester said as they reached the door. "Can I help you inside?"

Lisa grabbed his shoulder as her knees went out from under her. She let out a gasp, as did Chester. His strength returned to him, as did his police training, and he went into immediate problem-solving mode. He took the keys from her hand, almost dropping them as she buckled down with another spasm of pain, and let her inside. He stepped in with her, found a chair by the front hallway, and made her sit down. The house was very much like his own in design, but everything seemed dark. There was not a single light on.

"Let me call someone," he said. "You need to be around family if what I think is happening is happening."

"I am around family. That's the problem. That's—" Her voice cut out with another contraction of pain. They were all happening quite fast, quite close together. Chester remembered his sisters being in labor for days before they had this kind of momentum. Maybe she *had* been in labor for days. Maybe she'd been ignoring it, like he'd once seen her ignore a hole in her sneaker for an entire run.

Without waiting for another contraction, or Lisa's permission, he flicked on lights in her hallway towards her kitchen. He expected to find a phone on the wall where his own was, and he did—but he did not expect to find the table decked out as it was.

"Oh. I'm sorry. I…"

The table had been set, but now there were people populating it. Many of them, all dressed alike in Christmas colors, reds and greens and dark blue dresses with glitter on the edges. A woman with grey hair sat at the head of the table, a matriarch with a broach on her dress's lapel and a haughty expression over her pursed lips. An older man sat to her left, hunched over a bowl of something that no longer looked warm. Yet as he put the spoon to his mouth, over and over, nothing moved or changed. The rest of the table was filled with similarly aged people, complete with ceremonious holiday meal before them. The food was tangible enough to be held in their hands, to be chewed inside their mouths, and swallowed—but it would then materialize back on the table. No matter how hungry, no matter how much the family ate, nothing disappeared.

"Is that what I think it is?" one of the men at the other end of the table asked. He wore suspenders and was missing a front tooth. "The festive drink?"

"Yes, Uncle Maurice."

Lisa waddled into the kitchen, her face a tight matrix of pain. Dampness now stained the front of her dress, which now Chester realized matched the other outfits. She poured from the thermos of eggnog into everyone's glasses, and then topped off all who asked for it with some bourbon. As she finished pouring for the man with the suspenders, Maurice, another wave of pain came over her. She bent over, slicing through Maurice as if he was air.

Or a ghost.

"Oh." Chester looked around the table. Then he examined Lisa, wearing a dress from another era, before he regarded the people at the table once more. All of them chattering to one another in a cacophony of family and celebration, eating but never finishing anything. None of them real. "*Oh*. My God."

"Please leave." Lisa's voice was still hitched with pain. "I can handle this from here. Thank you for your eggnog, your kindness, but—"

"I can't leave," Chester said. "You're having a baby."

"About bloody time, too," the woman at the head of the table said. "She's been putting this off for years."

"Shut up." Lisa held her tongue as another flicker of pain passed. The matriarch said nothing, merely looked to Chester and gestured to Lisa, as if to ask, *see what I have to deal with?*

"Please," Lisa begged. "I know what I'm doing. I'll be fine."

Chester kept his hand on the phone on the wall. Every part of him told him to call for back-up. His training on the force, and the even slimmer training he'd been given as a security guard told him to call for help. For Jesus, even. *This is not a problem you can handle by yourself.*

And all of that was true. He needed help—but so did Lisa, so he couldn't leave. He repeated, "This is not a problem you can handle by yourself."

"I can. Women have been doing it for centuries, alone in the woods. I at least have indoor plumbing."

"No, I mean this." Chester gestured to the table full of ghosts. "You can't handle this by yourself."

Lisa laughed, though it ended prematurely by more pain. He left the phone to hold her in his arms, so she wouldn't fall on the floor where one of her relatives had already gotten drunk and spilled his eggnog. Or maybe he was already drunk, eternally drunk, because it seemed like whatever had happened to conjure this family, the worst parts of them had arrived for the holidays. Then again, wasn't that what always happened?

"You need help," Chester said, speaking in a low whisper. "So let me be a good neighbor, and a good person at the holidays, and help you. Or else God will be mad at me," he said, adding it as a joke though he was deadly serious, "and I've done too much bad stuff already to challenge Him again."

"Oh, me too."

"So, what should I do? Tell me and I'll help."

Lisa looked at her relatives at the table, then back to Chester as a contraction came through her body. "I can't leave them," she said in a low voice. "They come every year, no matter what, and they won't go until they've had dinner and I read them a ghost story."

"A ghost story?"

"Yes, I am aware of the irony," she said. "It's tradition in my family. And you don't fuck with that, apparently, even in death. And especially not as a single mother."

"Is your husband joining us or what?" the matriarch asked. "Because my soup is now cold, and my thirst has not yet been abated."

Lisa rolled her eyes. Then she dipped down in pain. And Chester saw an opportunity where others would have seen only fear. "Let me be your husband, then."

"What?"

"Not in real life. No, no. I'm too old. But I am a traditional man. Or at least, I've been schooled in the right traditions for the right causes. I'm sure I can handle these guys while you go and have your baby. In a hospital. Okay?"

Lisa's gaze darted between Chester's eyes. He saw fear mixed with elation mixed with relief. Then just pain. She nodded, knowing there was absolutely no choice. Chester slipped her the key for his house and whispered in her ear to call for an ambulance there. "As fast as you can," he said. "I know you can't run, but waddling is an excellent means of travel."

She smiled, and surprising him, kissed him on the cheek. Once Chester heard the door slam, he swallowed hard. Part of him hoped like hell that when he turned around all the ghosts would be gone, merely a strange hallucination, a kind of *folie-a-deux*, brought on by his *Rear Window* obsession with the pregnant lady across the street, and mixed with the guilt that he was not with his own family.

But no, they were still there. They all looked at him with a mixture of expressions—from boredom to bemusement to haughtiness—and he sighed. "Lisa is going to get us some more eggnog," he said. "But for now, how about I tell you guys a ghost story?"

"Not yet," Uncle Maurice said, his missing tooth whistling as he did. "I'm not done my meal."

"Hurry up, you fool," the matriarch said. She smiled at Chester and gestured to an empty seat on her right, where he assumed that Lisa had once been sitting. "Please sit here, my son-in-law. There is so much we have to know about one another."

Chester's blood grew cold. He oscillated between fear and revulsion, between absurdity and utter incredulity, before he finally treated this like any other holiday. It was boring. It was fastidious and often required alcohol to get through it. But he would get through it, the time would end, and these spirits would depart, and the entire world would awaken to a brand-new day.

Only this time, there would be a baby. Not a mythic babe, but a real live one, in the arms of the woman Chester had never truly met until tonight.

"Sit, sit." The matriarch patted the chair again. "And tell me whatever story—ghost or not—you would like."

Chester sat down. He sipped from the glass of eggnog, appreciating the strong kick, as he conjured up a real doozy. "Now,

I heard this at work. I'm a former police officer, and you know things can get very spooky around the full moon…"

The ghosts were gone at midnight. Each one faded in their own way, in their own time, with the matriarch—whose name was Bernice—last at the table to leave. She'd had her hand on Chester's the entire time, coaxing him into more and more stories from the police force, until he was just rehashing episodes of *NYPD Blue* from memory. No one knew any better.

Then, after a soft kiss on his cheek from Bernice, it was just him alone in the room.

"For ghosts," he said as he stood and surveyed the half-eaten food around him, "y'all make a hell of a mess."

He cleared the dishes into the dishwasher, put the tablecloth in Lisa's laundry room, and then set up a small plate of cookies and milk for Santa on the fireplace. Two stockings hung there, one that was a basic red that must have been Lisa's, because the other one was inscribed with the name James. Her boy. Chester was about to leave when he heard the phone ring on her wall, and something inside of him, yet another supernatural feeling, told him to answer it.

"Hello?"

"Chester?" Lisa's voice. Tired and strained, but Lisa. "Are they gone?"

"Left at midnight, after a lot of stories, just like you said."

"Oh, thank you. So much. There is nothing I can ever do to repay you."

"Yes, there is." When she was quiet on the line, and even Chester felt that tension, he quickly added, "Just raise a good baby. Have a good life."

"And invite you over for dinner next year?"

He laughed, and while they chatted like old friends about the baby, about birth and death and everything in between, he didn't think that was such a bad idea after all. A new Christmas tradition, dinner with ghosts and a nice young girl and her baby boy. There were worse ways of spending the holidays.

But he still wanted to think about it. "I'll let you go," he said. "You need some rest."

"Thank you again, Chester. Merry Christmas."

"You, too." He waited on the line until she disconnected.

Come morning, when Chester awoke, he set the table for two. He peered out his window, saw the lights on across the street, and decided to invite her over for breakfast. A new tradition, he hoped, now spared of old traditions and their ghosts.

About the Author

Eve Morton lives in Waterloo, Ontario, Canada with her partner and two sons. She reads tarot cards and coffee grinds for fun, while teaching university classes on the dangers of too much and not enough media consumption. Find more updates at authormorton.wordpress.com.

Earthly Angels
by
H.T. Ashmead

Earthly Angels

I know, Mom," Kate said into the empty car. "I wish I could be there too. But even if I didn't have a shift at the hospital today, I don't think I'd feel safe being around the whole family."

"We'll all wear masks if that gets you here." Her mother's whiny voice surrounded her from the car speakers.

Kate was glad they spoke over the phone and not via a video chat. That way her mom couldn't see her shaking her head. "I appreciate that, but it doesn't really matter because I've got to work today."

"Can't you call in sick?"

"On Christmas? You know I can't make someone else leave their family. This is part of the career I chose. Anyway, I just pulled into the parking lot, so I've gotta go."

"Love you."

"Love you too, Mom. Tell everyone Merry Christmas from me." Kate disconnected the call from her steering wheel.

She sighed. Missing holidays was part of the job, but that didn't make it easy. She missed the traditions and jokes and games with her family. But it's not like the patients chose to miss their traditions by being in the hospital on Christmas. In fact, they probably wanted to be home even more than she did.

She nodded once to herself for luck, then slipped her phone into the pocket of her dark blue scrubs and climbed from the car. Adjusting her N95 mask over her face and compressing it against the perpetually sore bridge of her nose, she walked to the back of her car and withdrew several large, reusable bags from the trunk. Looping the handles over her forearms, she hefted the canvas bags and walked across the lot, circles of light from overhead guiding her way. At six a.m., only a few cars sat at the far end of the lot, frosted windows glistening in the glow of the streetlamps, and she assumed they were all employees since visiting hours hadn't started yet.

Unsure how she would scan her badge at the doors and hold the bags, Kate was grateful when a doctor saw her coming and held it for her. After entering the elevator, she set the bags down and pressed the button. Sighing, she rubbed her muscles as she ascended to the fifth floor. When the doors opened, she gripped the bags and walked down the tiled hallway to the ICU doors, her sneakers squeaking across the shiny floor. With her shoulder, she pressed the access button.

"Yes, may I help you?" A woman's voice came over the intercom.

"Hey, it's Kate. My hands are full. Can someone let me in please?"

"Yeah, I'll send Juan."

A few moments later, the door opened, and Kate slipped inside.

"Here let me help with that." A dark-haired man in green scrubs reached for some of the packages.

Kate handed over an armful and readjusted the remaining bags. "Thanks. They're heavier than they look."

Juan looked inside the bags. "You wrapped them and everything."

She shrugged. "The ones that I could."

Juan jutted his chin at her. "You picked the wrong color today, Ms. Claus."

Looking down at her scrubs, Kate chuckled. "I guess you're right. But I don't think the patients will notice."

"You're probably right. Hey, thanks for doing this, by the way. It was a really great idea."

Kate shrugged. "I couldn't have done it without all of you. Everyone was so generous. I just did the shopping."

"I bet it was a battle on Christmas Eve."

Kate wasn't sure if the polite comment targeted her bloodshot eyes, so she shrugged again. It had been difficult to find everything on the list. And she stayed up until almost 1:30 wrapping it all. But it would be worth it.

The two of them carried the bags toward the center nurse's station. They finally relinquished them to a corner of the break room.

Brushing herself off, Kate returned to the central desk to receive the updates. She was glad to hear a couple of patients' oxygen levels had improved enough to move them to general recovery. The car accident victim was still heavily sedated. A woman who'd had a heart attack a couple of days earlier had improved enough that if the afternoon doctor approved, she could also be moved out. But Kate's heart dropped when she heard one of the older patients had been moved to a full breathing tube yesterday. She shook her head; it probably wouldn't be long now.

Another woman had been admitted late the night before with Covid-19. Kate held her x-ray to the light to examine the degree of damage to the patient's lungs. The distinctive haziness of "Covid Lung" stared back at her. Beyond that, there had been little change in the rest of the patients, most of whom were on high-flow oxygen to combat their respiratory struggles due to Covid.

With only a handful of clarifying questions, Kate took over the new shift. First things first. She made her rounds to her assigned patients, checking their vitals, adjusting IVs as needed, studying medications and dosages. She also erased the previous nurse's name on each whiteboard and wrote her own. At this early hour, most of the patients still slept, but she still had to wake one or two for scheduled meds. That was one irony she hated of the job. Everyone knew the best thing for healing was lots of rest, but then doctors and nurses woke some patients every three or four hours to give medicine, check vitals, or—worst of all—ask how they were feeling. Kate shook her head as a sardonic smile tugged at the corner of her mouth.

She moved back to the center desk and entered her notes into the computer. After a few minutes, the rest of the nursing staff finished their rounds as well. Jaden, the head nurse, requested everyone's attention. It wasn't hard since he was built like a bouncer, complete with a couple tattoos. But the more she worked with him, the more she realized he was just a big teddy bear.

"Alright," Jaden said, "from the pile of bags in the break room, it looks like Kate finished the shopping. Kate, what's the plan?"

Kate returned the gazes of the eight other staff members. Most sported dark circles and droopy eyelids because of the long hours, grueling work, and increased patient load over the past few months. But their eyes still sparkled and held an open honesty for this Christmas miracle. Even a few Santa or elf caps dotted the group. She blinked several times to keep back the tears.

"First of all, I want to thank each of you personally. Your help and generosity have made this happen, and for that, I'm so grateful." This idea had only occurred to Kate when the realization hit several patients a couple days ago that they would not be going home for Christmas. "You all helped gather information—some not as subtly as others—" Kate looked pointedly at Lucy, whose cheeks turned bright red. They all had a good-natured chuckle as Kate continued. "…about what each patient misses about Christmas.

"And then when I dumped the money from the jar to count it…" Kate trailed off, and she had to swallow three times before the lump in her throat shifted. "Just thank you," she said. "We all experience that nurses don't make a lot, but you'd never recognize it from your generosity."

One of the nurses called, "Hear, hear," and polite applause and quiet cheering echoed around the group.

Kate cleared her throat. "So, anyway, the plan. Unfortunately, we can't all deliver gifts because someone has to stay here and monitor the patients. But if some of you are willing to take on a few extra patients for a bit, then I think one person in each area could distribute."

They talked among themselves, sorting out who would deliver and who would remain behind. Three nurses stepped forward. "You should deliver for our section, Kate," Juan said. "After all, you did all the hard work."

Kate's heart swelled and tears pricked her eyes. She nodded. "One last thing. A bit later this morning, after everyone is awake, we've had several patients express how much they miss singing Christmas songs. So we'll all be caroling to each patient on the floor. I don't care if you're tone deaf." She smiled at Jaden, who sighed in return. "That's not the point of today. Today is for them." She gestured to the rooms. "And thank you. This has truly been a magical Christmas that I'm grateful to have been a part of. I think that's everything."

Leading two nurses to the pile of waiting presents, Kate sorted them according to zone, comparing the names against the room numbers. She had considered sorting them the night before, but she'd been so tired she was afraid she'd mix up who was in which room. She added an extra fuzzy blanket to another nurse's set for the newest patient. Repacking the bags, she handed each nurse a collection of gifts. Then she took her own sacks.

First stop: Alice's room. Kate quietly washed her hands at the sink in the corner. After all, this particular gift would be more effective if Alice awakened to it. And Alice's meds should keep her asleep. After thoroughly drying her hands, Kate withdrew a set of colored lights from the bag. Using a chair as a stepladder, she carefully wound the string of lights around the hooks of the privacy curtain. She made sure to keep them loose enough that they would stretch when the curtain was fully extended. Then Kate plugged them in. Bright spots of color dotted the fabric, sometimes small, focused circles, sometimes larger fuzzy ones. To be safe, she had made sure to get the cool temperature indoor lights. Kate pulled the curtain half-closed around the bed then moved to the sink to wash up again. She smiled as she scrubbed her hands, wondering what Alice would think when she awakened and found she had been sleeping beneath Christmas lights just like she'd told her nurse she missed.

Kate checked her watch. She could drop off another gift before Deshawna's room. Slipping into Isaac's room, she scrubbed in once again. She tried to remain quiet, but when she turned around, his blue eyes gazed at her. "Oh, sorry to wake you."

Isaac's gray hair stuck out at odd angles. "You didn't. I always wake early. A habit built over many years."

"Well, this is an especially great day to wake early. Merry Christmas, Isaac!"

"I'm sorry you have to spend your holiday taking care of an old fool like me." Isaac paused between every third or fourth word to take a deep breath.

"I'm not. It's my pleasure. In fact, I even brought something for you." Kate reached into her bag and handed him a box wrapped in shiny blue paper covered with shimmery snowflakes.

He narrowed his eyes. "What's this?"

Kate smiled, hoping it reached her eyes since he couldn't see under her mask. "Open it and find out."

His shaky fingers pulled at the edges of the paper, loosening it gently and unwrapping it in a single, whole sheet. He folded the tape back on the paper as he went. A murmur of pleasure escaped his lips when he finally revealed the contents. "Toffee. My favorite."

"I made sure to get the sugar-free kind. I know it's not quite as good, but I can't go breaking *all* the rules." Kate winked. "Just make sure you still eat breakfast when they bring it around. I don't want to get in trouble for ruining it."

"Thank you." His blue eyes pierced her through. Kate nodded then scrubbed out and left him to enjoy his candy.

Checking her watch, she snagged one of the tablets off the nurse station desk.

"How is it going?" Jaden asked, his hands clasped behind his head as he leaned back in the chair.

"So far, so good." She strode into Deshawna's room and scrubbed in. Already her hands were pink. Tipping her head to the side, she considered how it was going to be another long day for those hands.

Turning toward Deshawna, she smiled at the sleeping woman. Her tiny braids spread across the pillow, her face relaxed. Kate pulled up an email and clicked on it. Then she gently placed her hand on Deshawna's umber arm. "Deshawna, time to wake up. I have a surprise for you."

Deshawna's dark brown eyes blinked a few times before focusing on Kate. She reached up to her face, her arm knocking against the large cannula tubes of the high-flow oxygen. She rubbed the sleep out of her eyes.

"Merry Christmas." Kate smiled down at Deshawna and held the tablet toward her.

Deshawna's eyebrows creased as she took the device. Then her eyes widened. She tried to push herself upright, so Kate helped her adjust the bed.

"Hi, Mom!" a beautiful girl of about twelve called out on the video screen. She wore twin fluffy pigtails. "Merry Christmas!"

"Merry Christmas to you too, honey." Deshawna breathed heavily after speaking.

Next a younger boy appeared on the screen. "I miss you, Mommy. Are you feeling better?"

"So much better."

"When are you coming home?"

"As soon as I can, baby."

Then a handsome man, probably somewhere in his forties, came on. "Merry Christmas, my love."

"Merry Christmas." Deshawna's voice caught in her throat.

"Since you couldn't join us for Christmas morning, your nurse suggested we bring it to you."

"I'm so glad she did."

Kate tried to step away, but Deshawna grabbed her arm. "Thank you," she said. A single wet track on her cheek shone in the glare of the fluorescent lights.

Kate, not trusting her own voice, just nodded and patted Deshawna's hand. As she scrubbed out, she glanced back. The mother stroked the side of the tablet while squeals of delight from one of the children echoed through the tinny speakers.

Rob's room was next door. After scrubbing up, Kate stepped next to him. His eyes were closed, his head bobbing slightly. She'd learned in the past few days that he wasn't asleep but listening to music in his mind. "Happy holidays, Rob," she murmured.

His eyes snapped open. "What do you want?"

Some of the other staff had complained about how gruff Rob was, but Kate suspected it related more to fear than grumpiness. "Nothing. Actually, I brought something for you."

His eyes narrowed.

Kate handed him a small, thin package.

"What's this?"

She shrugged. "If I told you, that would ruin all the fun. Open it."

He glared at her before looking at the present. It had white wrapping paper decorated with gold stars. Finally, after studying her for long enough Kate thought her smile would permanently freeze, he looked back to the gift. He grabbed one edge and yanked, pulling a strip right out of the middle around the entire package. Rob gasped before turning to her. "Why?"

"Because it's Christmas, and even those of us who are stuck here deserve some Christmas joy too. Did I pick a good one?"

Rob's scowl softened. "Yeah. But how did you know?"

"How did I know what?"

"How did you know *Messiah* was the last concert I conducted before I retired?"

With a soft humph, Kate glanced up, then back at Rob. Sitting on the edge of the bed, she said, "I didn't. But it seems like you remember a lot of music. Sometimes you even hum when you think no one is around." Kate shrugged. "I don't know. It just seemed like the most appropriate CD for this time of year."

Rob's eyes flicked down to his lap. "I can't sing." Kate leaned closer, unsure if she heard him correctly. "My lungs are shot. Humming is the best I can do. I'm afraid I'll never sing again."

Kate didn't know what to say. Did he want her to acknowledge his fear? Or was it better for his pride to pretend she hadn't heard? He'd spoken so quietly, she went with the latter. "Well, a CD's no good if you can't listen to it." She withdrew a small boombox from the bag. "Now I'm sorry to say, you can't keep the player, but you can use it as much as you'd like while you're here." She helped him set everything up and plug it in. She pushed play and turned to walk out.

"Wait." Rob's voice wasn't loud, but it still commanded her attention. "Hand me my bag." His chin jerked toward a brown pleather briefcase sitting on the chair.

She gave it to him, then waited to return it to its place after he finished rummaging in it.

After almost a full minute, he grunted as he withdrew a small cylindrical tube. "Here."

Taking the lip balm, she asked, "What's this for?"

"You said it yourself. Even those of us stuck here deserve something for Christmas. It's new. I buy them in three-packs. Mint's my favorite, so I always save it for last."

Kate thought about rejecting the small gift, but when she looked back at Rob, he focused on the cover of the CD. His fist still stretched toward her, the tube sticking out between his fingers. Gingerly, she took the gift. "Thank you, Rob. It will feel great when I take my mask off at the end of my shift."

But he'd already leaned back against the bed with his eyes closed. His hands glided across the blankets in time with the music.

At the sink, Kate scrubbed the outside of the tube along with her hands before leaving.

When Kate exited the room, Jaden called her to the central desk as he hung up the phone. "Sheryl's gift has arrived."

Kate grinned and changed her next stop, snagging a pre-sanitized wheelchair along the way.

Most patients were awake by now, so Sheryl turned off the TV as Kate entered. "Merry Christmas," Sheryl said. She had curled her brown-dyed hair. The warm iron sat on the table near her bed.

"Merry Christmas, Sheryl. If you're feeling up to it, I have a surprise for you."

Sheryl cocked her head to the side. "What kind of surprise?"

"Technically, you're not supposed to leave your room, but do you feel well enough to sneak out for five, maybe ten minutes at the most? I'll hook you up to regular oxygen."

Sheryl nodded slowly, her eyes narrowed.

Kate replaced the larger cannula with a smaller one attached to a portable oxygen tank. Then she positioned a disposable mask over top of the equipment and helped Sheryl into the chair, tucking her robe carefully around her. She coiffed Sheryl's hair in the back where it had pressed down against the bed. "Are you ready?"

"I suppose," Sheryl answered. Kate heard a twinge of excitement in her voice.

Kate wheeled Sheryl down the circular hallway that wound around the nurse's desk. As they neared the end of it, Sheryl shifted in the seat.

"It's not safe for me to leave ICU."

"Don't worry, we're not leaving." Kate turned around the final bend before the secured doors of the wing. She scanned her badge, and the doors opened automatically. Kate parked Sheryl's wheelchair just behind the opening. Sheryl looked up and back at Kate with a question in her eyes. Kate gestured in front of Sheryl.

Sheryl scanned in front of her until she focused on a masked couple across the room. Then she squealed and covered her face with her hands, tears glistening between her fingers.

A young blonde woman stood maybe fifteen feet away. She held a bundle in her arms, and a taller dark-haired man stood next to her with his arm draped over her shoulders. "Hi, Grandma," the woman said.

Sheryl's arms reached out, but Kate wheeled her no closer.

The man spoke, his deep, rich voice rumbling across the room. "We aren't technically supposed to be visiting you, so we'll stay over here. But we wanted you to show you your first great-grandchild."

The young woman held the bundle at an angle while the man pulled the blankets away from the newborn's face. It had a pink bow in its hair and slept through the fussing. Sheryl's sobs were loud, but happy.

"We decided to name her Sheryl, Grandma," the woman said. "But we're going to call her Sherrie."

Sheryl's cries doubled. After a few moments, she regained control. "When are you taking her home?"

"The doctor released both of my girls just an hour or so ago," the young man said. "The best Christmas present ever." He squeezed his wife and they smiled at each other.

Sheryl nodded. "And you have given me the best Christmas present ever." She reached over her shoulder and found Kate's hand to give it a squeeze. "All of you." Then she started coughing and gasping for breath.

The young man stepped forward, worry in his eyes. "Are you alright?"

Kate gave him a reassuring smile. "She will be. She's healing well, but I'm afraid I've kept her off her oxygen too long. I'm going to have to cut this visit short." She turned to wheel Sheryl back.

Sheryl still couldn't catch her breath, so she blew kisses to her grandchildren instead. "We love you, Grandma," the couple replied. "We'll see you soon."

Kate helped Sheryl back onto the bed and replaced the portable oxygen with the high-flow. She waited until Sheryl's breathing returned to normal and her heart rate decreased. Sheryl never let go of Kate's hand the whole time, periodically squeezing it.

When she settled down, Sheryl thanked Kate.

"You can thank your nurse, Andy, the next time you see him. It was his idea when he overheard that phone call that your granddaughter delivered her baby."

"Well nevertheless," Sheryl said, "I have a poinsettia over on the counter there. It's not much, but please take it."

Kate looked at the large, bushy plant. It was a unique coloring, red leaves with white splotches. It was beautiful. "I couldn't. That was from someone else for you."

Sheryl squeezed her hand again. "Please. I insist."

Kate nodded once then patted Sheryl's hand before scrubbing out and leaving with the potted plant in the crook of her elbow.

The next two rooms would be quick. She wasn't sure if Oskar had days or hours left, but the whir and hiss of the ventilator controlling his breathing tube confirmed it wouldn't be long. For his family's sake, she hoped he'd at least make it until tomorrow. But either way, that didn't mean his last Christmas should be forgotten.

"Fröhliche Weihnachten, Oskar."

He dropped his head slightly, about all the movement he could make with the tube down his throat. His eyes were open but clouded. She wasn't sure if it was from pain or medicine.

"Your nurse said that your feet are always cold, so we thought we'd get you some really warm socks. Is it okay if I put them on?"

Another slight nod.

Kate folded the blankets back off his feet. Oskar straightened his legs—all the assistance he could muster. She scrunched the thick, gray socks all the way to the toes. Then she stretched them as she placed them over his feet, unrolling the sock as she moved up. They reached about halfway up his lower legs.

Replacing the blankets, she turned to leave. But a metallic clanking behind her startled her. She subconsciously registered that there were no beeps that indicated severe drops in any of his vitals, but still, she whirled quickly.

Then she chuckled. "That's not nice to do to a nurse, Oskar." He tapped his wedding ring against the metal frame of his bed. When he saw he had her attention, he gestured to the pen and paper on his table. She handed it to him. He tried to pull himself up, but he didn't have the strength. She lifted his bed until he could see what he wrote.

It took him several minutes to write the short note. Kate could tell he fought to maintain control of the letters so they would remain legible. Exhausted when he finished, he fell back against his pillow and panted. She lowered his bed before picking up the note: "Thank you for one last joy before I rejoin my beloved Marta."

Kate struggled to control her own breathing when she looked in his eyes. She wondered if her tears came because of his, or vice versa. It didn't matter. "It was my pleasure, Oskar. Tell Marta I said hi." Oskar nodded and Kate scrubbed and left.

She leaned against the wall between two rooms, hidden from either door. Sobs shuddered through her body, and she bit her lip to prevent them from becoming audible. Some days—and some patients—were harder than others. After she wiped the last of her tears, she stepped to the next room, glad for once for the washing ritual upon entering each room.

A young woman in her twenties lay in the bed. Her brown hair spilled around her face. Yesterday's shift must have brushed it for her because the last time Kate had seen Brittany, her hair had been matted and lifeless. Now it had a glossy sheen to it.

No one was really sure how much a coma patient heard, but Kate hoped it was a lot. So, although there was no response, she talked to Brittany like any other patient. She opened the blinds on the window. "There, that must be better. It's a glorious morning with a bright sun, but it's still cold. You'd probably like that. I'm sorry this accident got in the way of your annual ski trip. There still isn't any snow here, but

I bet the mountains would have been beautiful. Since you couldn't make it there this year, we thought we could maybe bring a little of them to you." Kate placed a small, stuffed snowman on the table beside the woman's bed. Whenever they stopped pumping the drugs into Brittany and allowed her to awaken on her own, Kate hoped the snowman would be the first thing she'd see. A little cheer amidst the sudden confusion, fears, and concerns. "Anyway, I have a couple more people to visit. But I hope you dream of the best powder runs you've ever had."

Kate's bags were significantly lighter when she entered Marie's room. But she'd still be glad to be rid of Marie's gift because it was probably the bulkiest. "Merry Christmas, Marie. What did you choose for breakfast today?"

"A ham and cheese omelet." She dabbed at the corners of her mouth with a napkin.

"And how was it?"

"Delicious," Marie said. "What do you have there?"

"Oh, just a little Christmas cheer."

Even in flannel pajamas in a hospital bed, Marie placed her hands on her ample hips and gave Kate a mock glare. "And what more could you possibly do for us than give up your holiday and time with your own family to take care of us old and decrepit folks? And on top of that, with a smile on your face." Marie flicked her hands toward Kate in a "forget-about-it" gesture. "There's nothing better than that."

Kate grinned. "I disagree. I'll bet you that I can make you speechless."

"Ha!" Marie burst out loud. "Impossible. I accept your bet. What are we betting with?"

"How about a candy bar?"

"Deal."

Kate turned her back to Marie and reached deep into her bag. "Alright, Marie, close your eyes."

Marie gave a humph, but then said, "They're closed."

Kate turned around, and wheeled Marie's bedside table closer, placing the empty breakfast tray on the chair out of the way. "Keep them closed. Almost done." Marie's gift couldn't be wrapped, so she placed it on the table carefully, then pulled out a couple smaller items to set beside it. One of them had to be plugged in, so she reached carefully for the outlet. She grabbed one last item but hid it behind her back. "Alright, you can open your eyes."

Marie gasped. "Well, I'll be. My very own Christmas tree."

Kate nodded. "That's not all. I remembered you talking the other day about how much you'd miss picking out the fresh tree with your family and decorating it on Christmas Eve. I'm sorry I'm a day late, but maybe this will capture a little bit of that tradition. Here are the ornaments and tinsel, so you can decorate the tree however you'd like."

"It's perfect," Marie said. She shook her head, her brown curls bouncing. "You've been so busy. I don't know when you would have found time to do all this." Then her eyes twinkled. "But you still lost the bet."

"I'm not done yet." Kate whipped the jar from behind her back. "You said your favorite part was smelling the fresh pine scent mixed with warm cider in the house. So, I also got a candle warmer and a pine-cinnamon candle."

Marie's mouth dropped open.

Kate set the candle on the warmer. "And on that note, I'm leaving before you can find anything to say." She didn't scrub out even though she was technically supposed to, but then she risked losing the bet. Outside the door, she used the sanitizer dispenser mounted on the wall to make up the difference. The alcohol stung her raw hands. But it was worth being able to say she won.

The last room on her list would take the longest, which is why she left it for last. She spent an extra-long time scrubbing in at Fernando's room. "Feliz Navidad," Kate said when she turned to him.

"Feliz Navidad," Fernando answered in a soft voice. He wore a white tank top, the skin loose on his brown arms. A cross rested on a thick, gold chain around his neck.

Kate taped a piece of paper that read 12:00 over his clock and closed his blinds, dimming the room.

"What are you doing?" Fernando asked in his deliberate English.

"Since my shift didn't start until 6:00, I'm making it midnight now."

"Mid-night?"

"Yes, so we can have Mass." Kate drew a box out of her bag that contained a small Nativity. Then she removed a Bible. Turning on a reading light in the headboard, she pulled the chair close. "The book of Luke, right?"

Fernando nodded, spots of light reflecting off his dark eyes as he watched her.

Kate read the scriptures that told of the Nativity, withdrawing each character in the story from the box as she read about it. She handed each small statue to Fernando, who arranged it carefully on his table. Occasionally he adjusted the placement of one while she read. But mostly he sat back with his eyes closed and fingered his cross. She only knew a few words and phrases in Spanish, and she wasn't really sure how much English Fernando actually understood. But he knew when to open his eyes for a new figurine.

When she finished, she removed the paper and opened the blinds. Fernando started to pick up the figurines and hand them to her. "No, no, Fernando." Kate gently pushed his hands away. "They are for you. A present."

"A pre-sent?" His eyebrows furrowed.

She wasn't sure if he misunderstood the word, or if the offer was confusing. Kate nodded. "A present. Um…" She scrunched her eyes in concentration, trying to remember some of the Spanish Juan had taught her. "Un regalo. I don't want them back."

Fernando's eyes widened. "A gift, si?" One hand clutched the baby Jesus, and the other held an angel.

"Si."

He paused, studying her. "Gracias, mi amiga." Then he turned away, gently replacing the two characters and touching each figure on the top of its head.

Kate quietly scrubbed out and left Fernando alone. She collapsed into one of the rolling chairs at the nurse's station with a big sigh. She felt physically exhausted but invigorated emotionally. It had been a long time since her emotions hadn't been in the dumps.

"How'd it go?" Juan asked.

"Great. Really great. I wish everyone could have done that." She fingered both the tube of lip balm and the note in her pocket.

"Don't worry, I got photos."

"What?" Kate asked. "When? How?"

"I've been following you little elves," Juan said with a wink. "I figured the other nurses who aren't on this shift would want to see how their donations were used too." He rolled his chair over to her side and started swiping through his phone. She found herself in several of the photos, obviously. But she also perceived some of the experiences the other nurses had. And she really meant perceived. Juan had focused mostly on the patients, sometimes the nurses, but he captured the precise moment when the emotion was clearly displayed on the person's face. Even Brittany—despite her coma—seemed to have a slight smile when he snapped her photo. And he'd somehow managed to include the gift in the corner of the image.

"Wow, Juan. These are beautiful. When did you learn photography?"

He shrugged. "I've dabbled a little here and there since high school."

"We should print these out and make a collage in the break room."

Juan nodded.

Tanya, one of the other nurses who had been delivering gifts, approached them. "Are you done, Kate?"

Kate nodded. "Yeah, I was just resting a moment before I gathered everyone for caroling."

"Could you help me with my last gift, please?" Tanya asked.

"Sure. Who is it for?"

"Elden."

"He missed playing games with his family, right? I think I got him a pack of cards."

"That's what I assumed by the size of the package," Tanya said. "And I figured rather than just give him the deck to play solitaire, maybe we could play Go Fish or something. Only he lost some of his motor control from the stroke, and probably can't hold his own cards."

"I see."

Tanya led the way to the sink in Elden's room. After scrubbing in, they both put gloves on. Tanya then walked to Elden's bedside. "Happy holidays, Elden. Kate and I have a gift for you."

"For me?" His voice was slurred.

Tanya nodded. "Here, grab right here." She led his fingers to the edge of the paper, and then pressed them closed tightly. While he held on, she twisted and turned the package until it tore open. She threw his paper away and held up the deck of cards for him to see. "We still have some work to do, so we can't stay all day, but I think we can manage a round of Go Fish. How does that sound?"

Elden's eyes lit up. "Sounds real good." His voice was gruff but childlike at the same time.

Tanya shuffled and dealt. Kate sat next to Elden with the cards angled so he could see them. When it was his turn, she'd hold out the hand to him and he'd point to the one he wanted. Then Kate would call out, "Do you have a four?" Or six, or jack, or whatever he requested. As Elden got sets of four, she'd arrange them on the bed where he could see them. At the end of the game, Elden had seven sets to Tanya's six.

"You won!" Tanya said.

Elden's face brightened, and his mouth hung a little slack as he cheered. His gray whiskers needed a shave, but that didn't detract from his joy. With shaky hands, he reached for both of them. "Sign."

"Sign?" Tanya asked. "What do you mean?"

"Sign cards." He gestured to the pen peeking from the edge of Kate's pocket.

Kate pulled out the pen and reached for the top card.

Elden's hand stopped her. "Not that one."

"Okay. Which one then?"

"Queen of Hearts," Elden said. "On the face."

So they both signed his Queen of Hearts. He told them he wanted every nurse on the floor to sign his cards. They promised to ask the rest of the staff to stop by as he blew sloppy kisses at them.

After scrubbing out, Kate grabbed a quick snack. Once all the nurses made their usual rounds again, she gathered them together to carol around the halls. Since it was circular, it didn't actually matter where they stood; the entire floor could hear their (off-key) singing. But they still started at one side and stopped at each room for at least half a verse before walking to the next room.

Kate tried to hide in the back, but more often than not someone (she guessed Jaden) pushed her forward to the front. They sang everything from "Rudolph" to "We Wish You a Merry Christmas" to "Jingle Bells." Some patients sang along, some hummed because it was the best they could do, and some merely watched and smiled.

While they sang in Alice's room—her lights twinkling above them—Alice beckoned to Kate. Juan nudged her and she stepped forward mid-song.

"I never got to properly thank you." Alice handed her a bottle of lotion. "It's new." She tried to whisper, but it was the whisper of the semi-deaf, so many of the other nurses chuckled amidst their singing.

Rob mustered enough breath to sing with a rich baritone when they visited his room. She missed his harmony throughout the rest of the hall.

As they sang at Isaac's room, he handed out origami figures to each of the staff members. Some got stars, others snowflakes, and even a few had Christmas trees. But only Kate received a small, white dove.

Fernando joined in as best as he could in his room. Though his singing voice was not much louder than his speaking voice, Kate could distinctly hear Spanish syllables over their English ones. Evidently, Juan could as well because he started singing along in Spanish, which made Fernando grin.

After they finished singing around the entire hall, Kate placed the lotion out on the desk counter where everyone could access it. And Sheryl's poinsettia brightened the break room table considerably. Kate wished she could share the lip balm as well, but that wasn't safe. As everyone compared their origami and she rubbed Oskar's note between her fingers, she didn't feel at all like she had given the presents. Instead, Kate knew this was a Christmas she would never forget because the gifts she had received were far better than the ones she'd help give.

About the Author

H.T. teaches secondary English by day, writes by afternoon, and sleeps by night. She writes whatever she darn well pleases, which usually ends up being flash fiction and YA fantasy. Her writing explores our humanity—the good, the bad, and the not-so-ordinary. You can find more by visiting www.htwrites.com or following H.T. Ashmead on Facebook or TikTok.

From the Editor

Thank you for sharing part of your holiday season with us. I hope you enjoyed these stories as much as I enjoyed collecting them for you. There were a couple of warm fuzzies in there, a couple of interesting surprises, some nostalgia, and some good, old-fashioned holiday cheer. Everything I want from holiday stories. (Well for this time of year, anyway!)

The Particular Passages anthologies are usually an eclectic collection of stories without theme or genre. The 2023 holiday season is the first time we have attempted to stick with themes, and, honestly, we are still amazed at the incredible variety of stories authors provide when we try not to restrict them.

As I've noted before, the Particular Passages Anthologies are curated and edited with a light touch, so if you see a difference in grammar, punctuation, or spelling styles, that may be why. We've gotten some negative feedback on that, but then, we've gotten some very positive feedback as well. There are not many places where authors get to share their story the way they like it, without trying to make it "fit in." Which means there aren't very many places where readers can find such varied authors in the same collection.

If you liked an author's story, reach out and let them know. The *best* way to make sure your favorite authors write more stories is to tell them you loved one of their stories. (Not to mention it will make their day!)

If you liked this kind of anthology, comments to us or to our authors on our social media, websites, or in an email are the best ways to make sure we do another one. The next best is to tell people about the anthology, so they buy the book. The third best way is to leave reviews.

May the rest of your holiday season be the stuff future (happy) stories are made of.

Sam Knight
October 1, 2023

Additional Copyright Information